MIDNIGHT KILL

FBI MYSTERY THRILLER

DEAN BLACKWOOD
BOOK 2

SAM JONES

INTRODUCTION

Wait until midnight, disable the alarm, and toy with the newlywed couple.

In San Francisco, a new breed of serial killer is on the loose —one who specializes in home invasions and crimes too dark to describe.

When the SFPD can't catch a psychopath, they call me.

I've got a talent for tracking down sadistic jackasses like this.

But this time, it's personal.

Threaten the ones I love, and the hunter becomes the hunted.

San Francisco's most wanted just made it to the top of my list.

And I always keep my list clean.

PROLOGUE

SAN FRANCISCO, CALIFORNIA

The killer held up his knife to the moonlight. The way the light glinted off the blade mesmerized him. His chest tightened with anticipation.

He was jittery.

Excited.

Ready.

Tonight it starts, he thought. *The game.*

Then, checkmate.

He caressed the spine of the knife with his gloved index finger. His senses were alert—on fire. His skin prickled as he fought his urge to smile.

He told himself it was not the time to feel pleasure. Not yet.

Begin, the killer thought. He slipped the blade into its sheath, tucked it into the back of his waistband, and pulled the black wool mask over his face.

Go.

He scanned the neighborhood—empty, no one wandering around. Dark. The only illumination was the dull glow of the streetlamps, pockets of light here and there.

Quiet, the killer thought. *Peaceful.*

He loved the game. The killer pinned his gaze to the target, the backyard of a two-story house.

He took another look around.

He lowered into a crouch and moved.

Silently, he reached the side entrance of the home. He'd learned how to approach a target undetected years before.

You made me, the killer thought as he pulled out his lock-picking tools.

All of you.

His breathing was steady and controlled. He slipped the tension wrench and pick into the door knob, moving them with ease until the knob was unlocked.

He moved inside.

The house was dark and still. He took out his knife and slithered almost weightless down the hallway.

I am a wraith.

He had steered clear of the only camera the home-owners had installed in the front.

Dummies.

He stopped at the first door on his left.

The killer closed his eyes.

Flexed his fingers.

Kill.

He stepped into the room.

Watched as the sleeping couple's chests slowly rose and fell with each breath they took as they dozed peacefully.

You don't deserve this life, the killer thought as he narrowed his eyes.

I will take it all away.

The man in the bed groaned in his sleep.

Turned onto his side.

The killer stepped closer to the bed.

The man's eyelids fluttered.

The killer raised the knife.

Then the man snapped open his eyes, his mouth dropping open as he looked up and stared deep into the fiery eyes of the masked intruder beside him.

"Undeserving," the killer whispered as he brought down the blade. "Unjust."

The deed was done.

Finished.

Both of the targets were dead.

The killer had accomplished the feat in under 10 minutes—exactly as he planned it.

Sixty seconds after he finished with the woman, he had sneaked out of the neighborhood. Ten minutes after that, he was back at his safe house.

No one would catch him on any cameras. If the San Francisco PD stumbled across *any* footage, all they would see was a figure dressed in black—no face, no discernable features.

The killer didn't use a car.

It would take weeks for the cops to catch up with him.

He just needed a few days.

Perfect, the killer thought as he closed the front door to his safe house. *Every last piece.*

He allowed himself to enjoy the success of his mission as he stripped off his black clothing, bagged it, and stored it for disposal.

Then he sifted through his gear, took out a burner phone, and dialed the number for the SFPD's Homicide Division.

The phone rang.

The killer closed his eyes.

On the sixth ring, the call went to voicemail.

"Your move, Blackwood," the killer said before he terminated the call, snapped the burner phone in half, and focused on the surveillance photo of Dean Blackwood pinned to his wall, a drawn-on bullet hole in his forehead.

1

VICTORVILLE, CALIFORNIA

The three meth manufacturers were polishing off their Saturday morning cups of coffee when the front door of their apartment detonated, blew apart, and knocked them to the floor.

One of them howled.

The other writhed in pain.

Then the third guy saw the entourage of black-clad FBI agents charging through a smoke cloud into the apartment.

"FBI!" one of the agents shouted. "Show me your hands!"

Eight Hostage Rescue Team members flooded the residence, their M4 carbines trained on the trio of men scattered along the floor. Two of the HRT members pinned the suspects' arms behind their backs. The downed men cursed as their wrists were secured with zip ties.

"Suspects secure," the team leader spoke into his mic. "Living room, clear."

The HRT members split apart.

Two cleared the kitchen.

Four more moved to their left and stalked their way

down a hallway with three doors, the one in the lead (Blythe) holding a fist to signal the men behind him (Stockton, Riley, Fitzpatrick) to stop.

"Riley. Stockton," Blythe whispered as he motioned his weapon toward the door on his left. "Boot it."

Riley and Stockton crept toward the door on their left.

Riley positioned himself by the door handle and cut a glance at Stockton.

Then Stockton took a step back, raised his booted foot, and proceeded to kick in the door.

He dashed into the room.

Riley followed behind him.

Gave it the all clear once they found nothing but a sagging mattress, take-out containers, and half of a molded pizza.

In the hallway, Blythe and Fitzpatrick moved toward the first door on their right, kicked it in, and cleared a small bedroom filled to the brim with Pelican cases, fertilizer, electronics, and several fifty-five-gallon drums.

"We got it," Blythe said into his radio. "Payload located."

"Copy," a team member responded. "Kitchen is clear."

Blythe signaled with two fingers toward the second door on the left. Riley and Stockton moved into position to clear it as Blythe and Fitzpatrick prepared to enter the room across from it.

Riley kicked open the door.

Stockton darted into the room.

Then a series of gunshots rang out. Twelve collective rounds stitched across both men's Kevlars as they fell to the floor.

"Shots fired!" Blythe shouted. "Agents down!"

Blythe angled his body toward the room where Riley

and Stockton were hit, his eyes widening as he pinned them to a man positioned in the doorway toting an AK-47.

The man swung with his AK.

Blythe put two rounds into his chest.

Then the door behind him flew open. Blythe's mouth dropped open as he saw a suspect with an Uzi who proceeded to squeeze off six rounds into his back.

Blythe's knees buckled.

He fell to the floor.

Then Fitzpatrick raised his M4 and took aim at the suspect with the Uzi. The suspect fired blind, one of the rounds clipping Fitzpatrick in his right shoulder that spun him around and dropped him onto his back.

"I'm hit!" Fitzpatrick hollered as he dug his heels and shuffled backward into the hallway. "I'm hit! *I'm hit!*"

The man with the Uzi emptied his magazine into the hallway, round after round boring into the walls and plaster.

Fitzpatrick's heart raced as he shot a look at Blythe, Riley, and Stockton bleeding out along the hardwood floors, the HRT members groaning and writhing in anguish.

"Agent down," Fitzpatrick whimpered into his radio. "Get some people in here now!"

Voices from the other team members came over the line, Fitzpatrick's brothers-in-arms putting out the call that they were on their way. Fitzpatrick then made out the racket of glass shattering from the room where the man with the Uzi was posted up, grimacing as three more HRT members entered the hallway and converged on the wounded team members.

"Get an RA unit here," the team member crouched down beside Blythe said. "We've got three agents down— multiple gunshot wounds."

A hand clapped Fitpatrick's shoulder. The young agent

winced as he looked into the goggle-shielded eyes of one of his fellow team members.

"Fitzy," the HRT member said. "You good?"

Fitzpatrick ogled the hole in his shoulder, a ribbon of crimson flowing freely from the wound. "Where is he? Where's the guy who hit me?"

Two team members charged into the room where the man with the Uzi was holed up, searching feverishly for signs of the suspect. They saw a busted-out window that spilled out onto the back lawn.

"He's on the move," one of the men said into his radio. "Does anyone have eyes on this guy?"

"Negative," another agent replied. "No visual."

Fitzpatrick gnashed his teeth, the pain in his shoulder pulsating like it had its own heartbeat. "Somebody find this guy, man," he said as he watched Blythe, Riley, and Stockton holding on for dear life. "Put one between his fuckin' eyes!"

A crackle came over the airwaves.

"Stand fast," an agent said. "I've got this son of a bitch."

"Who is that?" Fitzpatrick winced. "Who put that out?"

The team member applying pressure to Fitzpatrick's shoulder wound smirked. "That's Blackwood."

2

S   pecial Agent Dean Blackwood, flanked by several
          other agents, slipped out of the sedan. It was parked
          in the alley behind the house where the HRT
members had just been ambushed. A Kevlar vest was
strapped to his chest and a SIG-Sauer P320 was clutched in
his hand as he scanned the terrain for signs of the suspect.

Where are you? Dean's brain all but screamed out at him.
Show me that smiling face.

A rapping noise tickled his ears.

Dean whipped his body around.

He spotted the suspect with the Uzi vaulting over a
wooden fence.

"*Freeze!*" Dean raised his SIG and lined up the man's
chest between the sights. "On your knees, asshole!"

The suspect dropped to the pavement as he squeezed off
a series of rounds from his Uzi. A hailstorm of bullets
drilled their way into the pavement, FBI sedans, and nearby
homes. Dean and the other agents scattered and dived for
cover behind their cruisers. The suspect sprayed his weapon
wildly as he mounted the hood of an FBI sedan, scaled the

fence on the other side of the alley, and disappeared from sight.

"He's running," an agent shouted out. "He's on the move!"

Dean dashed out of cover, holstered his SIG, darted toward the fence, and climbed. He scaled over the top of it and dropped down onto a back lawn, drawing out with his SIG before he aimed it at the suspect who was in the throes of chucking a lawn chair into a screen storm door. The lawn chair struck the door and shattered it to pieces. The suspect sprinted through a shower of glass as he continued his retreat through the house and startled a woman inside the kitchen who proceeded to holler and cower behind a table.

"I'm on foot," Dean said into his radio as he pursued the suspect. "Suspect is headed east. Scramble nearby units, and try to cut him off."

Voices replied over the radio, but Dean couldn't make them out. He was too focused on the suspect fleeing 10 yards ahead of him through the house, homed in like a Tomahawk missile on his prey and resolved to take the man down no matter what the cost.

You're mine, dipshit.

I'm gonna rip your fuckin' heart out.

The suspect arrived at the front door and dashed through the living room, spraying a series of rounds over his shoulder. Dean rolled head over heels into cover behind a couch as the suspect fired his weapon, bullets whizzing past him, a swift pain throbbing in his shoulder as the suspect emptied the Uzi in the couch and flayed open the front door.

"How does that feel, *fuckhead*?" the suspect shrieked before he threw his depleted weapon to the floor and rattled off a smoke-choked cackle.

Dean glanced at his arm to find that a round had hit his left tricep, a superficial wound that merely grazed his flesh. Gritting his teeth, he peeked his head over the couch and saw the suspect dashing onto the front lawn.

He stood.

Tightened his grip on his SIG.

Then he bolted through the living room and through the front door.

The suspect slipped on the front lawn and glided across freshly watered grass, sliding like a ball player diving toward home base. Once he landed on his back, he shot a look toward the front door, a grimacing Dean Blackwood closing in on him with fire in his eyes and his SIG held up and at the ready.

The suspect cursed under his breath.

Pushed himself off the lawn.

Cut a glance toward the street that ran east to west where a pair of FBI sedans were attempting to close in on him from either direction.

"*Stop!*" Dean shouted. "Get on the ground!"

The suspect darted to his left toward the incoming sedan 10 yards away. Lungs on fire, he sprinted toward it, the vehicle's sirens blaring, the suspect making out the whites of the agent's eyes behind the wheel.

"Hands up," the agent behind the wheel commanded over his loudspeaker. "Do it, now!"

The suspect flashed his middle finger.

The agent behind the sedan slammed on his brakes and wrenched the steering wheel to the right, the vehicle bellowing to a halt before it lined up parallel with the suspect who glided over the hood before landing gracefully on his feet.

Dean shook his head as the suspect dashed down the

street. He arrived at the sedan and crooked his finger toward the agent behind the wheel.

"Get out."

The agent slid out of the driver's seat.

Dean nudged him aside.

Then he got behind the wheel, threw the gear shift into drive, and slammed his foot down on the gas.

The rear tires spun.

Smoke churned.

Then Dean wrenched the steering wheel to the left and aimed the front end of the car toward the suspect's back.

The suspect shot a look to his left and then to his right, his sights then settling on the lawn of a home 20 paces away.

A red-faced Dean tightened his grip on the steering wheel, the suspect now five yards out and closing to the point that Dean could make out the bald patches on the back of the man's scalp.

The suspect prepared to mount the curb.

Dean turned the steering wheel a few inches to his right.

Then he threw open the driver's side door, struck the suspect in the lower part of his back, and knocked him onto the pavement. The suspect grunted as an excruciating pain shot through his spine. He fell to his knees as Dean weaved the sedan around him, slammed on the brakes, and threw the shifter into park.

The incapacitated suspect pawed at his back, a gurgle slipping through his lips as Dean sauntered up to him like a man on a stroll in the park.

Dean got down on one knee.

Turned the suspect onto his back.

"How does *that* feel, shit bird?" he said as he produced a set of handcuffs.

3

FBI Field Office
Los Angeles, California

Cool AC lapped at Dean's face as he walked out of the elevator and stepped out into the hallway. He closed his eyes. Breathed a sigh. Took a moment to relish the climate-controlled environment after the five weeks he spent in the heat-soaked hellscape known as Victorville, California.

"Blackwood."

Dean snapped his eyes open and saw Kent Wilson, Special Agent in Charge, approaching him, lips twisted into a grin as he shot out his hand and slapped it into Dean's.

"What's good, Willy?" Dean greeted him.

"Good to see you." Wilson motioned to the bandage on Dean's left arm. "How's the arm?"

"It's all right."

"You taking anything for it?"

"Negative. Clean living means *clean living*, boss—no

booze, no pills. I'm not screwing up years of sobriety for a flesh wound."

"It's just Tylenol."

"I'll suck it up." Dean checked the time on the G-Shock strapped to his wrist. "Let's just get this over with so I can get the hell out of here, yeah?"

The two men strolled down the hallway. Dean glanced at the FBI agents posted up behind desks and cubicles, patriots doing their best to prevent the next disaster from hitting the homeland with unwavering spirits and hearts overflowing with American pride. But Dean didn't count himself among their ranks.

He didn't consider himself a patriot.

He wasn't Jack Ryan or Reacher or Tim Kennedy or any of those other rah-rah, jingoistic warriors who saluted the flag and did things because of a reverence for God and country. If anything, he was just a lackey doing the Bureau's dirty work because some asshole forced him to sign a contract a few months prior under duress.

He was just a guy.

A guy who wanted to be left alone.

Three years, Blackwood.

Dean shook his head.

Three more years of these cases and you're out.

For good.

Dean tailed Wilson through a door. A conference table was in the middle of the room. Several chairs flanked it, and one of them was occupied by a polished prick known as Sloane with pearly-white teeth and slicked hair—the same guy who recruited Dean to the Bureau's undercover division several years before.

"Agent Blackwood," Wilson said, his voice taking on a

more official, business-like tone. "You remember Mark Sloane."

Dean huffed.

Sloane offered his hand. "How's it going, Blackwood?"

"I got shot." Dean gestured to his bandage. "How do you think I'm doing?"

"Hell of a job you did in Victorville." Sloane withdrew his hand and took a seat. "On behalf of the director, I wanted to—"

"Cut the crap," Dean said as he stood to the side. "Three of our guys are in the hospital. One of them's got permanent nerve damage, that kid Fitzpatrick."

"Being in the HRT unit has its risks, Agent Blackwood." Sloane shrugged his shoulders dismissively. "Shit, as they say, happens."

Dean tapered his eyes.

Clenched a fist.

Tamped down the urge to clock Sloane across his jaw.

"Whatever," Dean groaned. "Just debrief me on this thing so I can go home."

"Agent Blackwood—"

"*Dean.*"

"Sure thing." Sloane held up his hands. "Again, I want to commend you on taking down that little operation that was being run out of Victorville. We managed to seize—"

"Over fifteen million in drug-related cash and other assets," Dean cut in, "and you now have a suspect in custody singing his heart out about his connections to the domestic terrorist cells he's connected to in Northern California. Congrats."

Sloane smirked. "You, uh," he appraised the files on the table in front of him, "ran this guy over with a car, correct?"

"No, I threw a door into his back."

"You fractured one of the discs in his spine."

"Good."

"He can't walk."

"*Sweet.*"

"Dean," Sloane said, "I feel the need to remind you that despite this agreement we have in place—"

"It's not an agreement," Dean clarified. "The director forced me to sign a slip of paper saying I would do jobs like the one in Victorville for a few years before you cut me loose. I didn't do it because I wanted to; I did it because you sons of bitches threatened to burn me for—" He waved his hand through the air, disinclined to talk about the case that caused his own son to be taken hostage by a deranged bastard, the same guy that had killed his brother when he was a kid.

Dean took down a corrupt faction of the LAPD during the course of the case.

The Armenian mob as well.

But he shattered the fragile trust he'd been building with the mother of his child in the process and, even worse, with his son, Jeremy. Dean was still reeling over the fact that his son was forced to lose his innocence much quicker than any kid should ever have to.

The Bureau almost threw Dean in jail because of his going rogue and taking down the men that he did, but then they offered him a deal: stay on the job for three years, kick in doors, and take down suspects the only way he knew how —hard—and then he could go and do as he pleased.

Three years.

Thirty-six months.

1,095 days.

Dean shook his head.

Don't think about that, Blackwood.

Not now.

Just focus on what's in front of you.

"If there's nothing more for me here, Mr. Sloane," Dean said, "then I'd like to go home."

Sloane furrowed his brow. "Home?"

"That's right. Everyone has one." Dean shrugged. "I assume your residence is in one of the seven circles of hell, you pearly-toothed dickhead."

"Well," Sloane chuckled, "last I heard, your ex-wife put you at arm's distance since that *SMASH* case you were on. My apologies, but," he flashed a grin, "it doesn't sound like you have much of a home to go home to at the moment."

"Okay, buddy." Dean felt the vein in his neck pulsate. "High-ranking member of the Bureau or not, if you talk about family again, I'll shove my foot so far up your ass I'll impale your brain."

"How colorful."

"I mean it."

"How's your kid?"

Dean took a beat. "What?"

"Your son." Sloane glanced down at his files. "He was taken hostage during that SMASH case, correct? According to the debrief, he had a gun to his head—"

Dean chucked a chair aside.

Charged toward Sloane.

Raised a fist but then felt Wilson grip him by the arm.

"Agent Wilson," Sloane said. "Control your agent."

"Kid," Wilson whispered into Dean's ear. "Take it easy."

Dean took a beat.

Lowered his fist.

He's not worth it.

Fuck him.

Just shut your mouth, let him talk, and then you can leave.

"Are you, uh..." Sloane said as he took a glimmer at his files, "keeping up with your mandated therapy sessions?"

"Yeah." Dean nodded. "Twice a week."

"Is it helping?"

"Some." Dean took out a nicotine toothpick—*Cut down, boss. You're up to four a day*—and placed it between his teeth. "I also got a punching bag at home with the Bureau's insignia stitched into it."

"Well, according to Doctor Rance," Sloane turned a page on his file, "you're a bit exhausted after the last case we put you on."

"No shit."

"Well, you need to rest up and get ready. We've got an assignment in Fort Lauderdale we want you to look into."

As Sloane droned on about the details of the case, Dean tuned him out. His head felt like it was filled with cotton. The muscles on the back of his neck constricted, and the notion that he had two-and-half years left on what amounted to a prison sentence left him feeling like his stomach was doing flips.

How long can you keep this up?

Dean clamped down on his toothpick.

You're gonna go nuts before your time is up.

"Point being," Sloane continued, "we think it's best if you take a few weeks off. We need you to take a break, refuel, and recharge, and then we'll get you back out into the field."

Dean said nothing.

"Agent Blackwood." Sloane scooted forward in his chair. "Are you reading me?"

"Yeah." Dean nodded, his brain teasing the onset of a headache. "I am."

"Good, then listen closely." Sloane tapped his finger on the files. "Because despite everything that happened with the last case, as thrilled as we are that you shut down this operation over in Victorville, you accrued a significant amount of damage in the process."

"It's like you said earlier about being on an HRT team," Dean said. "Shit happens."

"Don't sass me, son." Sloane narrowed his eyes. "You're in this for the long haul. You know what's at stake here in terms of your reputation, and if you keep approaching these operations with the same kamikaze mentality you had on the Victorville case, you're gonna wind up dead or in a cell before your three-year term with us is finished."

He's right, man.

You gotta relax.

You have to chill the hell out.

"The Fort Lauderdale assignment," Sloane said as he closed his file and stood, "is in three weeks. I recommend you take something in the way of a vacation in the meantime." He moved to the door. "Go to the beach. Get some sun. I *would* tell you to have a drink, but we both know you're on the wagon these days."

Sloane left.

Dean cursed under his breath.

A depleted looking Wilson sat down at the table.

"This fucking *sucks*, Willy," Dean said. "Top to bottom."

"I know." The SAC hung his head. "But like Sloane said, we've got three years—"

"Two-and-a-half."

"—two-and-*half* left with this little," Wilson grimaced, "*arrangement* they've set up. It is what it is. All that aside, though, Sloane is right. You can't keep attacking things on these cases with a hammer. I know you're pissed off, but you need to try to maintain your composure while you're on the job."

Dean thought of his son.

His ex-wife.

The gallery of victims that got caught in the crossfire during his last escapade.

"Life's a bitch right now, Willy," Dean said, the weight of his words triggering a lump in his throat. "I haven't seen my son in months. I've only spoken to him over the phone a couple of times."

"How's he doing?"

"He's all right." Dean's mind harkened back to the memory of a guy holding a gun to his son's head, one of a litany of memories he could recall with crystal-clear recollection thanks to what doctors had dubbed an eidetic memory. "All things considered."

"Has Claire—" Wilson took a beat. "Well, has she come around at all after—?"

"After my kid had a gun put to his head?" Dean rolled his eyes. "No, not really." He pulled out a chair and sat. "I've got a long ladder to climb before my relationship with my ex-wife resembles anything in the way of stability."

Wilson said nothing.

Dean rubbed the back of his neck.

The two men then shared the silence for what felt like an hour.

"As much as I hate saying it, kid," Wilson said, "Sloane is right. You need to take time off."

"And do what?"

"I don't know," Wilson gestured to his jaw. "Start with shaving that beard for starters."

"You don't like it?"

"You look like the Brawny Man."

Dean smirked. "Maybe you're right. I suppose a few weeks off puttering around the house is warranted."

"What about Layla?"

"What about her?"

"I don't know," Wilson said. "You sound like you've got a good woman in your corner is all."

"That I do." Dean couldn't help but beam at the thought of the one person in his life—aside from Wilson—who cheered him on day in and day out, one of only two human beings that accepted him for all his flaws, baggage, and bullshit.

"Well," Wilson stood, "take your time off, and take the lady out. Buy her a fancy dinner. Take her on vacation." He clapped Dean on the shoulder. "Just give yourself a break, okay? We'll pick this thing up in three weeks."

"Sounds good."

Wilson nodded.

He turned to leave.

But Dean called out his name before the SAC could make his exit.

"Boss," Dean said, the anxiety welling up inside of him so thick it could be sold by the pound. "Do you think I'll make it? These two years and change of kicking in doors for the Bureau, I mean?"

"Odds-wise, you mean?"

"Yeah."

Wilson took a beat, his eyes shimmering with a forlorn twinkle. "You have to," he finally said. "You just gotta suck it up, do the job, and then we can be done."

Two-and-half years, Dean thought as he left the room and headed to the parking garage.

Thirty months.

1,095 days.

Give or take.

4

EAGLE ROCK, CALIFORNIA

"Just the One (I've Been Looking For)" by Johnnie Taylor rang out of the Bluetooth speaker beside Dean, his eyes fixed to the marigold hues of the Southern California sunset off in the distance. He leaned against the porch railing of his one-story bungalow, scanning the skyline of downtown Los Angeles as his blue heeler Willy padded his way onto the porch. Willy grunted. Dean glanced at his four-legged companion as he rubbed the back of his neck. "What's up, bud?"

Willy whimpered and sat on his haunches, his gaze drifting toward the street before he laid down on his side.

"Yeah," Dean groaned, "the feeling's mutual."

As the intro to the song played out, a cobalt Honda Civic pulled up to the driveway. Dean flashed a smile as Layla Adrian got out of the car, the setting sun backlighting her with a dreamlike phosphorescence.

"Hey, you," Dean greeted.

"Hey, *you*." Layla climbed up the stairs to the porch, planted a kiss on Dean's cheek, and then wrapped her arms around his waist. "It's been a minute."

"That it has."

"Is your arm okay?"

"It's nothing."

"How'd the debrief go?"

"It's over," Dean said. "The case, at least. Still got some time left on my sentence."

"Don't think of it like that," Layla said as the two embraced, Dean squeezing his better half tightly as he noticed that her brunette hair now had a bit of an auburn tint. "Is that new?"

"My hair?"

"Looks like you added some color to it."

"No, it just looks like that when the sun hits it. Same with my eyes. When I'm crying—"

"They turn hazel," Dean said. "I noticed that when you started crying at the end of *Marley & Me*."

"I guess you've been around long enough to notice by now."

"Eight months, if we're keeping score."

"Nine, if we're keeping an *accurate* score."

"Sorry," Dean said before he kissed Layla on her forehead. "I'll pay better attention."

The two gazed out at the sunset for a moment. Dean's thoughts dwelled on the conversation he had with Wilson and Sloane back at the field office.

Sloane.

I'd kick you in the nuts if I could get away with it.

"Hey," Layla said as she squeezed Dean's hand. "What are you thinking about?"

"I shouldn't be thinking about *anything* at the moment. I mean, that's what a man on vacation is supposed to be doing."

Layla winced. "You taking a vacation is like telling an

elephant not to be heavy."

"Well, the orders came down straight from the top." Dean extended his arms in a messianic pose. "Yours truly has been officially placed on the bench."

"You're kidding."

"Three weeks."

"How come?"

"Direct orders," Dean said. "I'm being put on some case down in Fort Lauderdale, but the dipshits holding my leash told me to rest up for three weeks before I go back in the field."

Willy nestled his nose into Layla's leg. Layla stooped down to the dog's level and scratched him behind the ears. "That's good," she said. "You're never home for more than a day at a time anyway."

"Maybe I can make it a point to see Jeremy during my downtime."

"You think Claire will go for it?"

"I don't know." Dean sighed. "The last time I spoke with her, she said that Jeremy was acting a little withdrawn lately."

"That's understandable. I mean," Layla's tone softened, "after what happened."

The memory of the man who held a gun to his son's head, the same man who was responsible for killing his twin brother, Tommy, back when they were children, played back at high speed in Dean's mind. The fact that he had brought closure to that part of his life was something that brought comfort to his family, but the cost of obtaining that closure still kept him up at night.

The same went for his ex-wife, Claire. It took considerable time for Dean to repair his relationship with her, and what happened with Jeremy certainly didn't help. Still,

Claire wanted Jeremy to have a healthy relationship with his father, so part of the reason she was able to put the past behind her was for the sake of the child they shared together.

But there was still distance.

No physical visits.

How long that would last, Dean wasn't sure.

"I spoke to my dad right before you got here," he said in an effort to switch up the topic. "He's been having some heart trouble. I have to arrange a nurse to stop by his place twice a week now."

"I know," Layla replied. "He called me while you were still in Victorville."

"He did?"

"Yeah, he was just checking in."

"Since when do the two of you 'check in'?"

"You and I are an item now, Deano."

"An *item*?"

"We are."

"You sound like a character from a '50s teenybopper movie."

"Well, either way," Layla said as she gazed deep into Dean's eyes, "we're at that state where the two of us are supposed to have some kind of rapport with our parents."

"When you're right," Dean replied, "you're right. I guess that means I just need to hold up my end of the bargain then."

"I'm trying to get my mom to fly in from Italy for a visit. It's hard to get her to come back to the States after she retired there. I mean, I get it. If I had my own little villa for two grand a month, I wouldn't want to leave either."

"What about your dad?" Dean said. "Any progress in that arena?"

The lines in Layla's face slackened. "We're still not speaking. Honestly, I don't really have plans to do that for the foreseeable future."

If my father cheated on my mother, Dean thought, *I would pummel him into oblivion.* "I'm sorry, Lay," he said. "I can only imagine how tough that is."

"Let's not talk about it." Layla wrapped her arms around Dean's waist and rested her head against his shoulder. "I mean, I'll get to that point eventually, but it's just not now."

"What *would* you like to talk about?"

"Vacation plans, for starters. Maybe it's the stars aligning or something, but I'm taking two weeks off while my editor pitches my book to publishers."

Dean winced. "I'm not quite sure what a vacation looks like. I've never taken more than a day or two off at a time, like you said. It was always like that. Other than summer vacations at home, my family never went anywhere except church and the grocery store."

"We've both got a little saved up," Layla said. "I think if we do this right, we can find a nice little island spot to get sunburned on."

"Sounds fun."

"It will be." Layla kissed Dean on his neck. "Lean into your off time, Blackwood. Spend some quality time with me."

"Have we not done that before?"

"Of course we have." Layla took a small step back. "Look, I don't want to speak for you, but *I'd* like to think that things are progressing with us. I think it would be good for us if we try and, well, embrace the more mundane parts of life."

"Playing house?" Dean flexed his brow. "Arguing about who got the wrong coffee filters sort of thing?"

"Exactly," Layla said. "I mean, you and I started off our

relationship dealing with that whole SMASH case. It wasn't exactly ideal circumstances for a first date."

"Good point." Dean's mind drifted back to thoughts of taking down the corrupt LAPD squad, the case that culminated in his coming face to face with the man who killed his brother, Tommy. "We don't spend that much time indulging in the mundane."

"Exactly. It would be a nice change of pace to act like normal people for a minute, to keep things easy for a bit."

"Sounds good in theory."

"Well, practice makes perfect, Agent Blackwood. Just take it one day at a time. It's just like your workout routines. You used to be the scrawny kid all your life until you started picking up weights." Layla rubbed Dean's pectoral muscles. "This Captain America physique you've got going on didn't happen overnight, did it?"

"Captain America, huh?" Dean puffed his chest. "I'll take it."

"Good." Layla slapped Dean on his rear. "I'll make dinner tonight. I found this salmon recipe I want to try out. It's got a sweet chili marinade. The only catch is that I don't have the sweet chili."

"I guess that's my cue to go get some."

"That it is."

Dean pulled Layla in close and gently pressed his lips against hers, the moment forever cemented in his brain, one he would be able to recall until he was an old man.

"Hey," Layla said. "I love you. You know that, right?"

Dean's stomach twisted into a knot, his mouth open but the reply that he knew Layla craved was one he was unable to summon.

I can't say it.

Not yet.

As much as I would like to.

"It's okay," Layla said with a hint of a frown as the lines in her face slackened. "You're not ready. I get it. I hope you don't mind if I say it though."

"Not at all."

Layla turned toward the house, ordered Willy inside, and told Dean which brand of sweet chili he needed to fetch for her salmon dish. Minutes later, Dean, car keys in hand, thumbed the button for the roll-up garage door, watched it open, and pinned his eyes to the Plymouth Road Runner his father had given him.

Dean got behind the wheel.

Turned over the engine.

Backed out of the driveway, and cranked up the volume on Bob Seger's "Night Moves."

5

Dean tapped his finger on the steering wheel to the beat as the Plymouth cruised through the rolling foothills of Northeast Los Angeles. The driver's side window was open, the chilled breeze licking his face as he navigated his way toward Colorado Street. Despite the crisp weather and metronome-like putter of the music over the radio, Dean, as always, could not stop thinking.

Why can't you tell her you love her?

I mean, you do *love her, don't you?*

"*I* know why, laddie," Woody whispered, the prick bastard that served as a voice to Dean's subconscious. "The last time you told a lady you loved her, she divorced you."

Dean pulled up his shirt sleeve and glanced at the leprechaun tattoo on his arm, encased in a red circle with a slash that ran through him, something Dean inked into his arm not long after he rescued his son.

"Not now, dipshit," Dean said to Woody. "I'm not in the mood."

"Come on, laddie," Woody replied. "You *know* I'm right."

Dean recalled what his shrink, Dr. Rance, said—the

insurance he had through the Bureau covered the sessions, thank God—every week during their sessions.

"This voice, Woody," Rance said, "is just your subconscious, the voice of bad reasoning in a way. He's always going to run his mouth in your ear every now and again. When he does, just tell him to go away. Repeat that over and over. In time, he'll disappear."

"Oh, *come on,*" Woody hissed. "Don't listen to that head case."

"Go away." Dean clenched a fist. "Just stop."

"No way, my friend." Woody sighed. "You know how this little relationship of ours works. I'm here to help you. I've kept your arse alive more than you give me credit for."

Dean dismissed Woody and focused on the fact that he couldn't tell Layla that he loved her, which he did.

Well, why not just say it then, wonder boy?

This isn't junior high.

You've loved someone before.

All you have to do is say it.

"Because you've *lost* that love before, laddie," Woody suggested. "The moment you say it out loud, it opens up all kinds of bad doors for you."

Not necessarily, you pessimistic turd.

"You know I'm right."

Things are good with Layla.

"You'll probably screw it up."

Stop talking.

"Fine," Woody grumbled. "But if you keep this woman waiting too long, you *will* screw it up."

Noted.

"Have a good night."

You too, fuckwit.

Dean knew that subconscious part of his mind—for

once—was right. He had a good thing going with Layla—a *great* thing when he really took stock of their time together. Woody was right on the money in regard to having loved before, but with Layla, it felt different than it had with Claire. Dean held a special place in his heart for the mother of his child, the woman who helped him get his life back on track. But with Layla, it felt like he had been given a second chance, and saying those three words out loud to her ran the chance of hexing it.

"Not yet," Dean said with a sigh, coating his words. "*Not yet.*"

The cell phone in Dean's pocket buzzed. He fished out the device from his pocket and spotted his sister Sheila's name on the display.

Dear God.

When's the last time the two of us talked?

Dean answered the call and put it on speaker before he placed it in the cupholder beside him. "Hey, She," he greeted. "What's up?"

"Hey, little brother. How's tricks?"

"Oh, you know." Dean glanced at the wound under the arm of his leather jacket. "Same old, same old."

"Still getting into trouble?"

"Always."

Sheila snickered. "I figured."

"So, what's new? How're you holding up?"

"I'm hanging in there."

Silence settled over the line as Dean rummaged through his brain for topics of conversation.

This family only talks about work.

Heart-to-heart chit chats just aren't a part of our rapport.

"Are you working right now?" Dean said, rolling his eyes at his inability to ask about anything else.

"Yeah," his sister replied. "I'm at the office."

"Are you good? You sound a little off."

"I've been better."

Dean tapered his eyes. "Talk to me."

Sheila took a beat. "Something's up," she finally said. "I've got a problem, and I need your help, Deano."

6

Dean could hear the palpable strain in his sister's tone. Sheila—following in the footsteps of their mother—was one of the toughest women he had ever known. She rarely asked for help, and when she did, it meant that something of paramount importance was playing out.

"You've got that same tone," Dean said, "that you did back when you told Pop you totaled your first car."

"It's a bit more high stakes than that," his sister replied. "There's something playing out on my turf right now in San Francisco. It's a real mind-fuck, honestly, but as the SFPD's Robbery-Homicide Lieutenant, I have to act like my composure isn't being shaken."

Dean pulled the Pontiac off to the side of the road near the I-34 Freeway on ramp, put it in park, and settled back in his seat. "What's going on?"

His sister drew a deep breath. "Two murders," she said. "A couple. A man and a woman. Caucasian, early thirties. Signs of a break-in, but nothing was taken. The murder took place in an area of Presidio Heights, so it's an affluent neighborhood with a low crime rate. Needless to say, it's raised a lot of concerns."

"When did this happen?"

"Night before last."

"What do you have in the way of forensics?"

"That's the kicker," Sheila said. "We found no blood other than the victims'. There were no fibers. No fingerprints. My people are doing their third sweep of the place, but so far they've come up with zippo."

"What do your instincts tell you?"

"Knowing what I know by now as a result of my years of experience, I feel what happened is indicative of a bigger situation that's in the throes of playing out. The signs are there. What happened to these people is going to happen again."

Dean narrowed his eyes. "You're sure?"

"These people were *tortured*," his sister said. "The woman was beaten to the point that we almost needed dental records to confirm her ID. The male, we're pretty sure, was forced to watch it happen. And whoever did this is methodical, precise, and calculated with his MO. This wasn't a one-off, and like I said before, I have enough experience on the job that I have confidence in my ability to know the difference between a pattern and an isolated incident."

"You think this is the first in a series?" Dean said. "You think that whoever did this is going to do it again?"

"I do," Sheila replied. "So do a handful of my detectives. They've already coined this guy 'The San Francisco Reaper.' I mean, he'll have to get a few more under his belt before that moniker becomes official, but I can feel it in my bones, Dean. I know that this couple being murdered is just the first of many that might end up playing out."

"You have keen instincts, She," Dean said. "It's always

served you well. That's why you rose up the ranks as quickly as you did."

"I do have a great team of people I've assembled over at Robbery Homicide," she said. "They're solid cops. The only catch is that these guys know how to work a crime scene *after* the incident has played out, and I need someone who can look at the pieces of this thing and try to come up with some answers *before* it happens again."

"This isn't *Minority Report*," Dean snickered. "I can't predict crimes before they happen, She."

"Don't give me that," his sister said. "You and I both know that you have that magic eye. Your uncanny ability to sniff things out and piece together a narrative is a gift."

"You labeled me a freak show once when you described said gift."

"I did?"

"On several occasions."

"Well," Sheila said, "I could benefit from a bit of that freak show at the moment, Deano."

"I don't know." Dean shook his head. "I'm supposed to be on a bit of a sabbatical right now."

"What did you do?" Sheila laughed. "Run over your superior with your car?"

"I wish." Dean thought about the kid—Fitzpatrick—that got shot in the course of the last raid and the men like Sloane who wrote things like that off as nothing more than the cost of doing business.

Assholes.

Bunch of top-shelf motherfu—

"Dean," Sheila said. "There's something else."

"What is it?"

"Whoever did this left a message at the station. Their voice was masked by an app or something. They, uh—"

"Tell me."

"They said, 'Your move, Blackwood.'" The son of a bitch actually used my last name."

Some prick is threatening my family?

Dean tightened his grip on the phone as he stirred up the memory of when his son was held hostage.

Fuck that.

"All right." Dean's grip on the phone slackened, his passion replaced by a level-headed coolness. "How can I help?"

"I was hoping you could come to my neck of the woods," Sheila said. "Forty-eight hours at the most. I want you to look at the case and tell me what you think. The idea here is to get ahead of this thing before it ends up becoming head-line news. I even took the liberty of buying you a plane ticket for the effort. Plus, I don't know, maybe we could catch up."

Dean winced. "Catch up, huh?"

"I can't remember the last time we did."

"Same here."

"So," Sheila said, "will you do it?"

Forty-eight hours.

In and out.

Heck, Sheila is right. When was the last time we connected, just the two of us?

"Just go, you ingrate," Woody said. "You know that you're going to."

Dean took a beat.

Glanced at himself in the rear-view mirror.

Then he said, "I guess I should pack a bag" before he headed back home to break the news to Layla that their vacation would have to be put on hold.

7

"**Y**ou're sure it's okay that I leave?" Dean asked Layla, switching his cell phone to his other ear as he paced the polished floors of the terminal inside LAX.

"Of course it is," Layla replied. "She's your sister, and she needs your help."

"Still, I know you were saying I should lean into this whole time off thing."

"I feel like the circumstances warrant you getting a pass. Besides, we both know you'd just be sitting in the living room twiddling your thumbs until you got a call from Sheila saying they've arrested the guy."

A warm grin stretched from one of Dean's ears to the other. "I don't deserve you."

"Oh, I know."

"Then why do you stick around?"

"You're easy on the eyes. Plus, if things go south with the two of us, I'll throw a hissy fit and demand that Willy goes with me."

"How's he doing, by the way?"

"He's good. You want to talk to him?"

Dean shook his head. "No, every time he hears my voice over the phone he knows I'm not coming back for a while. Thank you for looking after him, by the way."

"It's my pleasure," Layla said. "The two of us will hold down the fort until you get back. I hope you don't mind if I raid the fridge."

"Go nuts."

"Talk soon?"

"Without question."

The two bid their goodbyes before Dean terminated the call. His gaze drifted toward the departure gate. The stewardess behind the counter announced over the loudspeaker that the flight was a couple minutes away from boarding. Dean, wanting to make one last call, pulled up his ex-wife's number, hit the dial, and held the phone to his ear.

"Hey," Claire greeted. "How are you?"

"I'm all right," Dean said. "I'm just about to hop on a plane."

"Are you gone for long?"

"Just a couple of days. I'm headed to San Francisco with Sheila to help her out with something."

"When was the last time you two saw each other?"

"Few years," Dean said. "But the two of us haven't had a one on one in a long time."

"I can't remember the last time the two of you spent more than 10 minutes in a room with one another."

"Me either." Dean adjusted the duffel bag slung over his shoulder. "Listen, I just wanted to check in real quick on Jeremy. Is he there?"

"No, he just stepped out. Geoff's taking him to counseling."

"How's it going?"

"I don't know." Claire sighed. "Jeremy's been a little distant lately. He hasn't talked much. The therapist said it could take some time, but she's confident that he'll start making progress soon."

"It's your fault, laddie," Woody said. "You're the one who—"

Don't.

"But you—"

Get. Bent.

Dean dismissed the intrusive thoughts in his head as he turned his focus back on Claire. "Is he sleeping all right?" he said. "Eating? It's been a couple of days since I talked to him. Even then, he didn't say much."

"He's had a hard time sleeping," Claire said. "It's the same with eating. It's also his disposition. He won't play with his friends, and he says all of two words to me and Geoff at any given time—same when he talks to you over the phone. Most days he just likes to play in his room by himself."

"He's only eight though. Shouldn't that be the case for kids his age?"

"No, not really. At least not as often as Jeremy does it."

Dean closed his eyes, the regret and anguish that plagued him over Jeremy's state of mind gnawing at him like a terrier had locked onto his pant leg and wouldn't let go. "As soon as I'm back," he said, "I'd like to spend some more time with him."

Claire took a beat. "Maybe," she finally said. "Let me think about it?"

That's something.

That's progress!

"Of course," Dean said. "You doing all right otherwise?"

"Yeah, I'm fine."

"You're sure?"

"I'm sure."

"Okay." Dean shrugged. "I, uh, I guess I'll talk to you when I'm back."

"Sounds good."

"Take care."

"You too."

Dean ended the call and stuffed the phone in his pocket. He rubbed the back of his neck, feeling like his life the past year was an endless game of whack-a-mole.

"Your life is a *bitch*, ain't it?" Woody said. "What's that saying? The one you always say?"

"Completely fucktangular," Dean replied, "on all sides."

"Right." Woody laughed. "*That's* the one."

The intercom in the terminal came to life. The stewardess stated that the pre-flight boarding had begun. Dean scooped up his bag, headed toward the gate, scanned the ticket on his smartphone, and padded his way through the jetway. Once he boarded, placed his bag in the overhead compartment, and took his seat, he gazed out the window and reminded himself that he'd be back in LA in the blink of an eye.

"It's never that easy," Woody said. "You *know* it never is."

"Yeah," Dean whispered to himself. "I kind of had a feeling."

8

T he moment Dean stepped out of the Uber outside his hotel on Mason Street, he counted that it had been ten years since his last visit to San Francisco. His nostrils flared as he picked up on the traces of saltwater air, closing his eyes as he recalled the memory when he and his late brother once rode a trolley just like the one cruising down the street.

One of the last vacations the family ever took.

And Dad was a top-shelf prick the entire time.

Dean thanked the Uber driver for the ride, tipped him, snagged his bag, and fixed his sights on the two-story, sixty-two-room hotel known as the San Remo. The hotel resided in a historic part of town, the Italian Victorian-style building and the ones that surrounded it making Dean feel like he had stepped out of a time machine and arrived somewhere in the 1930s. Once he checked in and received his key, the woman at the front desk—a descendent of one of the original owners—informed Dean that Fisherman's Wharf, the sea lion viewing area, and the piers were just a stone's throw away. Then she bade Dean a wonderful stay.

Dean headed to the second floor.

Pinpointed his room at the end of the hall.

Unfastened the locks and stepped inside.

The room was European-style, nothing modern in it save for the plasma television and the card on the night-stand that offered the instructions to log onto the Wi-Fi. Dean placed his bag down and made his way to the double doors that led out onto the balcony, stepped out, and took in the Golden Gate Bridge a few miles off in the distance. He breathed in the crisp, refreshing air, the wind kissing his face as it dried the thin layer of travel-triggered perspiration on his brow.

Not bad, Deano.

There's worse places to spend 48 hours of your time.

Dean headed back inside and then sent a text to Sheila, informing her that he was in town and ready to head over to her precinct. His sister quickly replied that she needed an hour to get settled, that she had to let the proper higher-ups know that he was going to take a look at the crime scene.

"Once I mention FBI to them," she said, "it shouldn't take too long."

Sheila followed it up by saying she was sending a PDF file to Dean's cell, a brief rundown of the case that she wanted him to look through before the two of them linked up. Dean opened the link his sister sent to his email and scrolled through the file, his eyes blinking like the shutter of the camera that triggered each and every word on the PDF to be logged away in his memory.

Peter Landsman and Ellie Walsh, Dean thought as his eyes perused the PDF.

Peter was an ER doctor.

Ellie was a nurse at a convalescent home.

Both were tortured before the killer stabbed them to death with a serrated blade and fled the scene.

No witnesses.

And the doorbell camera failed to catch anything at the front door.

Dean clicked out of the PDF file.

I need to get in that house.

I need to see those bodies.

Something will stick out to me that no one in the local PD has picked up yet.

Dean felt a tug in his stomach, that proverbial churn of his body signaling that the time had come to eat. He grabbed his wallet, slipped on his leather jacket, and then decided to go on a walkabout until he found something that piqued his interest. He walked for ten square blocks until he arrived on the outskirts of Chinatown, wondering why so many people had talked ill of San Francisco and the rampant crime that apparently plagued it.

Looks fine to me, Dean thought as he navigated a cramped street adorned with Chinese signs, lanterns, and other decor. *It doesn't look that bad at all.*

A deep, guttural grunt bellowed from the alleyway on Dean's right.

He angled his body toward it, the primal part of his brain switching on as he saw two brutes kicking a man across the slickened cobblestones of the pavement. The two men pummeled their victim with their fists, feet, and elbows, taunting him to get up as the man rolled around in agony.

"Wonderful," Dean whispered as he flexed the fingers on his hand and prepared to intercede.

9

"Get up, man!" the taller of the two men beating the third man said, his hair slicked back, a thin scar running down his left check.

The man on the ground cowered into the fetal position, pawing fruitlessly at his attackers as their assault drew blood from lacerations on his face and arms.

"Did you hear us?" the second attacker said, sucking air through his lips as he combed at the ragged beard on his face with his fingers. "Shit, why doesn't this guy talk?"

"He's Chinese," the tall one said as he delivered a kick to the victim's gut. "These guys only talk that *bing-bong* talk."

The two men cackled like hyenas as they continued their assault, the tall one raising his fist and drawing it back for a blow to the victim's cheek.

"*Yo*," Dean shouted out from the end of the alleyway, his hands stuffed into his pockets and his lips curled up into a sneer. "What's going on?"

The two attackers ceased their beating and stood back, the man on the ground backing up toward a dumpster and then gripping onto it for dear life. The tall man and the bearded man spread apart, their chests puffed and their focus fixed solely on Dean.

"All right," Dean said as he calmly approached the two men. "What the hell is this?"

The bearded attacker spit on the ground. "It's called none of your fucking business, shitstick."

His partner, tracing his fingers through his greased-up hair, flashed a crooked smile. "Now we got a two-for-one," he said. "Daily double, man." He crooked a finger. "Empty your pockets before you end up busted up like the Chinaman."

Dean shot a look at the curled-up man by the dumpster, anger swelling inside of him as he asked, "You okay?"

The fallen man shook his head, trembling as he inched away from his attackers and mumbled something under his breath.

"Empty your pockets, man," the tall one said to Dean. "I'm not going to ask you again."

Dean puttered his lips.

Slipped off his jacket.

Folded it once over and placed it on top of the lid of the dumpster

"Tell you what." Dean patted his jacket. "There's about 500 bucks in there. If you can take my jacket, you can have it."

The bearded man winced. "You shitting me?"

"Are you deaf or stupid?" Dean motioned to his jacket. "I said, if you can take my jacket, you can have the money. You just have to waltz your dumpy ass over here and pick it up."

The bearded man squinted.

His partner followed suit.

Both waited for the other to give the green light.

"Good *God*," Dean groaned. "Are you two married or

something? Come on, make a move, you breeze-brained dipshits. I'm trying to get a bite to eat here soon."

The tall one cracked his knuckles and moved in a slow stride toward Dean. "Okay, man," he said. "Let's do this."

Dean said nothing as the tall one made a beeline toward him, straightened his shoulders, curled his fingers into a fist, and shot it toward Dean's chin. Dean caught the incoming fist with one hand and squeezed, his bicep muscle flexing as he raised his foot back and then swung it upward into the tall man's groin. The tall man grunted, the whites of his eyes flashing as his legs folded and forced him to his knees. He spit out a gurgle, looking up at Dean as Dean flexed the digits on his left hand, made a fist, and then struck a downward blow across the tall man's cheek that knocked him to the ground and nearly put him to sleep.

The bearded man snarled, watching his cohort wriggle around on the ground as he pawed at his crotch.

"Well," Dean said as he stepped over the tall man and moved with slow, rhythmic steps toward the bearded man. "What now, playboy?"

Two options were weighed by the bearded man: stand his ground or flee. Splaying his feet, he opted for the former as he shot the cuffs off his long-sleeve shirt and jutted his chin at Dean.

"Let's do this."

"Oh, for the love of fuck's sake." Dean rolled his eyes as he watched his bearded foe throw his weight around like a boxer entering the ring. "Whatever."

The bearded man threw a right hook.

Dean ducked and dipped under it.

Then he spun around, cocked back his right elbow, and brought it down into the back of his opponent's neck. The bearded man howled, the hue of his skin changing to a shade of red as he angled his body toward Dean and took two steps back to maintain his distance.

Not bad.

Dean pouted his lower lip.

He's got a few street brawls under his belt.

Dean's bearded opponent spit on the ground, shooting his cuffs once again before he brought his arms up into a defensive position that shielded his face.

"*Really*?" Dean said. "Does the shooting the cuffs thing really help?"

The bearded man stepped in.

Dean took a step back.

Then the two men circled.

"Come on," Dean grumbled. "*Do it.*"

The bearded man threw a jab toward Dean's face, then a left hook followed by another jab. Dean blocked the first blow along with the second, but the third jab clipped his chin and nearly took him off his feet.

The bearded man flared a grin, a surge of ego swelling inside of him as he cocked back his right arm, appraised Dean's left cheek, and attempted to land a haymaker.

Dean drew up his left elbow and blocked the punch. Then he wrapped his left arm around the bearded man's right arm, cupped his right hand, and thrust it into his opponent's throat.

A wheeze dribbled through the bearded man's lips, his brain trying to process the blow as Dean planted his fist into his gut and keeled him over.

Dean grabbed a fistful of his opponent's hair and wrenched back his head.

Then he drew up his knee, struck the son of a bitch in his face, and split the bones in his nose.

Dean stepped back and did an assessment of the damage.

The pair of men he took down groaned and crawled away in retreat.

Dean then put his focus on the victim, spotted the man's wallet lying on the curb, picked it up, and handed it over.

"Split," Dean said. "And get those cuts looked at."

The man nodded.

He thanked Dean.

Then he hightailed it out of the alley, kicking one of the two men that assaulted him on his way out, and disappeared from sight.

Dean slipped his hands in his pockets.

He took one last look at his fallen foes clawing their way out of the alley.

Then he nodded his head, headed toward the street, and whistled the theme song to the show *Happy Days*.

10

Dean, a visitor's badge clipped to his shirt, stepped into the police precinct. He saw several desks corraled together in the center of the room, detectives huddled around them with cell phones held to their ears as they sifted through piles of paper. To the right of the detectives were a series of windows that overlooked the Bay Area, giving a stirring view of the Golden Gate Bridge 6 miles off in the distance.

Dean turned to his left and noted the open-area break room. Several plainclothes detectives and two uniformed officers rifled through the fridge. A pair of coffee pots churned up a fragrant aroma that filled the air around the station. Past the break area was a conference room. Beyond the detectives' bullpen were a pair of offices, and Dean's lips bowed into a grin when he spotted the name Lt. Sheila Blackwood stenciled in black ink on the glass above the door handle.

Dean threaded his way through the bullpen toward Sheila's office.

He rapped his knuckles on the door.

A quick beat later, his sister opened it and stepped out, a warm smile brimming from one ear to the other.

"Lieutenant," Dean said as his tone ticked down to a more authoritative octave. "I hope I'm not interrupting anything."

"Special Agent Blackwood." Sheila saluted with two fingers. "I'm pretty busy at the moment, so if you could just wait in the lobby, I'll get to you in a few hours."

They laughed.

They hugged.

Both of them realized it had been years since their last physical display of affection.

"Not bad," Dean said as he broke the embrace and shot a look over his shoulder to the Robbery Homicide Division. "Kind of reminds me of Dirty Harry's office."

"The place was a little derelict when I got assigned here," Sheila replied. "I managed to sweet-talk the department into giving the place a facelift. The whole place had a kind of sanitarium motif before."

"I like it."

"Thank you." His sister playfully nudged him in the shoulder. "I see that you still like dressing like a lumberjack."

"You look good too." Dean took in his sister, a spitting image of their mother made up of the same auburn, shoulder-length hair and sparkling blue eyes that could bore a hole through steel. "Very svelte."

"Svelte, huh?"

"No good?"

"You hear that term applied more to men than to women."

"Well, you *did* inherit Pop's paws there." Dean shot his chin toward Sheila's hands. "Could've fooled me."

"Okay, jackass." Sheila gestured for her brother to enter her office. "Come on in."

Dean moved inside and grabbed a seat in front of the desk.

"So." Sheila closed the door and slipped down in the chair across from him. "How's Pop?"

"The same." Dean tapped his chest. "After that crap a few months back, his heart's been a bit glitchy."

His sister nodded knowingly. "I talked to him a few days ago." She shook her head. "I still can't believe he was working with those SMASH assholes." She threw up her hands. "Who would've thought?"

"It definitely was a blitz." Dean's gaze drifted toward the window that looked out toward the city. "The only comfort I had was that they forced him to launder their ill-gotten gains out of duress. Still, Pop's lucky charges weren't filed."

"Why weren't they?"

Dean tapped the FBI shield clipped to his belt.

"I'm sorry, Dean," Sheila said. "For everything that happened, I mean."

"Is what it is. All we can do is move forward."

"What about Claire? How'd she take everything that happened?"

"Not well." Dean huffed. "I almost got our kid killed."

"What about Jeremy?" Sheila's lips twitched into a smirk. "How's he holding up?"

"As well as you would expect him to."

"I should call him."

"He'd like that."

"Then I will." Sheila sat back in her chair. "Thank you for doing this, by the way." The timbre of her voice became less playful and more systematic. "I know we've never seen each other that much, so it means a lot to me that you're taking the time to do this."

"Family is family, regardless of time or distance." Dean held up a finger. "That sentiment doesn't apply to Uncle Joey though. I won't even give that guy my Netflix password."

"The feeling is mutual." Sheila settled back in her chair. "Well, getting down to brass tacks, where do you want to start? I've got a few case files we can sift through."

"I'll want to see it all," Dean told her. "I'd want to start at the crime scene."

"We can roll by there now, if you want."

"We can?"

"I'm in charge around here." Sheila curled her lips up mischievously. "Perks come with the job."

11

Six minutes of drive time later, Dean and Sheila arrived in the affluent Presidio Heights area. The neighborhood rested flush against a hillside, ground zero to a series of manicured, Tudor-style homes flanked with palm trees, the bay, and the towering Golden Gate Bridge in clear view off to Dean's left.

Dean was halfway out of Sheila's navy blue sedan as she brought it to a stop in front of a cream-colored, two-story Tudor home. Dean saw the red tape strip that had been secured over the door. The yellow "DO NOT CROSS" tape stretched across the fence that opened up into the front walkway. A breeze nipped at the back of his neck as he approached the home, the hairs bristling as the sensation struck him that all eyes on the block were watching.

"You hear that?" Dean said.

Sheila shrugged. "Hear what?"

"No noise." Dean did a scan of the neighborhood. "People pay for peace and quiet in a place like this, but there's a morbid stillness about it."

"That's weird to you? You've walked your fair share of crime scenes by this point in your life."

"I just never got used to it," Dean said. "It always makes me feel like I have to take a hot shower afterward to scrub off the residue."

The lines on Sheila's forehead slackened into a glower. "This place doesn't have a high crime rate. The fact that a pair of murders went down here has put people on edge. This is one of a handful of places in San Fran that's untainted, for lack of a better way of putting it. It's a well-known fact that the city has its problems right now. It's hard to go anywhere in certain areas without getting mugged."

The recently cemented memory of the two men Dean took down in the alley flashed in his mind. "Tell me about it," he said as Sheila guided him toward the house.

Dean took mental pictures of the residence. The homes that flanked either side of it were so close that all you had to do was open a window and reach out and touch the neighboring house.

Someone had to have seen something.

These homes are too close together.

Sheila opened the front gate.

The two of them climbed up on the porch.

Then Sheila dug out a pair of house keys from her pocket, unfastened the locks, and swung the door open, the hinges creaking as Dean walked inside and winced at the lingering scent of copper that clung to the air.

"Okay," Sheila said, her tone sounding like a Realtor showing a client a potential buy. "Follow me."

Dean tailed her to the left into a living room, a spacious area with a couch, love seat, recliner, big-screen television, and an outline on the floor where an oriental rug had once been. The edges where the rug had been were caked with a thin layer of blood, the remnants of it in the throes of changing to a shade of black. On Dean's right was a hallway that spilled into the kitchen and the back bedrooms. Streaks of blood smeared along the polished wooden floorboards that trailed from the master bedroom and into the living room.

"Both of our vics were found here," Sheila said as she pointed to the area where the rug had been. "Peter Landsman and Ellie Walsh."

Dean stooped down by the outline of the rug, cocking his head to the side as he drew a deep breath. "Talk to me."

"Landsman was stabbed twice in his sternum," his sister said, "once in his trachea, and a final laceration across his windpipe. That's what killed him. Walsh was severely beaten across her face and torso. She also received two stab wounds to her sternum, one in her trachea, and four in her back. She bled to death. She wasn't killed as quickly as Landsman was. Both of them also had markings on their legs and wrists. The bruising and swelling the medical examiner found indicates that their arms and legs were bound."

Dean nodded along.

The woman suffered more than the man did.

The killer wanted her *to suffer the most.*

"How'd this guy get in?" Dean said. "What was his point of entry?"

His sister gestured toward the kitchen area. "There are two points of access into the house—the front door in here and the side door in the kitchen. The only witness who gave us anything of value was the next-door neighbor in the house on the right. She said that Landsman took out the trash to the bins at the side of the house around 10:00 p.m.

Landsman waved to the neighbor, she waved back, and that was the last time she ever saw him."

"When was the time of death established?"

"Between midnight and 2:00 a.m."

"Who found the bodies?"

"An employee at the convalescent home Walsh works in," Sheila said. "When Walsh failed to show up after 3 hours, someone sent this employee to knock on their door around 11:00 a.m. When no one answered, she walked around the outside of the house and spotted the bodies in the living room through the window. Then she called 911, a patrol unit arrived, and then my department was called in."

"Okay." Dean stood and motioned to the blood trail in the hallway. "That smear there looks like they were killed in another room."

Sheila nodded. "In the master bedroom. The blood we found there indicates that they were assaulted in there and then dragged into the living room."

"How do you think it went down?"

"From what my detectives gathered, it sounds like our guy entered through the side door, slunk into the bedroom, and then assaulted Walsh and Landsman in their sleep. There was no sign of forced entry. The lock on the side door had been picked."

Dean furrowed his brow. "The lock was picked?"

His sister led him into the kitchen. Both of them stepped around the blood trail that snaked from the living room to the master bedroom door.

The two of them entered the kitchen.

Sheila peeled open the side door and motioned to the locks.

Dean made out the faint scratches around the lock and

logged the visual away to memory. "Yeah," he said. "Son of a bitch picked it."

Sheila made her way into the master bedroom across from the kitchen.

She nudged open the door.

Sheila stood aside so Dean could see the residual blood splotches on the bed frame and the pool of dried blood on the mattress.

"All right, wonder boy," Sheila said. "Tell me what you think."

"I'm not the murder police, She," Dean replied. "I'm an undercover flunkie—a door kicker."

"You took courses at Quantico for stuff like this." Sheila nudged her brother. "You know more than you think you do."

Supportive as always.

Even if you gave me a swirly once when we were kids.

Dean mulled it over. "He enters the room in the dead of night," he said. "Walsh and Landsman were asleep." He furrowed his brow when a thought popped into his brain. "The stab wounds on their sternum—if our suspect incapacitated them, they wouldn't have been able to move or speak."

His sister nodded approval. "That's *exactly* what he did. Both victims were stabbed in their trachea with what the medical examiner deduced as a 6–9 inch serrated blade. The killer entered the bedroom, stabbed them both quickly in the throat, and then proceeded to stab them several more times before he zip-tied their hands and legs. By that point, they were in the throes of bleeding out as our killer then dragged them into the living room one at a time. The bodies were found facing one another on the floor, both of them spaced about 2 feet apart."

"They couldn't move." Dean winced as he pictured the crime in his mind. "They were beaten and bleeding to death. Walsh took the brunt of it, so she was the primary target. The killer was really taking his hate out on her."

Doesn't matter how many times I've done this.

Dean narrowed his eyes.

It never gets any easier.

"I have officers questioning everyone on the block," Sheila said. "We're pulling all the footage from every available door camera to see if there were maintenance workers, delivery guys, cars that repeatedly drove by, or anyone else who stood out in the days or months leading up to the crime. It's going to take some time." She pointed to the front door. "The only doorbell camera that Landsman and Walsh had was in front, but it didn't register anything, so that confirms that our killer made entry through here. Walsh and Landsman also didn't have any alarms, so nothing went off when the killer made entry."

Dean shook his head.

They should have put a camera on the side door.

We would have at least gotten a glimpse of this guy.

Woulda-coulda-shoulda.

"Well," Dean said, "our guy definitely cased the house beforehand; he knew they had one camera and no alarms. He hand-selected Walsh and Landsman because they were easy prey. The guy took his time picking them too. Are you rounding up known prowlers, B&E suspects, people of that nature?"

"As we speak," Sheila replied. "So far, everyone checks out. No one on the list of usual suspects so far could have done this."

Dean moved out of the bedroom. It didn't matter how long he'd been with the Bureau, how much training he had, or the number of corpses he was forced to come face to face with in his lifetime. He knew how to compartmentalize, but he was still human at the end of the day. The loss of innocent life always instilled him with an anger so palpable that he felt like he could sell it by the pound.

"I want to see the bodies," Dean said. "And I want to know all about Peter and Ellie. I want to know *everything*."

12

"Landsman was thirty-two," Sheila said as she and Dean pinned their eyes to the corpses on the cold metal slab in the medical examiner's office, "and Walsh was twenty-nine. They bought their home where the murders took place about eight months back. Landsman actually proposed three months prior to the murders. The friends and family I've interviewed so far spoke highly of both of them as well as the relationship. 'A match made in heaven' were the exact words that Walsh's father relayed to me."

Dean circled the bodies, both of them pale and streaked with shades of cobalt. "Have you managed to pull anything off the bodies?"

"Traces of talcum powder."

"So our guy used gloves when he committed the crime. What about the crime scene? Did you guys find anything?"

"Like I told you before," Sheila said, "it looks like our boy wiped things clean other than the blood—assuming he *is* a man, that is."

"He is."

"You're sure?"

"You're saying you're not, *Lieutenant*?"

"No, I am." Sheila rattled off a chuckle. "Just wanted to hear a member of the FBI confirm it for me. And to answer your previous question, I'm gonna have the techs do another sweep to see if they missed anything."

"What about Landsman and Walsh's friends?" Dean said. "Their acquaintances? Anything noteworthy?"

"Landsman and Walsh had a small group of people they were close with," Sheila said. "Both of them had busy schedules, so it was hard for them to find time to socialize. From what I've gathered so far, they spent two weeks out of the year traveling between June and July—Hawaii, Mexico, camping trips to Yosemite, places like that."

"You said Landsman worked at an ER."

"That's right."

"Get your people to talk to anyone over there that knew of any patients that Landsman had interactions with that stood out," Dean said. "The guy who killed him and his fiancée isn't some run of the mill whack job."

Sheila huffed. "I thought the FBI refrained from using that type of lingo."

"They do," Dean said, "but I don't. Listen," he crossed his arms, "the unsub here is not some off the wall crazed person who kills on a whim. He's thorough. Meticulous. Still, maybe Landsman treated him at some point. Maybe that's how our killer targeted him."

"My people are also questioning everyone at the convalescent home Ellie worked at too," his sister said. "Employees, patients, people that deliver equipment—anyone who walked in or out of that place is in the throes of being questioned."

Dean did an appraisal of Ellie Walsh's body. Her flaxen

hair was matted, her mouth agape, the rest of her face mangled to the point that she looked nothing like the photo Sheila had provided earlier.

Unnecessary.

Dean shook his head.

Excessive.

He shifted his gaze to Peter Landsman's body, the young man's chestnut hair matted like Ellie's and his eyes partially rolled back into his head.

Things like this should never happen.

But they do.

Man, the world can be a giant bummer.

"Landsman and Walsh's friends you mentioned," Dean said. "The ones that you interviewed. Does anyone in that group stand out to you?"

"No, not really." Sheila replied. "They're all upstanding citizens. Every single one of them. They're liberal types with medical or law degrees, and every one of them has alibis for the night of the murder. This wasn't personal, Dean. Whoever did this didn't know them—we just have to prove that."

"I'm inclined to think you're right." Dean sighed. "And I'm also inclined to agree with another statement you made not that long ago."

"Which one?"

Dean took one last look at the bodies. "This is going to happen again," he said. "And whoever is doing this has already picked out his next set of victims."

13

Bay Area mist peppered Dean's face as he stood on the balcony outside his hotel room. He shuffled through a series of images in his mind, memories that flickered one after another like he was seeing them through one of those View Master toys he had when he was a kid.

Dean recalled the blood from the crime scene and Peter Landsman and Ellie Walsh's bodies.

Then he thought back to the litany of corpses he'd seen before.

His brother's.

The friends he lost during his time as a Ranger.

The people he was forced to shoot at, the ones that shot at him.

There was no shortage of memories for Dean, and the luminance of the eternal flame of his recollections never diminished, no matter how much time had passed. The collection just seemed to grow.

"That's your gift, laddie," Woody said. "*And* it's your

curse. You can remember it all—you can remember *everything.*"

"Yeah," Dean replied. "That I can."

"Doesn't it get to you?"

"Stop."

"I'm just saying that—"

Dean, implementing a move Dr. Rance taught him to drown Woody out, fished out his phone and opened a streaming music app.

He pulled up a list he had curated with Layla a few weeks prior.

Pressed play.

Slipped a toothpick into his mouth.

Then he nodded approval as "Hot Fun in the Summertime" by Sly and the Family Stone percolated through the phone's speakers.

Dean grinned warmly as he thought back to last time he played the song, a memory just as vibrant as all the others stored in the vault in his mind he had dubbed his "Home Movie Collection."

He remembered Layla.

His arms around her waist.

Her hands coiled his neck as they swayed to the beat of the same song, and his dog Willy gawking at them in the corner with an annoyed set of eyes.

Hit her up, Deano.

See what the better half is doing.

Dean opened the text message app on his phone. Pulled up Layla's number. Texted her: *How's it going?* and waited for a reply.

Layla texted back a moment later, Dean snickering in amusement as he laid his eyes on a photo that Layla sent of her hugging Willy on his couch.

Just hanging out. Layla's text read. *You?*

Same. Dean texted back. *Need to get out of here soon.*

That bad?

A little bit.

What are you doing now?

Listening to that song.

Layla sent back the "heart" emoji.

Dean replied in kind.

Missing you, she said.

Missing you, he replied.

Dean stared at the phone, Woody pressuring him to say the three words that he knew Layla wanted to hear—but he couldn't bring himself to do it.

Dean's fingers hovered over the "I" key.

He tried to rally the courage to write the next two words.

Instead, he pocketed the phone, shook his head, and called himself an "idiot."

The end of the song played out, Dean's phone then ringing and his eyes catching Sheila's name on the display. "Howdy," he answered.

"Howdy back," his sister said. "Ready to get back to work?"

Dean headed back into his room, reached for his jacket, and then replied, "I'm on my way."

14

Dean's gaze was fastened to the view of the ocean outside the Beach Chalet Brewery and Restaurant, the tides elucidated by the gleam of the moonlight, the waters churning with a serene and pleasing quality as they teased the edge of the shore.

"I gotta hand it to you, She," Dean said to his sister. "I'm starting to understand why you moved here."

Sheila, seated across from her brother, nodded her head. "It has its moments—if you exclude something like that crime scene I made you walk through."

Dean reached over toward his leather jacket that rested on the seat beside him, pulled out a series of folded papers stuffed inside of it, placed them on the table, and slid them over.

"What's this?" his sister said.

"My initial assessment," Dean told her. "My tentative thoughts on what we saw and what I think it means."

Sheila picked up the papers and sifted through them. "When did you have time to do this?"

"Not long after you dropped me off at the hotel."

"That was fast. It used to take you two weeks to finish your homework back when you were a kid."

"Just keep in mind that my assessment is just one man's opinion," Dean said. "I'm sure your detectives are more seasoned at this type of work than I am, so don't put too much stock in what I have to say. I've done undercover work most of my career. It's a different field entirely."

"Oh, *please.*" Sheila brushed off the comment with a swipe of her hand. "You took all those nifty little courses at Quantico—behavioral science, reading body language, all that fun stuff."

"Still, if you need another Bureau goon to help you out, I can recommend a few people. They actually assisted in helping foster some of the skill sets that I have. They're real pros, the cream of the crop."

"I want *your* initial assessment," Sheila said as she placed down the papers. "Tell me who you think did this."

"Off the top of my head," Dean shrugged, "he's a white male. Early to late thirties. He's in pretty solid physical shape. He's got former military or possibly police training, based on the way he stabbed and bound your victims."

"You're sure?"

"Yep." Dean nodded. "The way he stabbed and tied them up was the way *I* would do it if I were him." Saying the words out loud triggered a shudder to snake up his spine. "You'll want to look into places that sell the kind of gear your medical examiner deduced as being the kind that was used during the murders. He picked this stuff up somewhere."

"What's the MO?" Sheila said. "Why is he doing this?"

Dean narrowed his eyes and then put them back on the waves outside of the window. "He targeted a couple, so that might indicate that our killer has a kind of pent-up aggression toward people in a relationship, *women* specifically, hence why Ellie Walsh was forced to watch Peter Landsman expire. It's possible that your unsub has been unable to maintain healthy relationships, and because of that he's developed this, well, *urge* to violently 'dispatch' the people he's stalked."

"And you're sure that he's white?"

"Statistically speaking, it lines up with the profile, based on the kind of crimes that have happened before. And there was no sexual assault, no signs of anything along those lines, so I have a feeling it's the optics that this guy's obsessed with." Dean flexed his brow. "He *loathes* seeing happy couples. It drives him mad. It's possible that your guy was in a relationship that turned sour. I have a sense based on what I've seen that he might have even been married before."

"You know, you say all of this stuff in pretty plain speak for an FBI agent," Sheila said. "Usually agents tend to drop ten-dollar words every chance they get when they talk about this stuff."

"They do," Dean replied, "but I don't. I'm not that guy." He winked. "I'm just a blue-collar dude from LA who's good at kicking down doors."

"It gets results."

"That it does."

"So," Sheila said, "I should look at cases in the state or others where a woman was murdered and the spouse or ex was a person of interest. It's possible that there was a case where a guy got off or couldn't be convicted due to a lack of evidence."

"It wouldn't hurt," Dean replied. "I can make some calls to help you expedite that. Some of my colleagues at the Bureau can help you pull those files. Again, you'll want to confer with agents who do this every day—the *professional* profilers. My opinion will only go so far."

"What about the fact that it was a wealthy neighborhood? Does that have anything to do with it?"

"It might reflect this vehemence your suspect has toward a lifestyle he either had and lost or wants to have and cannot achieve," Dean said. "Again, it's about the optics here. This guy wants to tear down and obliterate the life of a happy couple, and his fixation, his *thrill*, is to make sure the woman watches that play out before she dies."

"What about the part where he mentioned my name?"

"You said he called the station and left a message."

"He did," Sheila said. "We couldn't trace the call; it was an unknown number. He just phoned into the station at Detective Leary's desk and left a voicemail. All he said was, 'Your move, Blackwood.'"

Dean took a beat to think. "He could have looked you up easily," he finally said. "It's disconcerting, yeah, but these dipshits like to get off toying with the police. If anything, I'd take it as a good thing."

"How do you figure?"

"It's a lot like the BTK killer," Dean explained. "One of Dennis Rader's biggest thrills was fucking with the cops. He *wanted* them to chase him. The same applies here. Whoever is doing this wants to make a game out of it. He'll probably call again. That being the case, that means your odds at catching him will increase. Sooner or later, he'll slip up. The more he reaches out to your department, the better the odds are of you pinpointing who he is and where he is."

A deep exhale trickled out of Sheila's mouth, her focus on the tides outside the window. "This is going to get worse before it gets better," she said. "I just know it."

"You've got this one, She," Dean said. "That's why you

were promoted to your position. If anyone can figure this thing out and take this guy down, it's you."

"You sound like Dad."

"*Yikes.*"

"I meant that in a good way. Pop has his moments. Same as you." Sheila smirked. "I suppose we all do. It's the Blackwood method of living."

"You really did inherit Mom's ability to dish out cheesy sentiments in any given situation, didn't you?"

"What was that one thing she used to say to you and Tommy?" Sheila's eyes glossed over with remembrance. "She said it all of the time when you guys started going at it with each other."

"'Don't measure, boys,'" Dean said, "or you'll always come up short.' She said that whenever Tommy and I got into pissing contests with one another. Not *literal* pissing contests, that is, but I think you know what I mean."

Sheila nodded along. "She had things she used to say to everyone. We all had our own little unique 'Mom phrase' that she would tell us whenever we were all worked up or having a hard time. Dad's was, 'Breathe and think.' Mine was, 'Ask yourself if you think it's worth it.'"

"They weren't that clever, were they?"

"They didn't need to be. They worked, and that was the point." Tears glazed Sheila's eyes as she thought of her mother. "How long has it been since she passed away?"

"Nineteen years," Dean said, "eight months, five weeks, six days, four hours, nineteen minutes, and fifty-two seconds."

Sheila whistled. "How the hell do you do that?"

"It's not a skill I learned; it just sort of happened."

"And to think if you had just applied that to a more nefarious way of living, you could have," Sheila thought about it, "I don't know, turned into an arch criminal or something."

"There were times I came close to it." Dean averted his gaze. "Believe me."

His sister leaned in close. "What's it like?"

"What's what like?"

"Being able to remember everything that ever happened in your life? It must drive you crazy."

"Sometimes, yeah." Dean huffed. "I think about it every day. It's just a matter of keeping it in check and making sure to stay away from certain vices I used to use as a coping mechanism."

"How long has it been since you had a drink?"

"Nine years, four months, twelve days, six hours, two minutes, and thirty-one seconds."

"Congrats."

"Thank you kindly."

"So," Sheila said as she appraised her brother's face, "how are you doing otherwise?"

"I'm hungry." Dean searched for signs of their server. "I saw a guy chowing down on a burger over at that table that looked intriguing."

His sister rolled her eyes. "No, I mean in general. We haven't really connected in a while. The last time I saw you," Sheila held her hand to her waist, "Jeremy was yay high."

"Last time we were together was 2017."

"That long?"

"Yeah." Dean nodded. "That long."

"Well," Sheila's expression was a study of revelation, "how *are* you doing?"

"Good enough, I suppose."

"Claire's still keeping you at arm's length?"

"Unfortunately."

"Well, I know I said it before, but," Sheila's lips shifted downward into a frown, "I'm sorry about what happened. I can't imagine how tough that is, not seeing Jeremy as much, I mean."

"It's my fault."

"How so?"

"I let my anger get the better of me," Dean said. "I did what I do best. I charged head first into a situation that nearly got my kid killed because of it."

"But he's alive," Sheila replied. "Dad is safe. I know all of that came at a cost, but it could have gone a lot worse than it did."

"I suppose."

"What about work?"

"It sucks."

"Why don't you quit?"

Thirty months.

1,095 days.

"It's a long story," Dean said, "but I'm working on," he thought of a way to phrase it, "a kind of contract basis with the Bureau. After what happened in LA on that SMASH case a few months back, I cut a deal with the higher-ups to do some door kicking for a few years. That's a big reason Pop and I were able to evade having any charges leveled against us after what happened."

"Good God, Dean." Sheila sat back. "What the hell did you do?"

Dean gave his sister a brief rundown of the time he took down a corrupt facet of the LAPD, the Armenian mobsters they were working with, and the shootout at the Long Beach docks that had signaled an end to the ordeal.

"I kind of went a little nuts on that one," Dean said.

"Cutting the deal I did with the FBI was the only way to sweep it all under the rug."

"And now they've got you playing *Starsky and Hutch* out there in the streets," Sheila replied. "After your stint in undercover, you made it a point to steer as clear as you could from that kind of action."

"I did—for a while, at least." The angst triggered by his deal with the FBI and his fragmented relationship with his son prompted Dean to grind his teeth. "I was a different guy back in those days, She. I didn't give a damn about what happened to me. I lost a wife and a life because of it."

"I remember you back then." Sheila tugged a strand of her hair behind her ear. "You had that whole grunge rock vibe. Half the time you were sleeping off the night before."

"Therapy and clean living helped me do a 180. I'm still a bit wired. That'll always be the case, but I've found healthier outlets for my angst."

"You've always needed something to keep your mind occupied, Deano," Sheila said. "You're constantly thinking, always remembering, and doing stuff that requires your full attention to help you tune out the noise."

"You must be a cop."

"It's true, though, isn't it?"

It is.

Dean sighed.

But let's switch topics.

"What about you, She?" he said. "How's things going with Michael?"

"*Michael*?" His sister laughed. "The guy I dated nine years ago?"

"I take it that you're no longer together."

"Man, you really are out of the loop, aren't you?"

"I guess I should try picking up the phone more often."

"That you should. I guess I should too." Sheila straightened her back. "And to answer your question, no, Michael and I are no longer together. Last I heard, he got married and moved out to someplace in Jersey."

"You got any prospects right now?" Dean asked. "You're still young enough. I mean, you're a friggin' *pill* to deal with, but you've got some redeeming qualities."

"Thanks for the ego boost, dipstick." Sheila's gaze drifted. "But honestly, I don't think I'm going to step back into that particular arena ever again."

Dean laughed. "I guess Michael really did a number on you."

"No." His sister winked. "But men like him made me realize that my interests lie *elsewhere*, if you know what I mean."

Dean's eyes widened. "You mean—"

Sheila nodded. "I figured you would have picked up on the telltale signs back when I was a kid, FBI guy."

I didn't.

My God, how could I not have seen it?

"Does Dad know?" Dean said.

"No," his sister replied. "I know he wouldn't care but he's got bigger things on his mind right now. I'll be sure to bring it up the next time I'm with someone I feel might make it through more than just the first couple rounds of dates."

"So there's no one?" Dean's heart swelled with concern for his sister. "You shouldn't be going through life alone, She."

"I just don't have the time. Frankly, with all of *this* going on," Sheila gestured to the papers her brother gave her, "I don't know when I'll ever have the time again."

"You will. Trust me. If someone like me can manage to

find someone like Layla, that leads me to believe there's still hope left in this world."

"Does she make you happy?"

"She does." Dean smirked. "I really got lucky with that one. I just hope I don't screw it up."

"What makes you say that?"

"The past. My history."

"You mean your inability to get out of your own damn way?"

"I see you inherited Pop's knack of getting right to the point."

"It's true," Sheila said. "After Tommy died, you always—"

The comment triggered Dean to play back the memory of his twin brother's death, avert his gaze from his sister, and then pin it to the view outside the window.

Sheila winced. "I'm sorry, I didn't mean to..." Her voice trailed off.

"You're good." Dean waved his sister off. "You were always as tough on me as Dad was. I guess we can chalk that up to the both of you fulfilling that whole older sibling role bit."

"I mean, we did bail you out of trouble more times than not."

"You can't be serious."

"Sean Lipsky," Sheila said.

"What about him?" Dean replied.

"You mean you don't remember?"

"Of course I do." Dean scoured through the memory of him striking a student across his jaw after the kid talked ill about his late brother. "And that buck-toothed idiot had it coming."

"You almost got expelled for that." Sheila held up a finger. "If I didn't step in and run interference for you with Ms. Keesey—"

"Is there a point to this, She?" Dean cut in as his complexion turned a shade of crimson.

"I'm just saying," his sister surrendered her hands, "you've always been a bit of a troublemaker, that's all. You hit first and ask questions later, and because of that I had to come to your aid a few times to, I don't know, knock some sense into you."

"It's nice to know that even as an adult, you're still talking down to me."

"I'm not talking down to you."

"You are."

"Let's not do this."

"I'd appreciate it if you didn't act like we're still on the schoolyard, She," Dean said. "I'm a grown-ass man, in case you didn't notice."

"I didn't mean to offend you," Sheila replied. "I'm just saying that—"

The phone in Sheila's pocket buzzed and prevented her from finishing the thought. Dean welcomed the interruption as he exhaled a deep breath. Sheila gave him the "one-minute gesture" as she answered the call.

"Lieutenant Blackwood," Sheila greeted.

Several seconds ticked by.

Dean watched the color drained from his sister's face.

Oh, man.

This can't be good.

"Understood," Sheila said into the phone. "I'll be right there." She terminated the call, stood up from the table as she fished around her messenger bag for her wallet.

Dean shrugged. "What's up?"

"It happened again." Sheila looked him square in the eyes as her bottom lip trembled. "Two of my guys just discovered another pair of bodies."

15

The crime scene was exactly the same as the first one that Dean had encountered. A couple had been murdered inside of their home in the Marina District of San Francisco, and the MO of the slayings had been executed in the same fashion as before. The killer entered through a basement door, pierced the couple's throat as they slept in bed, and stabbed them repeatedly. Then he proceeded to assault the woman before he bound both of their hands and legs, dragged them into the living room, and killed the male victim by slitting his throat as the female watched him bleed out.

"Nicollete Ashton," one of the patrolmen standing over the body said, "and Eric Alper."

A tech snapped a picture of the bodies positioned on their sides and facing one another, the corpses swathed in copious amounts of blood with terror-stricken expressions etched into their faces.

Dean, as he lingered near the front door and took his own mental snapshots, could not help but feel a sense of sickly déjà vu overcome him.

This is whacked.

Completely fucktangular on all sides.

"Do you *feel* that, laddie?" Woody said. "Something big is happening here."

Not now, shithead.

I'm busy.

Dean watched on from the corner of the living room as Sheila spoke with a pair of detectives and dished out orders. Told a patrolman to speak with the neighbors. Assigned another one to cordon off the outside of the house with yellow caution tape. Despite the fervor of the situation playing out, Dean couldn't help commend his sister for her diligence and composure in light of what was happening.

She looks like Mom the way she holds her head high like that.

The apple truly doesn't fall too far from the tree.

"We don't like apples, laddie," Woody said. "They're too firm."

Quiet.

"Save for a honeycrisp, maybe. I do like those."

Fuck off.

Several minutes ticked by as Sheila worked with her people. As she did, Dean, toothpick clenched between his teeth, walked the perimeter of the two-story Tudor, making sure to steer clear of anyone who was working the scene and flashing his badge when questions were raised as to who he was and why he was there.

Dean's gaze drifted to the blood trail that snaked from the living room and came to a stop at the first door on his left at the end of a hallway, the gears in his brain turning as he did an assessment of the scene.

He approached the door.

Pushed it open.

Peeked inside the master bedroom.

Saw that the bedsheets were doused in blood just like the first crime scene.

"Same thing," Sheila announced from behind Dean. "Same exact circumstances as the last one."

Dean angled his body toward his sister. "The stab wounds," he said. "Were they the same number of wounds in the same places?"

"Exactly the same—just like the first crime scene."

"Not exactly."

"How so?"

Dean motioned over his shoulder with his toothpick. "This place has a doorbell camera on the front, back, *and* basement door where this guy entered."

"Well, hopefully we caught a break then. Maybe we'll catch this guy on candid camera this time."

"I doubt it. I mean, *two* series of murders in the span of 96 hours?" Dean shook his head. "That's a record that hasn't been broken in quite some time. It's not the era of Ted Bundy or Berkowitz or any of those guys anymore. Serial murders occurring at such rapid succession are virtually unheard of. Point being, if the suspect is as savvy as he is, he probably found a way to deal with the cameras." Dean cut a glance at his sister. "But don't quote me on that."

Two more hours ticked by.

Sheila worked the scene with her detectives.

Dean dawdled in the background and stood out of everyone's way as the scene was worked and evidence was collected.

Another hour had passed by the time the coroner came to collect the bodies, and after a solid 6 hours had been spent on the scene—the 3:00 a.m. hour had rolled around—Dean stepped outside with his sister for a breath of fresh air.

Neighbors flooded the street, all of them bleary-eyed

and exchanging whispers as they tried to catch a glimpse inside the house. Two news crews held court on the sidewalk at the bottom of the pair of steps that led up to the house where a cameraman was in the throes of trying to get a shot of the bodies.

"There's no keeping a lid on it now," Sheila said. "The press is going to run wild with all of this." She raked her fingers through her hair. "What's that thing you say?"

"What thing?"

"When something is messed up."

"Fucktangular," Dean said.

"Right." Sheila nodded. "Completely fucktangular on all sides."

Dean hung his head. "I'm sorry, She." He took out another toothpick from his pocket and slipped it between his lips. "I was hoping I'd be able to offer something that could help you get ahead of this thing."

"It's not your fault. It's like you said inside when you mentioned how something like this happening this fast is unheard of." Sheila sighed. "I guess I figured we would have more time." She motioned to the toothpick jutting out of Dean's lip. "What is that?"

"It's coated with nicotine."

"I figured. Last time I saw you, you were still smoking."

"I'm trying to cut back." Dean flicked the toothpick with his finger. "Helps with my nerves though."

"Just quit." Sheila snagged the nicotine-glazed stick out of her brother's mouth. "You'll add years to your heart's shelf life."

As Dean flexed his brow, a patrolman approached Sheila and informed her that interviews with the neighbors were still being conducted, but so far, no one saw or heard a thing.

"Get Captain Horne on the phone for me," Sheila ordered the patrolman. "Tell him I need to know if he wants a statement made to the press."

The patrolman nodded and hopped to it.

Sheila turned her back on the crowd that had gathered on the street as she rubbed the muscles in the back of her neck. "Times like this," she said, "makes me wish I hadn't quit smoking."

Dean grabbed her by the arm. "Let's walk the scene again. Maybe we'll find something that stands out. Let's just work with what we have on hand and go from there."

Sheila followed her brother inside the house as she cast one last look over her shoulder toward the street. "I'm sure that the SFPD higher ups will want to bring the FBI into this in an official capacity now."

"Most likely," Dean said. "This whole thing is definitely going to turn some heads. Last time a serial killer reared his head, it was that guy who started shooting people in Sacramento. The PD over there ended up catching him in a little under a month."

"You're telling me there's hope."

"There's *always* hope, She," Dean said. "Guys like this always get caught."

"Not always. Sometimes they get away."

"Sheila Blackwood wasn't working the case in those instances."

"Cheesy, Deano," Sheila said. "But appreciated nonetheless."

The two padded their way back into the home, Sheila tailing her brother as they moved through the scene, went over the details again line by line, and then entered the kitchen.

"I'll get one of my people to take you back to the hotel," Sheila said. "There's no reason for you to be here."

Dean furrowed his brow. "To hell with that. I'm in this for the duration—if you'll let me, that is."

"You don't have to do that."

"Yes, I do. Look, I know this wasn't what we were hoping for when we said we needed to spend some quality time together..."

Sheila snickered.

"...but regardless," Dean continued, "I want to help you out any way that I can. An FBI shield goes a long way. Consider this a 'what's mine is yours' type of scenario in regard to my resources."

Sheila closed her eyes. "It's going to be a long few weeks, Deano. I just need to focus and figure this out. I also need to get some chow so I'm not operating on an empty stomach."

Dean glanced at the fridge. "If all this stuff in here wasn't evidence, I'd say we should raid the icebox."

"That's not funny."

Dean opened his mouth to offer his apologies, but then he spotted something at the bottom of the fridge—scratches on the floor tiles where it appeared like the fridge had been pulled out before being put back in its original place.

Well, well, well.

Am I seeing things, or am I seeing things?

"She," Dean said, "get a load of this."

His sister came up alongside him, both of them moving into a crouch down by the bottom of the fridge.

Dean stuck out his hand. "You got gloves?"

Sheila dug into her pockets, produced a pair of Latex gloves, and palmed them over. As Dean slipped them on, Shiela did the same with a pair of her own as she watched as her brother examined every inch of the appliance.

"You see anything?" she said.

Dean moved to the back of the fridge, his cheek an inch away from making contact with the wall.

He squinted.

Surveyed the area behind the appliance.

Requested a flashlight from his sister.

Dean clicked the flashlight on and directed the beam toward the wall behind the fridge, his eyes widening as he said, "I think there's something here."

Once Sheila had confirmed a tech had taken the pictures of the kitchen, she assisted Dean in pulling out the fridge six inches away from the wall. Her mouth dropped open when she saw one word scrawled on the paint on the wall behind the appliance.

WRATH.

"Wrath," Sheila said. "What the hell does that mean?"

Dean huffed. "I don't believe it."

"You've seen this before?"

"I have but not in real life."

"What do you mean?"

Dean gestured to the writing. "That's from the movie *Se7en*," he said. "The killer in that movie did this exact same thing."

16

"The word *WRATH*," the tech said, "was written in grease that was obtained from the bottom of the fridge. I'm going to analyze it a bit further, but don't hold your breath in terms of getting anything in the way of prints."

Dean, seated in the chair across from Sheila's desk in the Robbery Homicide Office, shook his head. "I'm telling you," he said. "It's from that movie *Se7en*."

The tech, a slim man with Buddy Holly glasses, furrowed his brow. "Is that the Brad Pitt movie?"

Dean nodded. "Brad Pitt, Morgan Freeman, and Kevin Spacey."

A look of disgust washed across the tech's face.

"Don't let Spacey's misdeeds turn you off from seeing it," Dean said. "The movie's outstanding."

Sheila thanked the tech for the report.

Dismissed him.

Then she slipped down into the seat behind her desk. "So," she said, her breathing loaded with strain, "our suspect is now reenacting shit from David Fincher films."

Dean motioned to the tech before he left. "Did you guys do another sweep of the first crime scene to see if he left a clue there after we called you about this *WRATH* thing? If he's following the beats from *Se7en*, he might have left something at the first scene."

The tech shook his head. "We didn't find anything. We checked high and low. We can look again, but I don't think we're going to find anything."

Dean stroked the stubble on his chin. "This is so odd. It's completely out of left field. I'm not really sure what the hell this guy intended to say by putting that on the wall. If he was reenacting that movie, he would've followed what the killer did in it to a T—but he didn't. It's almost like this guy has no rhyme or reason. It's like he's just whipping up a beef stew of film references."

"What part of the movie *was* he reenacting?" Sheila said. "I only saw it once when I was a teenager."

"Yeah, Mom freaked out on you because you rented it without permission."

"Be serious—what part of the movie was this from?"

"The killer in that movie," Dean said, "made an obese man eat himself to death. The idea he had was to make him pay for his sins of gluttony, and when the deed was done, he wrote the word 'Gluttony' on the wall behind the fridge in grease. The 'Wrath' killing came later." He shook his head. "I don't get it. What is this guy trying to say?"

"That's why you're here." Sheila's face became a study of frustration. "Tell me what you think this means."

"I'm thinking."

"Well, think harder." Sheila threw up her hands. "You offered me a profile that seems to be a bust at this point."

"The profile is solid," Dean said. "This whole 'wrath' thing just puts a new twist on it."

"The last thing I need is more twists," Sheila replied. "The phones have been ringing off the hooks in here, and now I've been tasked with going before the press in a couple of hours to state officially to the world that some lunatic is running around San Francisco emulating crimes from '90s thriller movies."

The word written in grease behind the fridge was the sole image in Dean's mind.

What's the point?

Why reenact a movie?

And if so, why put a twist on it?

"I don't know, She," Dean said. "This may be a bit out of my depth. It might be good to get someone else from Quantico to come down here to check this out, someone who might have a better insight into this."

Sheila rested back in her chair and pinched the bridge of her nose. "The deputy chief said the same thing. Whoever's doing this is moving fast. Not only that, but he's ruthless, brutal, and trying to send some kind of cryptic message I'm having a hard time deciphering. My people are having a hard time trying to keep up with his pace." She widened her eyes and then pinned them to her brother. "I've never seen anything like this before, Deano."

A thick silence lingered throughout the room as Sheila gazed out the window that looked out to the Robbery Homicide Division, surveying her troops as they ping-ponged between desks and fielded phone calls. "Be real with me, Dean," she said. "Wager a guess as to how this is going to play out."

Dean stuffed his hands in his pockets as he sifted through the hypothetical scenarios. "It'll happen again. This guy is clearly building up to something, and it leads me to believe these two murders are like a teaser trailer he's presenting for a bigger picture."

"This family is just a magnet for psychos, isn't it?"

"Yeah." Dean couldn't help but think of the SMASH case. "That's a notion that's been on my mind as of late."

A few seconds ticked by.

Telephones rang.

Officers shouted over each other.

Then a thought occurred to Dean.

"There's one thing that might help you out here though," he said. "If you're up for hearing it."

Sheila furrowed her brow. "What?"

"The press conference," Dean said. "More times than not, killers tend to—"

"Attend the funerals or press conferences for their victims." Sheila nodded approval. "Yeah, you're right. There's a good chance this guy is going to be there."

"Put out a description to your guys—white, male, thirties. Post them up around the scene, and get eyes on every single person that's there. If you can turn the press conference into a bit of a parade, you might have a better shot at luring him in." Dean approached Sheila's desk and braced against it. "You gotta make it a *scene*, She. You have to make it hard for this guy to not want to attend."

"And I take it that you're going to be there too?"

"Well," Dean flashed a toothy grin, "that goes without saying."

17

Over a hundred people had gathered at the press conference at San Francisco City Hall. The crowd had congregated in front of the French-inspired dome that served as the building's focal point, a dozen cameras directed toward a podium where Sheila, the mayor, the SFPD's Deputy Chief, and several patrolmen were placed in the background.

In the back of the crowd, viewing the press conference, was Dean, his eyes shielded by a pair of Ray Ban Wayfarers as he surveyed the crowd, sizing up each and every person in attendance for signs of someone who fit the profile.

Okay, Deano.

Where's Waldo?

Six minutes after noon, Sheila approached the microphone. Dressed in a pantsuit for the occasion, she adjusted the badge on her hip, gripped the sides of the podium, and then looked directly into the cameras with a stern expression.

"Good afternoon," Sheila said. "As you are all aware, the Presidio Heights and Marina District have experienced several murders in the span of 96 hours. The victims, Peter Landsman, Ellie Walsh, Nicollete Ashton, and Eric Alper, were brutally slain inside their homes."

Dean nodded subtly.

That's good.

The more she plays it up, the more the guy who's doing this is going to relish the attention.

He continued to survey the members in the crowd, hoping to suss out someone who stood out in the worst of ways.

The press conference continued, Sheila ending her address to the cameras and signing off by announcing that justice would be "swift and without fail." She then turned the podium over to the deputy chief, a robust gentleman with salt and pepper hair, who took his position behind the microphone. He assured the public that the crimes would be investigated thoroughly, that the culprit would be prosecuted to the fullest extent of the law. He then dished out information about the murders to the news cameras, leaving out pertinent tidbits, including the fact that the word "Wrath" had been found behind the fridge.

Good.

Dean refrained from giving the guy the thumbs-up gesture.

Keep it simple, slick.

Don't tell the media what they don't absolutely have to know.

Reporters volleyed questions to the deputy chief after he finished his speech. As the questions flew and the DC did his best to field them, Dean started to move through the crowd. The reporters and deputy chief's voices were drowned out as he examined every white male over the age of thirty.

Are you here, buddy?

Dean slowly moved into the crowd.

I know you are.

Come on, you gotta be here somewhere.

Several minutes went by as Dean snaked his way through the audience.

No one in his sight piqued his interest.

Then the thought occurred to Dean that maybe the plan was a bust, that the suspect—who almost certainly had a police or military background—was tactful enough to refrain from showing up.

Dean huffed his frustrations.

Put his focus back on the crowd.

Then he saw a white male in an Army jacket staring at the deputy chief with a crooked smirk on his face.

18

The hairs on the back of Dean's neck went rigid as he pinned his sights on the man. The primal part of his brain signaled that a threat was on his radar.

Dean's skin flushed.

Time felt like it had slowed to a creep as he honed in on the man and slowly threaded his way through the sea of people toward him.

Is that you, shitbird?

Dean assessed the man from 10 yards out. The man's eyes narrowed, and his body swayed slightly from left to right as though his brain was being flooded by endorphins as a result of the press conference.

Cautiously optimistic, Blackwood, Dean told himself. *Cautiously optimistic.* He approached the man and pulled his hands out of his pockets 5 yards away from him, close enough that Dean could make out the sun-cracked quality of the man's skin.

Dean peeled off his glasses.

The man in the Army jacket shot a look in his direction.

The two of them stood their ground for the next several moments.

"Hey, there," Dean said. "How's it going?"

The lines in the man's face slackened into a frown.

The fingers on Dean's left hand curled into a fist.

The man in the Army jacket then spun around and broke out into a sprint toward his right.

The second the man took off, Dean's booted feet pushed off the pavement, the ground feeling like an ice rink that he coasted across with ease. The man in the jacket pushed people in the crowd out of his way, shooting frantic, wide-eyed looks over his shoulder as nearby patrolmen put the call out over the radios. Dean, 12 yards behind the suspect, dipped and dived and weaved his way through the crowd, fixated on the suspect he was pursuing with a heated gaze.

"*Stop!*" Dean yelled. "Freeze!"

The man in the jacket continued his retreat as he shoved a woman violently to the ground. The woman shrieked as other people came to her aid, a reporter in the crowd attempting to grab onto a fistful of the suspect's jacket but to no avail.

Dean pumped his arms as he closed in on the man in the jacket, his boots slapping against the pavement as he closed in the distance. But the suspect managed to get through the crowd and spill out onto the street where he continued his retreat.

Lungs on fire, Dean, 10 yards away from the suspect, drew a deep breath and continued his pursuit. He tailed the man into a steady stream of traffic, cars from either direction blaring their horns and snaking around the suspect as he navigated his way through the traffic.

Dean glanced to his right as he stepped onto the street, an incoming vehicle slamming on its brakes and missing him by just a couple of inches. Dean, mid-stride, glided across the hood of the car, the man in the jacket now 5 yards ahead of him and halfway through the intersection.

The suspect stopped as a car passed in front of him, his hands held high in the air as the driver behind the wheel shouted a stream of obscenities. The man in the jacket then ran behind the car, the sidewalk a few paces away where a group of pedestrians were in the throes of getting out of his way.

Dean's eyes were on the man's back, close enough now that all he had to do was reach out and grab his jacket. The pace of his run intensified, Dean gnashing his teeth as the suspect prepared to mount the curb.

A civilian on the sidewalk, brawny and built like a powerlifter, spun around and attempted to assist Dean in taking the suspect down. Cursing under his breath, the man in the jacket dipped to his right, evading the brawny man's attempts to snag him as he ran back into the street before his eyes widened the moment he spotted a green Mazda closing in on him.

The man in the jacket ceased his run.

The Mazda caterwauled to a halt.

Dean leapt toward the suspect and then went into a dive.

The suspect spun around as Dean tackled him into the windshield of the Mazda, the glass splintering into a spider-web series of cracks as the suspect let out an air-depleting huff of his lungs.

19

"Here you go," Sheila said as she held up an ice pack and tossed it over to her brother. Dean caught it with one hand, bidding his sister thanks before he put his focus on the two-way mirror that looked into the interrogation room. Seated behind a desk, his hands shackled and gaze on the ceiling, was the man that Dean had chased down. An EMT dabbed at the cuts on the left side of the man's face, a by-product of Dean tackling him into a car windshield.

"Any luck on getting a name?" Dean said. "The guy didn't have anything in the way of an ID on him."

"Not yet." Sheila leaned against the two-way mirror and shook her head. "We're running his fingerprints right now." She rolled her eyes. "The driver of the Mazda you crashed into is pissed, by the way. He's already filed a grievance with SFPD."

"Tell him to call Safelite Repair." Dean rested the ice pack against his shoulder, the pressure triggering him to wince. "They'll get him fixed right up."

"You know," Sheila crossed her arms, "between the press

conference and that little sideshow that took place with you and this guy on the street, everyone from the mayor to the chief of police to—"

"—the guy mopping the floors is concerned. I get it." Dean flexed his tender shoulder and grimaced. "I've heard this spiel plenty of times before, She. It's as exhausting as it is cliché."

"Well, it's good to know you're still handling things with an unsparing approach as opposed to a more surgical one, Deano."

"Yeah." Dean tossed the icepack onto the table beside him, took out a toothpick from his pocket, and popped it in his mouth. "Story of my life."

"This doesn't look good, Dean." Sheila inched closer to her brother. "Look, I brought you here as a consultant. I figured you'd be in and out before anyone was the wiser, but now I'm having to explain to everyone who you are and the nature behind your participation. We agreed you would help out and look at evidence, not chase people down on foot through the city. You've practically gift-wrapped a lawsuit to this guy you took down."

"And we managed to get a suspect in custody who might possess information pertaining to these murders," Dean said. "I chalk that up to a win."

"Same old Deano," Sheila sighed, "same old bull-shit." She rubbed the back of her neck and paced the room. "I asked you to lend me an assist here, brother. I thought that enough time had passed that you were through with this whole," she thought of a way to phrase it, "*brazen* approach you have to this line of work. You secure results, yeah, but it's been at the cost of your reputation—and now it's potentially at the cost of mine too."

"She's not wrong," Woody said. "Remember what Sloane said?"

Fuck him.

"Still—"

And fuck you.

"I'm sorry, She," Dean said. "After I'm finished up here," he held up his ice pack, "I'll head out."

"Yeah," Sheila said as she removed the toothpick from her brother's mouth and snapped it in half. "That might be for the best. You definitely gave me some things to think on, but I think I need to take it from here."

The two didn't speak. Nothing was audible but the static buzz of the fluorescent lights overhead. Dean felt like he did back when he was a kid during those moments when Sheila had to step in and clean up his messes.

Knuckles rapped on the door that led into the room.

A bearded detective entered the room, a file in his hand and a defeated look on his face. "Nicolas J. Rosen," he said before he jutted his chin toward the suspect. "Thirty eight. He was just released from his job at PacBell two months ago for a drinking problem. He has an outstanding bench warrant for public indecency, so I think that's why he ran."

Dean faced the detective. "Military record?"

"Negative," the detective said. "Guy barely got his hand on his GED back in '05. According to his old supervisor at PacBell, Rosen is, in the supervisor's words, 'about as dim-witted as a guy can get.'"

Dean put his focus on Rosen on the other side of the room. The guy's eyes were bloodshot. He was burping and cradling his stomach as he put his eyes on the EMT beside him and said, "I think I need to puke."

It's not him.

He's nothing more than a run-of-the-mill drunk.

Dean puttered his lips.

He definitely isn't our guy.

"Put him in a cell to sleep it off," Sheila said to the detective. "Get Weiss or Plemmons to talk to him once he sobers up. Find out why he was at the press conference. I'll think about booking him on something if I can figure out a reasonable charge in the meantime, but until then, just," Sheila threw up her hands, "get him out of my sight."

The detective bowed out of the room.

Dean turned and faced his sister. "That's not your guy."

Sheila nodded. "I know."

"I'm sorry, She. Really, I—"

"I know. It's fine. Listen, I have a lot to do, so—"

Dean held up his hands. "Say no more." He moved to the door and reached out to palm the handle, but he stopped halfway, his shoulder slackening as he turned back to face his sibling. "Look," he said, "I didn't mean to throw a wrench in the works here. If there's anything I can do—"

"I'll catch up with you later, Deano, okay?" Sheila replied. "I'm not mad. I just need to keep my focus on this." She narrowed her eyes. "You did mention something about forwarding me the info of an agent who specializes in this kind of thing, so if you want to do that in the meantime, I'd appreciate it."

Dean nodded.

There's nothing more to say.

Just go home.

Leave before you do any more damage.

"*Fuck* that, laddie!" Woody said. "Let's *stay*."

Don't.

"We can—"

Enough.

Dean twisted the door handle and prepared to make his

exit, but when he opened the door, he saw the same detective from before trying to get back into the room.

"Lieutenant," the detective said. "There's a call on the line for you."

Sheila furrowed her brow. "Who?"

"I think it's the guy."

"You'll need to be a little more specific."

"The guy that's doing this," the detective said. "There's a person on hold right now claiming responsibility for the murders."

Dean saw four detectives corralled around a phone in the bullpen, their gazes pinned to it like it was outfitted with C4. They turned around as Dean and Sheila approached them, clearing out of the way as Sheila splayed her fingers and inched them toward the receiver.

"Who's running the trace?" Sheila said.

A detective, hunched over a computer with headphones draped over his ears, held up a finger, mouthing to Sheila, "I'm on it" before he put his focus on his monitor.

Dean leaned into his sister's ear, his eyes fastened to the desk phone and the blinking red light, indicating that there was a call waiting.

It's him.

I can feel it.

Sheila scooped up the receiver and pressed it to her ear, clearing her throat before she greeted the caller with "Lieutenant Sheila Blackwood."

The members of the Robbery Homicide Department fell silent, their collective curiosity manifesting itself to the point that the entire room felt like the heat in the room had kicked up several degrees.

Sheila waited for the caller to speak, several seconds ticking by as she heard nothing but the slow ebb and flow of his breathing. "Hello?" she said. "Are you there?"

"I'm here," the caller replied, his voice masked and leading Sheila to deduce that the guy was using some kind of software to equalize his voice.

Sheila palmed her hand over the mouthpiece, placed the phone on speaker, and cut a glance at the officer tracing the call, who shot a thumbs up to signal that the trace was being made.

"Is he with you?" the caller said.

"Is who with me?" Sheila replied.

"Your *friend*."

Dean inched closer to Sheila, his brow wrinkled as he pinned his eyes to the speaker. "Do I know you?" he said.

"Maybe," the caller huffed, "maybe not."

"So, we're playing games, huh?"

"I like games. Don't you?"

"That depends, mystery man." Dean crossed his arms. "What game are you looking to play?"

"Birds of a feather, flocked together," the caller said, "so do pigs and swine. As nice as their chance as well as I had mine."

Sheila looked at her detectives. All of them shrugged or shook their heads.

"Dude," Dean whispered to his sister. "This guy is a trip."

Sheila winced. "What are you talking about?"

"You're a big movie buff," Dean said into the speaker-phone, "aren't you?"

The caller snickered. "How could you tell?"

"That last quote was from *Die Hard 3*. Jeremy Irons said it when he was playing Simon Says with Bruce Willis."

"Very good," the caller said. "*Very* good."

He's talking to me like he knows me.

Dean's eyes narrowed.

Strange.

"Who are you?" Dean said.

"Where's the fun in telling you that right off the bat?" the caller replied. "We have to go a few more rounds before I let that slip."

Dean braced the sides of the desk, staring at the phone as if the suspect was right in front of him. "If it's really you, if you're the guy that's responsible for this, then what was scribbled on the back of that fridge at the second crime scene?"

"*Wrath*," the caller replied without skipping a beat. "I figured it wouldn't take long for you guys to find that."

Sheila tensed her jaw muscles as she looked at the detective tracing the call. "It says the call is coming from Oslo," he said as he looked at the monitor and huffed. "And *now* it says it's coming from Bridgeport, Connecticut."

"Screw around with the phone lines all you want," the caller said. "You're not going to find me."

"You pulled that scrambling the phone lines trick from the same movie, didn't you?" Dean said.

"It's a good one, all plot holes and leaps of logic aside."

"Well, if you're taking cues from a *Die Hard* villain," Dean looked at his sister, "do we have to worry about you setting off bombs around the city now?"

"As a matter of fact, yes," the caller said. "In less than an hour, I will be detonating a series of devices I've planted throughout the San Francisco Bay Area."

The detectives in the room scrambled. Some barked

orders, a few made calls, and the rest issued directives to the plainclothes officers scattered throughout the room.

Dean flashed his hand. "He's bluffing."

Sheila gripped his arm. "What the hell are you doing?"

"This guy is blowing smoke up our asses." Dean shook his head. "He doesn't have a bomb."

"Are you sure about that?" the caller said. "No doubt in your mind?"

"You're pulling my leg," Dean said. "You've got no intention to try to pivot from your MO. You're not about to start blowing up half the city."

One second ticked by.

Two more followed.

Everyone in the room held their breath.

"Well, you got me there," the caller said. "Bombs were never my forte."

Remember every word he says.

All of this is going to come in handy later.

"All right," Sheila said as she slipped her hands in her pockets. "Let's get real here. Tell us who you are. Tell us what you want."

"Well, I'm keen on killing a few more folks," the caller said, "for starters."

"Why?"

"I have my reasons."

"Do you care to share them?"

"No. Not *yet* at least."

"Why are you doing this?" Dean chimed in. "Give me something to work with here. You called us." He flicked his gaze toward Sheila. "You threatened the Lieutenant of the Robbery Homicide Division for a reason."

"I consider this a courtesy call, if we have to call it anything," the caller said. "I just wanted to speak with the pair of you before I floated another set of bodies your way."

The pair *of you.*

Dean tensed his jaw muscles.

He knows us.

Somehow, he knows about me ... and Sheila.

"Something tells me," Dean said, "that you and I might have crossed paths before."

"Maybe we have," the caller said, "and maybe we haven't." He took a beat. *"Dean."*

Dean closed his eyes.

Oh, hell.

"You know," the caller said, "you've had an illustrious career, Agent Blackwood. You've been around the block. Taking your reputation into consideration, I'm surprised you've managed to last this long without getting booted from the Bureau, much less killed."

"Same here."

"What is it? Luck?"

"I ask myself the same question all the time."

"Well, it's only a matter of time until it catches up to you. Don't you think?"

"I take it that you've got some kind of personal vendetta against me."

"What makes you say that?"

"A hunch."

The caller took a beat. "Maybe," he finally said, "maybe not."

"Alright, cut the crap," Dean groaned. "If you want to talk this out, maybe we can—"

"Enough," the caller snapped. "We're done here. I just wanted to hear your voice, *and* to let you know that I'm the one responsible for what's happened in the last several days.

Lastly, and this is the most important thing, *know* that I am nowhere near finished with my little sideshow." With that, the call was terminated, a long beep ringing over the line as Sheila ended the call.

Dean looked at his sister.

Sheila looked at her brother.

The two of them turned toward the window overlooking the bay, curious if the man who had called in was watching them at that very moment.

21

The hour that went by after the suspect called in was marked by Sheila addressing her officers, updating the mayor and the deputy chief, and giving herself a moment to indulge in a cup of coffee. More traces were run on the origin of the suspect's call, but the efforts turned up nothing.

Despite the fact that Dean called the suspect's bluff of planting bombs around the city, Sheila put in a call to the bomb squad to do a sweep to make sure the false claim was nothing more than that. After she hopped off the phone with the bomb squad's captain, she made her way into her office with two fresh cups of coffee and handed one to Dean who was posted up behind her desk.

"Well," Sheila said after a few moments to break the silence, "that took a series of left turns that I wasn't expecting."

Dean put down his cup. "He knows who I am. He knew my name. He knew that I worked for the Bureau."

"You can turn up all kinds of things on the Internet, little brother. Anyone with a smartphone and two thumbs can turn up just as much information as the NSA and the CIA combined."

Dean shook his head. "It's more than that. The guy was talking to me in such an informal way, like he *knew* me somehow." He stood and paced. "Nothing right about that phone call. I've been on the other end of negotiation-based chats before, and *this*," Dean threw up his hands, "this is a new one."

Sheila gazed out at the bullpen, the officers dashing from one desk to the next. "Why would he call us?"

"Because it's personal," Dean replied. "This guy is dropping the first hint that whatever he's doing has something to do with me, maybe with the both of us. He knows that we're involved in this case. In a lot of ways, it's like a basketball game. The guy was smack-talking us before the start of the first quarter. He was looking in our eyes and dishing out that first chest bump before the whistle."

"Wonderful." Sheila reclined back in her chair. "So, someone you might have pissed off has decided to carve up victims in my territory in an effort to what? Get *even* with you? Why the theatrics? Why not just target you directly, if that's what his endgame is?"

"I don't know," Dean said. "All I do know is that none of this is over by a long shot." He pointed at his sister. "We do need to get someone up here from the Bureau who can craft a deeper profile on this guy. I went ahead and left a message for my boss Wilson to give him an update of the situation so he can get the ball rolling on that."

"Good," Sheila said, "because the FBI field office over here in San Francisco phoned in about 20 minutes ago asking if we needed their assistance. I told them that there was an agent on site at the moment." She laughed. "I refrained from telling them the part that we were related to each other."

"You should have told them that I'm not involved in an official capacity anymore."

"Well, you're not going anywhere, either way. Now that we know that the suspect has you lined up between his sights, for whatever reason, that's keeping you on the playing field."

Not the first time that's happened.

Something tells me that it won't be the last, either.

"I'm sorry," Dean said. "It's like you said before. Chaos clings to this family like a curse."

Sheila batted the comment aside with a swipe of her hand. "Let's refrain from the Freudian stuff until we figure out what's going on. In the meantime, I need you here. If this guy has some kind of vested interest in you, we have to keep you around."

"So, I'm the bait," Dean said, "in a manner of speaking."

"I wouldn't phrase it like that."

"But it's true."

"Well, if this guy has a hard-on for you, it'll help having you close by then."

"Don't say hard-on, She." Dean winced. "It's unbecoming."

"Grow up."

"Likewise."

The phone in Dean's pocket buzzed. He pulled it out, saw Claire's name on the display, and answered. "Hey."

"Hey," Claire said. "Do you have a second to talk?"

"Is everything all right?"

"I just had to pick Jeremy up from school. Something," Claire sighed, "something happened."

22

Dean's heart skipped a beat. "What's going on?" he asked Claire as he stood from his chair, worried that some terrible fate had befallen his one and only son. After everything that happened with Jeremy, it was hard for him to not assume the worst.

"Jeremy's fine," Claire said. "He got into a fist fight with someone. I'm still trying to find out why, but Jeremy punched another student in his face."

Dean pinched the bridge of his nose.

Like father, like son.

"Is he all right?" he said. "The kid that he hit, I mean."

"The kid has a bit of a shiner, but he's fine. I just spoke with the vice principal a moment ago. Geoff is on his way to pick up Jeremy right now."

"What about Jeremy?"

"The vice principal was leaning toward something drastic after she spoke with the parents of the kid Jeremy hit. Long story short, I stepped in and finessed the situation a bit, so they're going to let us handle it internally."

"Thank God you're a lawyer."

"Agreed," Claire said. "Anyway, I just wanted to give you the heads up. I know you said you'd be back in town after a couple of days, so it might be good if you sit down with Jeremy and have a little talk. I know I asked for some distance, but I think he," she took a beat, "needs his father on this one."

Dean looked at his sister. "I might be a little longer than I expected. Things are a little more complicated here than I initially thought."

"Is everything okay?"

"More or less. I just need to help Sheila sort some stuff out before I hop on the plane. I'll call you tonight once you guys are settled so I can have a little FaceTime with Jeremy."

"Just get back here as soon as you can. I'm worried that this thing is indicative of something bigger rearing its head, if you know what I mean."

"We'll cut this thing off at the pass before it escalates. You have my word. I'll call you guys in a little bit before he goes to school, if that works."

"Yeah, that's fine."

"Are you okay?"

"I'm hanging in there," Claire said. "We'll talk to you soon."

"Talk soon," Dean replied before he ended the call and put the phone in his pocket.

Sheila furrowed her brow. "Everything good?"

"Jeremy clocked some kid in his class."

"You're kidding."

"That I am not."

"Kind of a full-circle moment, no?" Sheila flexed her brow. "I believe you socked someone in class when you were Jeremy's age."

Memories of the past when Dean went toe to toe with

other kids in school drifted through his mind. "Yeah," he said. "My thoughts exactly." He drummed his fingers on the desk. "I'm going to call the kid later to have a talk with him. Honestly, I'm not surprised this happened considering what went down a few months back. It was only a matter of time."

"You're doing the best with what you've got," Sheila said. "Try to keep that in mind."

Dean said, "I'm trying to," before he felt his cell phone chirp to life once again. He fished it out, spotted Wilson's name flashing on the display, answered the call, and put the device on speaker.

"So," Wilson said, "even during your downtime, you still manage to find something to keep you occupied."

Dean shrugged. "I don't know what to tell you, boss."

"Well, let's not waste time commenting on your knack for acting like a bug light to the cretins of this world. Just bring me up to speed on everything."

Dean gave his boss the full rundown—the victims, the MO, the press conference, the call the killer made, and the fact that the killer seemed to have a particular interest in Dean.

"Okay," Wilson said. "What do you need from me?"

"Someone of a better mind to map up a blueprint of this guy's mind," Dean said. "Unfortunately, I can't really distance myself from this situation now that the suspect has my name in his mouth, but we'll still need one of the brainiacs over at Quantico to try to get a read on this individual."

"Understood. I'll need to get everything you have on hand so I can send it up the ladder. I'll also put in a call to the people out there at our San Francisco office. I assume they've already put in some calls to the SFPD by now."

Sheila perched forward in her chair. "That they have,

Agent Wilson. This is Lieutenant Sheila Blackwood, by the way."

"A pleasure," Wilson said. "So, what has the field office out there said?"

"They've asked if they need our assistance," Sheila said. "I relayed to them that we have an agent on site, my brother, attempting to get a read on the situation."

"I'll have a chat with SAC Schultz. He runs the field office out there. I'll also get the Deputy Chief to put in a call to the mayor's office *and* the governor's office so everyone is on the same page. Consider this my effort to make sure you're holding onto the reins of this investigation for as long as humanly possible. No promises though."

"Thank you, sir."

"Dean," Wilson said.

Dean held his head high. "Yes, sir?"

"It goes without saying that the nature of your relationship with your sister will cause some problems in terms of your level of involvement."

"I know," Dean said. "I'll be deferring to you and Sheila from here on out. If either of you issues a directive, I'll follow it. Last thing I want to do is dick up the works here."

"Good," Wilson said. "I just have one more question before we hop off the line."

"Shoot."

"Do you have *any* idea who this guy is? If this truly is a personal vendetta, who do you think is behind it?"

"I hate to say it, sir," Dean said, "but the list of people I've pissed off is pretty extensive."

Wilson sighed. "Well, stay on it. Use that big brain of yours. Work the angles, and figure out who the hell this person is."

"Will do."

Before he ended the call, Wilson told Dean that he'd be in touch.

Sheila went about fielding several more calls as Dean fetched a refill on his cup of coffee. His sister coordinated with her officers and put out one fire after the next. When Dean returned to the office, Sheila asked him, "Do you have any tricks up your sleeve? Is there anything you can think of that might help us out before the next pair of bodies get dropped off on our doorstep?"

One name popped into Dean's brain. "There's one guy that might be able to help," he said as he pulled out his cell and pulled up a name from his contacts.

23

"Bazz's Brazzer Boutique," Cliff Bazz greeted Dean over the phone. "Our office hours are from 9:00 to 9:30 every other Wednesday."

Dean, leaning against the doorway that led into Sheila's office, flashed a smirk. "Are you busy?"

"I'm right in the middle of watching *Matlock*, so this better be good."

"If I told you that the suspect in a quadruple murder just called and threatened me over the phone, would that pique your interest?"

"Very much so."

"Good," Dean said, "because I need you to start hitting up some of your old Agency contacts in a bid to find out what's going on. The suspect rang us up about an hour and a half ago, and the SFPD can't pinpoint the origin of the call. The son of a bitch managed to scramble the phone systems like it was his job."

"Impressive," Bazz said. "The guy would have to be working with some top-shelf equipment to pull that off."

"My feeling is that he's former military or law enforcement, the kind of person who could not only access that kind of stuff but also has extensive history in using it."

"I'll need some specifics to help you out there, boss."

"Would a chat with the head of Robbery Homicide help?"

"It wouldn't hurt."

Dean handed the phone to Sheila and told her who was on the line. Sheila spoke with Bazz for several minutes, confirmed that she would provide him with what he needed to trace the call, and then handed the phone back to Dean.

"All set?" Dean said.

"We're good on my end," Bazz said. "By the way, your sister has a lovely speaking voice."

"Steer clear, my friend."

"Duly noted," Bazz said before he ended the call.

Dean placed the phone in his jacket pocket. "If anyone can figure out this whole screwing with the phone lines business," he said to his sister, "it's Bazz."

Sheila narrowed her eyes. "The guy sounds like a spy or something."

"Because he was. I'm not sure the specifics of exactly what he did for the Agency back in the day, but I do know that Bazz is my go-to when I'm in a pinch. Just don't ask him too many personal questions."

"Well," Sheila said, "while your spy buddy works on figuring out where the suspect made the call from, we should—"

Knuckles rapped on the door to Sheila's office.

The siblings turned their heads and pinned their eyes to a young detective who rushed into the room and grumbled through labored breaths, "It happened again."

24

The blue and red lights on top of the police cruisers painted the two-story home that resided in Potrero Hill. As Sheila rolled onto the scene in her cruiser, Dean, seated beside her, did a scan of the block and saw that it was yet another affluent part of the city that the suspect had picked for his traveling circus of horrors.

After this week, the real estate prices are going to drop way *down.*

"It's been less than a day since his last kill," Dean said. "He's speeding up his timeline."

"He had to have pulled this off during daylight hours. He's getting more brazen." Sheila shook her head. "God, I've never seen anything like this before."

Sheila parked her car in front of the house, a two-story Victorian painted in a canary yellow hue. A pair of steps led up to the front door where police officers and technicians filtered in and out of the home, a cameraman with a local news station attempting to get a shot of the door only to be nudged away by one of the uniformed patrolmen.

"This has to be some kind of record," Sheila said. "The

tempo of the kills, I mean. No one has knocked off people this quickly since, I don't know, Bundy, maybe."

"No," Dean replied as he piled out of the car. "They haven't."

He took out a toothpick.

Sheila slapped it out of his hand.

Once Dean and his sister were in the home, they were led by a detective to the bodies of Angela Vayo and Mark Pickering. Like the previous set of murders, Angela and Mark had been stabbed in their throats while they were asleep. After that, they were assaulted, bound, and then dragged to the living room where Angela was forced to watch Mark die before succumbing to her wounds.

Dean stood near the bodies, snapping away mental pictures of the blood-swathed victims to add to his home movie collection.

"*Yikes*," Woody said. "Not a great sight to behold."

Nope.

"A drink would help it go down easier."

Quiet.

"Just think it over."

Goodbye.

"Doorbell cameras were shut off in the front and back," a detective said. "No signs of forced entry. No witnesses as of yet."

"He probably left us some kind of sign like before," Dean said to his sister. "He wrote 'Wrath' on the last crime scene. He's made it clear that he wants to play games with us, so maybe it's safe to assume that he's left something else for us to find."

The two began to work their way through the home, scouring every inch of it for something that looked out of place.

They searched the kitchen.

The living room.

The bathrooms.

After nothing of interest was found, they pivoted their efforts and cleared every inch of the second floor only to find the same result.

"He should have left *something*," Sheila said as she paced the second floor hallway. "Don't you think?"

"I'm not sure." Dean rubbed the back of his neck as he eyeballed the bodies in the living room. "Man, this son of a bitch is good. He kills these people with militaristic precision."

The siblings were intent on doing a second sweep of the first floor. A patrolman intercepted Sheila and then nodded over his shoulder. Sheila's eyes narrowed as she spotted a man and a woman in muted business suits standing behind the officer.

"Ma'am," the patrolman said, "the FBI is here to speak with you."

Dean laid eyes on the agents. The woman was 5 feet 4 inches, her chestnut-colored hair pulled back into a rigid bun, her face devoid of any wrinkles due to—from what Dean deduced—her persistent lack of any facial expressions. The man beside her, a 6-foot tall gentleman with broad shoulders and raven-colored hair, was someone Dean was more familiar with—Special Agent Aden Greer.

"Well, well, well," Dean said. "How's it going, Aden?"

Greer flashed his badge to Sheila. "Blackwood," he said as though it elicited a sour taste. "Word through the grapevine was that you were running around the crime scene."

Sheila nudged her brother. "You know this guy?"

"That I do," Dean said. "Sheila, this is Special Agent

Aden Greer. We were rookies together back at Quantico. He came in *second* behind my running time at Quantico, still the highest to this day, I believe."

"Not anymore," Greer said. "Some new kid who was there last year smoked your time."

Damn.

I thought no one could beat me.

"Special Agent Karen Dewitt," the agent beside Greer said. "Our SAC sent us over here to assess the scene."

"You were supposed to speak to SAC Wilson," Dean said. "He was supposed to give you the head's up that—"

"We spoke to Wilson," Greer cut in. "We also had a word with the governor. Election season is about to rear its head, so he's not looking to leave anything up to chance, especially when a quadruple," Greer glanced at the bodies in the living room, "well, now a *sextuple* set of murders has hit the Northern California area."

Dean crossed his arms. "Cut to the punchline, Aden."

"I'll keep it simple," Greer stepped closer to Dean. "We're taking over from here. I suppose it looks like Wilson running constant interference for you like he has for the duration of your career isn't going to fly anymore." He glanced at Sheila. "*And* I'm afraid that from here on out, the Bureau is going to take the lead with this investigation, Lieutenant."

Sheila huffed. "You're kidding me."

"I'm afraid not," Dewitt chimed in. "This situation is unprecedented. The governor has good reason for us to step in to take over from here. It's nothing personal."

"Call your deputy chief," Greer said. "He'll tell you all about it."

Sheila held up one finger, took out her cell phone, and then plugged in a number. She stepped away from the group, shooting a heated glance at Dean who proceeded to stand right in Greer's path.

"Go-Get-Em Greer," Dean said. "Do they still call you that?"

Greer's eyes shimmered. "They do. You know as well as I do that my closure rate is unparalleled—*and* I managed to pull that off without my SAC stepping in every 15 minutes to clean up my messes."

"Are you sure about that? I mean," Dean sucked air through his teeth, "the last time I checked, you were never cleared on that case you tackled back in 2019."

The lines on Greer's face contorted into a grimace as his partner grabbed him by the arm.

"What is he talking about?" Dewitt said.

"Oh, she doesn't know?" Dean said as he clapped his hands together. "Your boy here got pulled in by the Office of Professional Responsibility a few years back for breaking a suspect's jaw during an interrogation. Last I heard, the DOJ had to dismiss the charges and dish a hefty payout to the guy you tuned up."

"It was a load of malarkey, Blackwood," Greer said. "And let's not start dredging up each other's past misdeeds. Your slights far outweigh any of mine."

"Fair enough." Dean clapped his hand on Greer's shoulder. "But just to be clear, I think you're a shoddy agent whose personality and approach is on par with a frat boy looking for someone to roofie at a party."

Dewitt pressed a hand against Greer's chest and pushed him back. "That's enough," she said. "The both of you. I have no problem writing this up officially if you don't terminate this exchange right here and now."

"Smart move," Dean said as he nodded to Dewitt. "Last thing I want to do is have Greer explain himself to OPR."

Greer tensed his jaw muscles. "You got a big mouth, Blackwood."

"And you've got a big penchant for those nifty little suits you wear, *Aden*. You look like a walking advertisement for *DoucheBag Quarterly*."

Dewitt pulled Greer aside for a sidebar. As the two spoke, Sheila returned and stood beside Dean, the color draining from her complexion.

"What's up?" Dean said.

"Your friend Greer wasn't blowing hot air," his sister said. "I just got off the phone with the deputy chief. It looks like your SAC's efforts to keep us on board were worth nothing. As of now, we've both been pulled off of the case."

"You've got to be kidding me."

"'Steer clear, and let the Feds handle it, Lieutenant,'" his sister said. "Those were the deputy chief's exact words."

Dean looked over his shoulder at Greer.

The agent saluted him with two fingers.

Dean offered a sardonic smile in reply.

All right.

What the hell do we do now?

25

Two knocks sounded on the door to Dean's hotel room. He opened it and greeted the delivery service kid clutching a bag of burritos, over-tipped him for the effort, and then put his focus on Sheila. His sister stood out on the balcony, her cell phone pressed to her ear, a forlorn expression masking her face.

"Understood, sir," Sheila said. "I'll make sure everything is turned over right away." She shook her head. "No, I understand." She nodded. "Yes, sir. I will."

"So," Dean said as he made his way out onto the balcony, "what's the status?"

"Your buddies Greer and Dewitt," Sheila said, "now have complete authority over the investigation. My people are turning over all the evidence to them as we speak. The entirety of the Robbery Homicide Department is now a veritable FBI convention."

Dean pulled out the sparkling soda from the takeout bag and twisted the cap that triggered a long sizzle. "I just spoke to Wilson too. He said there was nothing he could do. Governor Slauson pulled out all the stops on this one."

"Guy's a top-shelf prick." Sheila gripped the balcony railing tight to the point that the whites of her knuckles protruded. "He's the state's most stealthiest politician. That son of a bitch only surfaces when there's something that directly affects his interests."

"He can't run the risk of having this thing go south." Dean raised the bottle to his lips. "To be fair, Dewitt was right when she said this whole thing was unprecedented."

"Did you mention the part where the killer mentioned you by name?"

"I did."

"So, what did your federal buddies have to say about that?"

"Greer managed to convince his SAC that the guy could have seen me and pulled my information off the Internet," Dean said. "The same theory you had back when the guy first called."

"I can't believe this." Sheila closed her eyes. "I've been stonewalled from partaking in an investigation in *my* territory. I'm supposed to field questions from the local news stations and partake in press conferences for the duration of this thing. By the time your buddies figure this thing out, I'll have to stand in front of a camera and thank them for the effort."

Dean furrowed his brow. "I don't get it."

"What's there to get?" Sheila threw up her hands. "We're off this thing until someone nails the guy who did this."

"No," Dean said, "I mean, I don't get why the guy didn't leave something in the way of a clue at the last scene. After that phone call, he seemed intent on turning this whole thing into a game, so if that's the case, why didn't he leave a bread crumb?"

"I don't know." Sheila kneaded her neck muscles. "All I

do know is that six people have died—three families whose lives have been irreparably destroyed, and I don't have any answers for them, and I'm not in the position anymore to try to find them."

It had been years since Dean had seen his sister's composure shaken. She was the tactful one, the headstrong one. Rarely had he ever seen her at her wits end, and for the first time in his life, he had a front row seat to the inaugural event.

"I hate to say it," Sheila said as she turned and faced her brother, "but I feel like I'm going to be screwed after this thing is over. I've been in charge of this department for just shy of a year, and the first big case that ended up landing on my doorstep got hijacked from me in less than a week."

"Don't think about that now."

"You don't get it, Dean," Sheila said. "I'm not like you. I don't possess the lucky streak that you have when it comes to ducking out of the way of consequences."

"You think I haven't suffered my fair share of that, She?"

"You're pretty good at screwing up and managing to walk away scot-free."

Dean's nostrils flared. "I've got one divorce under my belt," he said, "a litany of career problems, an alcoholism issue, *and* a kid who ended up going through an ordeal that might have screwed him up for the rest of his life. I've got a dead brother," he winced, "*we've* got a dead brother, a mother who was taken from us too soon, and a father whose reputation is fucked for life because of what he did to protect our family. I'm not free and clear of my troubles, Sheila, so don't fool yourself into thinking otherwise."

Sheila's shoulders slackened.

She hung her head.

Then she flattened her hand across her chest. "I'm sorry,

Deano," she said. "I didn't mean to shortchange what you've been through. I'm just—"

"You're frustrated," Dean said. "And you've got every right to be." He waved his hand through the air. "And forget about it. I think if anyone is allowed to throw me any shade, it's you. You stepped in for me more than once when we were younger. In a lot of ways, you've earned the right to take a shot or two at me."

"This is the longest we've been together in a while," Sheila said. "You know that, right?"

"You're right." Dean traced his thumb on the lip of his water bottle. "And I still don't understand why you called me in the first place."

"I needed your help. It was that simple."

"No, it wasn't."

"Is that a fact?"

"Yeah," Dean said. "It is. We've barely spoken to one another since I left for basic all those years ago. We've had, what, two or three interactions since then? Maybe a few phone calls?"

"I mean," Sheila said, "you're right, but I don't know what that has to do with me ringing you up for an assist with the case."

"Come on, She." Dean laughed. "You were plenty capable of figuring this thing out on your own."

"Cut to the chase, smartass." His sister shrugged. "What are you getting at?"

"I think maybe you were trying to find a way to reconnect with me. Maybe not consciously, but the fact that this case got slapped down on your desk gave you an excuse to lure your brother out to your neck of the woods."

"Not bad, kiddo," Sheila smirked. "You really do this for a living, don't you?"

"I have my moments," Dean replied. "And to be honest, and as morbid as it may sound, I'm kind of happy you used this situation as your excuse to call me. Aside from Dad—and I have to call him up 75 percent of the time—I don't hear from the family. The ones still standing, that is."

"Dad's on his own wavelength. He comes around when he wants to."

"The same could be said for us."

"Yeah," Sheila said. "I guess all of us have spent our lives running from what happened that day with Tommy."

"Not me," Dean replied. "Not anymore, at least. Once I found the guy who did it, I decided to put that all to rest."

"You still are who you are, though, Dean. That won't change. You've curbed your bad habits, yeah, but you're still the same guy you've always been."

Is she right?

Even though I found justice for Tommy, am I no different than I was before I found the guy who did it?

The telephone on the nightstand started ringing. Dean scooped up the receiver. "Yes?"

"How's it going, Blackwood?"

The color drained from Dean's face.

He tightened his grip on the phone.

Then he angled his body toward his sister.

"It's him," Dean said. "It's the same guy who called the station."

26

"I just missed you two at the last scene," the caller said, his voice distorted by software like it had been in the previous phone call. "I left right before the cops rolled in. I actually thought about sticking around, but I knew that wouldn't be a wise move on my part."

Dean snapped his fingers. Sheila lingered close to the receiver so she could hear.

"Is *Lieutenant* Blackwood there?" the caller said.

"Yeah," Dean replied. "She's here."

"I take it by now that the FBI has forced her to recuse herself from taking the lead on the investigation."

"You're really up to speed with everything, aren't you?"

"Well, this whole thing is by design, after all. I mean," the caller laughed, "it is a *loose* design that I might deviate from at certain points soon, but a solid design nonetheless."

"Well," Dean took his personal cell out of his pocket and palmed it to his sister, "the kind of effort you have to exert to kill six people in several days has got to be taxing."

The caller huffed. "You have no idea."

Sheila, ogling Dean's cell in her palm, mouthed, "What am I supposed to do with this?"

Dean cupped his hand over the mouthpiece of the phone. "Call Bazz. Tell him what room we're in. Tell him what's going on, and to try to pinpoint the call. It's a long shot, but do it anyway."

Sheila ducked out onto the balcony, feverishly scouring through Dean's contacts before she located Bazz's name.

"Okay, bud," Dean said to the caller. "The first question I've got is why you didn't leave another note for us at the last scene."

"That would have been too easy," the caller replied. "I thought a phone call would be more appropriate."

"So what is this one going to entail? You gloating about what you did? To tell us that this is going to keep happening? What?"

"All of the above. If anything, I just wanted to express that since the FBI has excused you two from taking part in the case, I'm quite thrilled that I've got the two of you all to myself."

"Fat chance," Dean said. "The moment we wrap up with you here, we're going to tell them about this call."

"Oh, I know you will," the caller said. "I'm counting on it. And after you tell your buddies at the Bureau about this little conversation, they'll waste their time chasing their tails. There's not going to be any record of this exchange once I hang up."

"So you're banking on them thinking that this phone call never happened? Something like that?"

"Exactly. This whole thing is about you and me, Dean. *You're* the reason this is happening."

Dean paused. "Who are you? What did I do to piss you off, huh?"

"In time," the caller replied. "I really want to make you *feel* this before the final curtain call."

Final curtain call.

Man, this guy is obsessed *with his theatrics.*

"Okay, asshole," Dean said. "So what happens next? You seem to have a master plan all laid out, so tell me."

"Like I said, this is about you and me, Blackwood. I want you all to myself. And if you try to rope *anyone* else into this aside from that sister of yours, heads will roll."

"Then arrange a place." Dean smirked. "I'd be happy to have a little one on one with you."

The line fell silent for a moment. Dean looked at the receiver and worried that the call may have dropped. A second later, he heard a soft *click* followed by the smoky voice of a woman saying, "To the ships at sea who can hear my voice, look across the water, into the darkness."

I know that voice!

Where have I heard that before?

"That was a great broadcast," the caller then said. "If I could retire anywhere, it would *definitely* be there."

The line clicked off.

Dean stared at the receiver like the device was coated in grime.

27

Sheila reentered the room as Dean replaced the receiver in its cradle, handed her brother his cell, and informed him that she was unable to get hold of Bazz. Dean took back his phone and sat on the edge of the bed, shaking his head and trying to piece together the caller's cryptic riddle.

"So," Sheila said, "what did he say?"

"He played a recording," Dean said. "It was a woman's voice. I know that I heard it before."

"What did the recording say?"

"'To the ships at sea who can hear my voice, look across the water, into the darkness.' Then the guy said, 'That was a great broadcast. If I could retire anywhere, it would *definitely* be there.'"

His sister wrinkled her brow. "I don't get it."

"Yeah," Dean said. "Me either." He turned up his gaze and pinned it back onto the room's phone. "We need to call Greer and some of your people. We need to tell them what happened. The guy who called said we wouldn't be able to trace the call, but we need to try anyway."

One hour later, Greer, Dewitt, and one of Sheila's detectives—a woman with auburn hair named Crawford—held court with Dean and Sheila inside the hotel room. Dean and Sheila proceeded to give Greer and Dewitt the full rundown of what happened, Crawford taking notes as Dean gave a full recitation of the story.

"Well," Greer said, "to be frank, this all sounds a little farfetched to me."

A flustered Dean narrowed his eyes. "Are you kidding me, Aden?" He stretched out his arms. "Do you think I'm making this up or something?"

Greer gestured to the phone on the credenza. "We're pulling the call logs as we speak, but according to the profile we're working off of, it's outside the suspect's MO to just ring you up like this. It doesn't line up with how guys like him operate."

"This son of a bitch isn't operating by a normal playbook, Greer," Dean said. "He's got some kind of personal beef with me, and he's going to great lengths to make sure he's got me isolated."

Greer shrugged. "It could mean anything. All the guy had to do was implement a Google search to figure that one out, Blackwood."

Dean inched closer toward Greer, the fingers on his right hand curling into a fist. "You can't be that dense," he said as he motioned to the room phone. "The moment this sucker first called the station, he made it pretty clear that he's got his sights set on me, maybe even Sheila."

"He's obfuscating the investigation," Greer explained. "He's just trying to confuse us so we're looking in all of the wrong places. He simply figured out who you were and is using your, how should I phrase it," he snickered, "less than stellar reputation as a means to deflect. He wants us to *think* that he's got some kind of interest in you as a way to toy with us so he has time to stalk and plan his next attack."

"Oh, *Christ*," Dean groaned. "You really are a gem, you dimwitted shitbird."

"I'm inclined to agree with Greer on this one," Dewitt said. "There's a shred of truth in your statement that this individual doesn't operate off a run of the mill psychological template here, but I think he's toying with you. He's simply trying to frustrate us and divert our focus while he goes about selecting his next victim."

"He's leaving clues," Sheila said. "You heard what Dean said about that message he played."

"And we'll look into that," Greer said. "Until then, it's clear to us that any level of involvement from either of you is going to significantly impact this investigation."

Dean shot a look at the agent. "What are you trying to say?"

"I'm saying that the two of you need to steer clear of San Francisco for the time being." Greer motioned to Sheila and then swept his hand toward Dean. "We need both of you off the playing field. If we remove you from the equation, that will increase our chances of finding this guy."

Dean looked at his sister. A look of defeat washed across her face as the two of them moved toward the corner of the room, the siblings feeling like outcasts who had just been stripped of their badges.

"In the meantime," Dewitt said, "if this man contacts you again, you need to let us know immediately. As soon as we make some headway on this, you'll be brought back into the fold."

"Get out of town, Blackwood," Greer said as he picked at his manicured fingernails. "Let us handle this. The last thing we need is your penchant for wanton mayhem screwing this up. This is coming straight from the top. If you interfere with this case in any capacity, you'll be formally reprimanded and put on suspension. Those were the deputy director's exact words."

Dean crossed his arms, shook his head, and then put his focus on the Golden Gate Bridge outside his window.

That's it.

He clicked his teeth.

We're officially on the bench.

28

"Well," Sheila said as she sat on the bed beside Dean. "What now?"

Dean held up his cell phone, lassoed it in the air, and then tossed it on the bed. "Wilson just confirmed everything that Greer and Dewitt told us. He said I need to get back to LA and lie low until they figure this out."

"There's nothing he can do?"

Dean shook his head. "Not a damn thing. Wilson tried, but the people above him on the pecking order tied his hands. This is nothing new, She. The FBI has a track record of fouling things up like this. Greer is just one of a long line of asswipes who possess a knack for screwing up cases. It's like the Oklahoma City bombing. There were other people besides Tim McVeigh and Terry Nichols involved in the plot, but the ATF, the Bureau, and the DOJ had to pin it on one man simply to satisfy their interests. It's about their bottom line. It's not about the truth; it's about finding someone to pin it on so they can wrap it all up with a neat little bow, no matter what the cost."

Sheila let out a deep sigh, perched forward on the bed, and tapped her fingers. "I can't sit still knowing that Greer and Dewitt are way off the mark here. I know you're right. The person who's doing this wants to go head to head with you."

"Well," Dean said, "he got what he wanted." He closed his eyes. "I just can't figure out what comes next."

"It's got to be in the message he played for you," Sheila said. "*That* was the clue. If we can figure out what he was trying to say, that will lead us to the next stop."

"You're saying you want to keep going?"

"You're saying that you *don't*?"

"I'm thinking about it."

"Same here."

"Well," Dean said, "then we need to answer that question before anything else." He looked deep into his sister's eyes. "Do we keep going? Or do we walk away? We have a choice to make, and we have to make it right now."

Sheila stood up and paced the room, her mind spinning and feeling like it was being pulled in several directions at once. "If we walk away now, we run the risk of this guy going ballistic. If we don't give in to what he wants, he might escalate things. If we simply drop off his radar, he might start killing other people just to make a point."

"And if we stay on," Dean said, "if we go after him ourselves, it'll just be the three of us. We'll be able to take him out of the city and save other people from falling prey to his little sideshow. There's no guarantee that will happen, but going after him together and playing by his rules might spare other lives from being taken."

"But if we do this," Sheila replied, "if we go off the reservation like this, there's a strong chance we'll lose our jobs after this. Our careers, our reputations might be destroyed."

"This wouldn't be the first time I've put my rep on the line," Dean said. "I have no problem making that choice. You told me before that I am who I am, and I'm the kind of guy who rolls the dice. I have to. It's the only way I know how to operate. And to be honest, this is the only way I know how to get things done." He motioned to his sister. "But I'm not going to pressure you into making that same choice. If you want to stay behind, I'll take this guy on myself."

Sheila shook her head. "You're not going after him alone, Dean. You're my brother. I can't live with thinking that you're out there on your own."

"I can handle myself."

"I know you can." A fiery twinkle glimmered in Sheila's eyes. "But I want this son of a bitch. I want him to answer for what he's done. And if we can nail him, *if* we can bring him in, that will make all of the difference. We might be able to salvage our jobs if we pull it off."

"My thoughts exactly," Dean said. "That being said, it sounds like we've landed on a decision."

"It sounds like we have, little brother."

"Then the next step is figuring out what the hell this guy meant when he played that message."

"You mentioned that you had heard it before," Sheila said. "You told me you recognized the woman's voice."

The litany of files in Dean's home movie collection surfaced in his mind, his cerebral recollections fluttering about like a pack of pigeons.

He closed his eyes.

Tried to pinpoint where he heard the voice before, pacing the room as he snapped his fingers like he was clicking together Dorothy's ruby red heels.

"What are you thinking?" Sheila said.

"I've heard that voice before," Dean said, "but it wasn't in person. It's familiar, but it's not the voice of someone I've ever actually crossed paths with before." He smirked. "This guy definitely knows who I am. He has to. He's leaving specific clues only I can figure out. He wants *me*."

"To the ships at sea who can hear my voice," the woman's voice whispered in Dean's ear, "look across the water, into the darkness."

It's not a person I know.

But it's a voice I've heard before.

Dean's eyes widened.

This guy has a knack for movies. That's an actor's *voice on the recording.*

'60s-era cinema?

No, that's not it.

The '70s?

Yeah, we're getting closer.

Wait.

The 1980s.

John Carpenter!

That voice belonged to his ex-wife Adrienne Barbeau.

"Dean," Sheila said, "it would be great to know what you're thinking."

"That voice," Dean replied, "the one the guy played for me. It's Adrienne Barbeau; she was the wife of John Carpenter, the guy who did the first *Halloween* movie."

"The guy who called was playing you a clip from a movie?"

"He was. I'm just trying to remember which one it was."

Dean replayed Adrienne Barbeau's voice again and again and again as he thought back to the days of his youth, back when he rented videotapes from Blockbuster every Friday with his late brother Tommy.

"*Escape from New York*," Dean said. "No, that's not it." He thought of more titles. "It's not *Halloween*. She wasn't in that one." His mouth dropped open when another film title popped into his head. "Holy shit."

Sheila shrugged. "What?"

"I've got it."

"Then tell me!"

Dean snapped his fingers. "The guy who called me played a sound clip from the movie *The Fog*. It's a film that takes place in the Bay Area. Adrienne Barbeau played a disc jockey in that movie."

"Okay," Sheila said, "then what about the part where he said, 'That was a great broadcast. If I could retire anywhere, it would *definitely* be there'?"

Dean pulled out his phone, opened the Internet application, and plugged in "trivia for the movie *The Fog*" in the search bar. "Adrienne Barbeau's character worked in a lighthouse in that movie," he said. "It's where she did her radio broadcasts."

"*Broadcasts*," Sheila said. "That's what the guy said over the phone."

Dean nodded. "It was a real location. I remember Dad walking in on Tommy and me while we were watching it. He said, 'Look at that place, boys. That's a slice of paradise if I've ever seen one.'"

Sheila rolled her eyes. "Reminisce later. Where's the location of the lighthouse?"

Thumbs scrolling through the trivia pages, Dean landed on a section that read *The Fog: Filming Locations* and focused on a picture of a lighthouse jutting out in the middle of a bluff.

"Point Reyes Lighthouse," Dean said. "It's in Inverness, California. That's where they filmed those scenes." He handed Sheila his phone. "And it's only 1 hour and 50 minutes away from here."

His sister appraised the photo on the phone. "Do you think that's it?"

"I'd put the 6 grand in my savings account on it. This suspect has a thing for movies, and I think it's safe to say that this is where he's leading us."

"You only have 6K in your savings account?"

"Alimony is expensive."

"I thought Claire made six figures a year."

"Let it go, She."

"Sorry," Sheila said. "Look, I'm inclined to put in a call to my people, maybe yours. Backup might be good in this case. If this guy is trying to get us out in the open—"

"We have to do this ourselves, She," Dean replied. "You and me. No one else. This guy has been ten steps ahead of us the whole time. He'll sniff a blitz if we try to get anyone else involved."

"It's risky."

"And I'm a good shot." Dean nudged his sister. "How about you?"

"I'd put you to shame, Deano." Sheila patted the Glock 47 stuffed into her hip holster. "Not that it's a contest or anything."

Dean rolled his eyes as he took the phone from Sheila and fixed his gaze on the picture of the lighthouse. "Inverness, California," he said. "I guess we're taking a little road trip."

29

The sedan threaded its way up the 101 through Sausalito, California. Sheila, behind the wheel, cranked up the AC and kept the needle just above 65 miles per hour. Dean, seated beside her, took in the sight known as Richardson Bay off to his right. Boats skimmed the water off in the distance, and the faraway clang of a foghorn prompted Dean to recall stories of old sea captains he read about in his youth. He cranked the window down. The breeze wafted inside the car and cooled the thin layer of perspiration on his brow.

"For all of California's problems," Dean said, "it sure is beautiful."

Sheila motioned to the car radio. "You wanna listen to something? We've got about 2 hours before we get to the lighthouse."

"Sure." Dean fiddled with the radio knobs. "I'm curious to hear what your presets are. Ten-to-one says your choice in music hasn't changed even in your waning years."

"*Waning*?" Sheila's eyes widened. "I'm only eight years older than you, you pepped-up little shit."

Dean laughed as he switched on the radio and pressed the first preset. A moment later, the opening riff to "Black Hole Sun" by Soundgarden pumped through the car's speakers.

"Just like I thought," Dean shook his head. "You're stuck in a time capsule, She."

"I don't have time to sift through the current music catalog, brother."

"You're not missing much. Everything today is mumble-rap or autotuned nonsense."

"Spoken like the proverbial old man on the porch, Deano. Having a kid really did leave you with a bit of a salty disposition."

Dean nestled his head back against the headrest as thoughts of his only child floated through his mind. "I hope that kid is going to turn out all right, She," he said. "I tried to do my best to make sure he never has to live a life like I did, like *we* did."

"I'd like to think that I turned out all right."

"That you did."

The sedan hugged the upward curve in the road, the outro of the song playing out before it was replaced with "Zombie" by the Cranberries.

Sheila let out a deep sigh.

Dean noticed a contemplative twinkle in her eye.

"What?" he said.

She shook her head. "It's nothing."

"No, it's not. We've got time to kill, She, so we might as well kill it."

"I just remember Mom coming into my room one time when I was playing this at full blast," Sheila said. "I thought I was the only one home at the time. I was standing on my bed screaming the lyrics when Mom came in and stood in the doorway. She must've watched me belt out half the song. When I turned around, all she did was smile."

"No talk?"

"No, she didn't say anything." Sheila turned the steering wheel to the left and eased the sedan into the next lane. "She wasn't like Dad; she was the soft-spoken one. She just smirked, and then I turned the music down."

"When was that?"

The lines in Sheila's face slackened. "About a month after Tommy died."

Memories of the past played back at high speed in Dean's brain—Tommy's funeral, the silence his family shared in the weeks that passed.

The lack of sleep.

The pain they shared and coped with in different ways.

"We all dealt with it in our own way," Dean said. "I guess I kind of retreated into myself afterward." He glanced at his sister. "I never really checked in with you to see how you were doing."

"I was the older sister," Sheila said. "I was supposed to be the headstrong one because I was older or something, at least that's how Dad phrased it."

"He actually said that?"

Sheila nodded. "A couple days after Tommy passed, Dad came into my room and said to me, 'She, you need to be strong right now. Everyone in this family is in a bad spot, and you're the oldest. You need to set an example for your brother.'"

The comment elicited a grimace from Dean. "He didn't have any right to put that on you."

"It was *always* that way," Sheila said. "School, work, my personal life. I had to set the standard for you, according to

Dad, that is. After Tommy passed away, Dad put it on me to lead the charge, I guess."

"That's bullshit."

"I was never really bitter about it."

"I would have been."

"You were hurting." Sheila cut a glance at her brother. "You really wore your heart on your sleeve after what happened, kiddo. I think that's why I mentioned that thing about stepping in for you all those times when we were younger. I guess I thought I owed it to you to try to, I don't know, soften the blow that had been dealt to you. You were in pain for such a long time because of what happened. I mean," she shook her head, "you had to *watch* what happened to Tommy. I guess I just wanted to help you any way I could. You were like a zombie for so long."

"I was too consumed by my own bullshit, I guess."

"I understood why," Sheila said. "I just wanted you to feel better. Sometimes it felt like no matter how I tried, though, you couldn't pull yourself out of your funk."

"It wasn't on you to fix me, She," Dean replied. "It was on *me*. It took some time, but each day that passes, it gets a little easier."

"Nailing the guy who did it had to help."

"That it did." Aram Sarkissian's mugshot popped into Dean's brain. "That prick is rotting away in San Quentin for the rest of his natural life, or what's left of it, that is. Last I heard, his heart's been giving out."

"Good."

"You really do put the burdens of the entire world on your shoulder, She," Dean said. "You should find a little time for yourself."

Sheila huffed. "I wish I could."

"That's a load of bull. If *I* could manage to start a family, you could damn sure pull it off. Granted, I'm sort of starting all over with Layla, but," Dean closed his eyes. "*Damn it.*"

"What?"

"I need to call her."

"Then call her."

Dean fished out his cell and drafted a text to Layla. "I can't screw this one up, She," he said. "I got a second chance with this woman, and I can't foul that up like I did with Claire."

"Just don't overthink it. Get out of your own way. You'll be surprised at the results."

Dean laughed. "There it is again."

"What do you mean?"

"You gotta focus on *yourself* every once in a while, lady. I mean that in a nice way. There's someone out there for you. You just need to carve out some time to find them."

His sister rolled her eyes. "Bleeding hearts of the world unite."

"I mean it," Dean said. "I don't like seeing you ride solo your whole life. You've been so focused on your career and looking after your family that you've never taken a moment to find something just for you."

Sheila tightened her grip on the steering wheel, the sunlight outside filtering through the windshield and casting a radiant glow on her face. "I'll make you a deal," she said. "When this thing is finished, when it's all done, let's make each other a promise. The two of us will *both* take some personal time for ourselves. No work. We'll just take time to live our lives."

"Like a family trip or something?"

"Maybe."

Dean huffed. "Good luck getting Dad to go on a plane. Remember what he said that one time we flew to Phoenix?"

Sheila flattened her hand over her chest as laughter welled up inside of her. As her eyes misted, she conjured up the best guttural imitation of her father's voice that she could, and said, "I hate stewardesses. They're always grinning all the time. What the hell do you have to smile about?"

Dean, nodding, implemented a similar imitation of his father's voice and followed up with, "Those glossed-up nitwits are stuck in a metal tube in the sky all day."

The two siblings looked at one another and said in unison, "They're nothing more than a bunch of make-up-caked sky floozies."

Dean and Sheila laughed, Dean drying his eyes as the music on the radio changed over to "Run-Around" by Blues Traveler.

Sheila tapped her finger on the steering wheel to the beat.

Dean did the same with his foot.

"It's good to see you again, Deano," Sheila said, "circumstances of the reunion aside."

"Yeah." Dean nodded. "It's good to see you, too, She."

The siblings said nothing as Sheila cranked up the volume on the radio, both of them mouthing the lyrics and momentarily forgetting about what awaited them at the lighthouse 60 miles away.

30

Dean piled out of the car. The chilled breeze cooled his face and tousled his hair as he glanced left toward a long staircase that led down to a bluff. Situated on the edge of it was a lone lighthouse shrouded by a dense thicket of fog. The ocean waves slapped against the rocks, clapping like a slow rolling thunder. The wind current that blew through whistled like the sea itself was hissing.

"This is it," Sheila said as she closed her door and took a scan of her surroundings. "Do you see anyone?"

Dean flattened his palm against the SIG-Sauer P320-AXG in his appendix holster.

His eyes narrowed.

The hairs on the back of his neck prickled.

Then a switch flicked on in his brain, the one that triggered all the predatory skills ingrained in him by his rigorous training with the Army's elite Rangers unit to kick into high gear.

Dean winced as the tendons in his knee squealed.

Despite the years of physical therapy, cold weather still had a knack for causing the injury to flair up.

Suck it up, man.

Keep moving.

Sheila stood beside Dean, caressing the trigger guard of her weapon as she tailed her brother to the staircase that led down to the lighthouse. "It's beautiful," she said, "in a freaky, film noir kind of way."

Snapshots from the film *The Fog* flickered in Dean's mind. He saw Adrienne Barbeau's character Stevie Wayne sauntering down to the lighthouse, mozying through a thick blanket of mist much like the one that blanketed the landscape in front of him.

"What do you think?" Sheila said. "Should we call in local cops?"

"I wouldn't be surprised if this guy has eyes on us already." Dean gestured to the lighthouse. "I say we check it out."

"You sure?"

"If he wanted to kill us, he would have done it already."

"That place is a kill box, Dean." Sheila fastened her gaze on the lighthouse. "If he's hiding out there, he's got the drop on us."

"You're right," Dean said. "You stay here. I'll check it out." He pulled out his cell phone. "If you see something, call it in. I'll do the same."

"Good God, man," Sheila groaned. "With such defiant instincts, it's a miracle you've managed to survive this long."

"Yeah." Dean pulled out his SIG. "I think about that all the time." He made his way toward the staircase, his index finger brushing the trigger guard as the waves crashing against the rocks howled in the distance.

31

Each step Dean took toward the lighthouse left him feeling like he was navigating a series of land-mines. His eyes darted from left to right as he closed in on the front of the building, the rumble of the sea growing louder the closer he came to the front door.

Are you here?

Are you watching me right now, you son of a bitch?

As he placed a nicotine-coated toothpick between his lips, Dean appraised the Brazilian cedarwood and ghost gum trees peppering the bluff across the terrain, towering in their height and offering perfect cover for whatever—or *whoever*—might be hiding among them.

Dean approached the front of the lighthouse holding his SIG with both hands as he padded his way down the last steps that led to the front door. He took a moment to survey the structure in front of him, a relic of the past that towered like a mighty tyrant gazing out on its vast empire known as the sea.

Dean shook his head as he heard the ominous piano score from *The Fog* playing in his mind.

He reached his hand out to grab the door handle.

Then he molded his hand around it and twisted, the creak of the knob letting out an ear-piercing shriek as Dean slowly pushed the door open.

"All right," Dean whispered. "Slow and easy."

Dean quickly slipped into the lighthouse, scanning with his SIG from left to right as his heart drummed inside his chest. On his left, he made out a spiral staircase that led to the service room on the top level. The sound of his booted feet echoed against the structure's walls as he cleared the first floor and then made his way toward the staircase. Dean kept his weapon trained on the balcony on the upper level as he started his climb, moving with slow, fluid strides as he ascended each step until he stepped one foot onto the second floor landing.

Dean relaxed his posture upon seeing that the service room was void of anything save a small metal table and a series of empty wooden shelves. He furrowed his brow, his gaze fixed on the diamond-like prism beacon of the lighthouse 10 feet above his head. The wind whipped in through the awning-style windows, the ear-piercing whistle prompting Dean to close them all.

Silence held sway.

Dean implemented one last scan of the room.

Then he holstered his weapon and placed his hands on his hips.

"Nothing," Dean whispered to himself. "*Zip.*"

32

Sheila breathed a sigh of relief when she spotted her brother emerge from the lighthouse. She threw up her hands, shrugged, and then received a thumbs down from Dean in reply. It took 7 minutes for Dean to make the journey back up the staircase, and the moment he was back at Sheila's side, he told his sister, "There's no one there."

"Nothing?" Sheila said as she flicked the toothpick out of Dean's mouth. "No note? No clue?"

"This is real life, She," Dean said. "Maybe Greer and Dewitt are right. This guy might be pissing on our leg and calling it rain."

"You didn't see anything?"

"Feel free to take a look if you want. I think this whole thing was a bust."

Sheila and Dean said nothing as they stood by the sedan, Dean doing another scan of his surroundings as the denseness of the fog began to dissipate.

Why here?

Why bring us out to the middle of nowhere?

Is he toying with us?

Misdirecting us?

Dean huffed.

Maybe the guy is just an asshole who wanted us to waste the gas money.

"This is off," Sheila said. "If this whole thing is a game to this guy, why drag us out here?"

"I don't know, She," Dean said. "Maybe—"

His sister shrugged. "What?"

Dean felt a tug in his gut, a sensation that was triggered whenever he felt the eyes of a lingering predator fixed on him. It was a sense that was drilled into Dean back when he was a Ranger, an ability hard-wired into him that told him when some*thing* or some*one* was waiting in the wings, fixated on him like a panther readying itself to pounce on a potential meal.

"He's here," Dean said as the wind chilled the back of his neck. "He's *watching* us."

Sheila's eyes widened as she spun around and noted the cedarwood trees, the nearby structures, and the lighthouse, her hand inching toward her service weapon and ready to draw it out at a moment's notice. "You're sure?"

"Oh, yeah." Dean focused on the wind blowing through a grouping of trees 100 yards away. "He's scouting us out."

"How do you know?"

"You can't feel that?" Dean said. "You can't feel that there's a pair of eyes glued to the back of your neck? This guy has his sights on us *right now*. He's doing nothing more right now than enjoying the view."

Sheila pulled out her Glock and draped it by her side. "Why isn't he making a move? Should we get back in the car? Maybe he's got our heads lined up with a long-range rifle on us."

"He would have taken a shot at us already if he did. He's just watching us." Dean gnashed his teeth. "*Screwing* with us. He wants us to know that he's here. He's not ready to move in for the kill. Not yet. Yeah, this creep is going to take his sweet time getting to that point."

"We should search him out," Sheila said. "Let's find this guy and take him right now."

"He'll leave before we get to him. We'll never find him," Dean said. "No, he'll come to us when he's ready." He motioned to the ghost gum trees off in the distance. "This is just his way of saying hello."

Nothing but the roar of the ocean tides, the hiss of the wind, and the distant caw of a pelican were heard as Dean and Sheila took in the sights around them. Shaking his head, Dean stared at the ghost gum trees and offered the concealed suspect a rigid middle finger in reply.

33

Two steaming mugs of coffee were placed on the table. Dean looked up and thanked the server, placed an order for a burger—medium rear—and then put his focus on the parking lot outside the diner window, the melodic thump of Kenny Rogers' "Lucille" pumping through the jukebox in the corner.

"So," Sheila said, "I feel like a broken record saying this, but what happens next?"

"I don't know," Dean replied. "What are you thinking?"

"Well, I just got off the horn with some of my people back at the division. Your FBI buddies have been tag teaming the forensics end of the investigation. Luckily, I still have a couple of people on my side willing to throw me a bone."

Dean hooked two fingers around the handle of his ceramic mug. "What did they say?"

"Nothing's changed in terms of them finding anything of value. There are no fibers or anything in the way of residual DNA. It looks like your friends Greer and Dewitt are bringing in some people to pick apart each of the crime scenes to see if they can find anything. They're bringing in their full technical arsenal."

"They'll focus on the duct tape that was used on the victims," Dean said, "the rope that was used to bind them, the knife that was used to kill them. Those are the only cards they have to play with right now, but by the time they get a hit on anything—"

"What?"

Dean took a swig of his coffee. "This guy is killing these people for a reason, like we said, but all of it has something to do with me. He kills these people. Then he gets us pulled off the investigation. He's got us all to ourselves now while the FBI and the SFPD are occupied elsewhere."

"And after that little scene at the lighthouse," Sheila said, "it's possible that he might be following us." She flexed her brow. "We're going off just a hunch that you have, but those have a sick proclivity for being on the money more often than not."

Dean angled his body around and took note of the other patrons in the diner. A burly man dressed in denim sat at the counter. Beside him was a scrawny gentleman hunched over a beer. In the corner, Dean saw a young couple, early twenties, laughing about something as they picked at a pair of meals on their plates.

"You're right," Dean said. "He *is* tailing us now. But I don't take this guy for a fool. He's not going to try to make a move on us while we're out in the open." He winced. "*Maybe*."

"So we stick together," Sheila said. "Neither of us leaves the other's sight. We stay in the open, in areas of high traffic, if possible."

Dean drummed his fingers on the table. "In the meantime, we have to figure out who this guy might be. It's someone who knows me, but the question is *who*."

"Any ideas?"

"I've ruffled a lot of feathers in my lifetime, She," Dean said. "I'm certain that this guy is a cop or former military. Greer and Dewitt will reach that conclusion, too, but they won't land on that or announce it officially for the next day or so." Dean huffed. "I'm just trying to rummage through the list of people I've slighted over the years. Unfortunately, I can't get anyone at the Bureau to assist me in sifting through my old files now that we're on the bench. If anyone gets a whiff that I'm working something, they'll pull me in."

"Well," Sheila perched forward in her seat, "let's go through the list of people you've got stored away in that noggin of yours, line by line."

"There's no shortage of people. That's what I'm trying to get at."

"It's the only thing we have to go on until my people or yours uncover something in the way of a lead."

"By then, it'll be too late." Dean threw up his hands. "*That's* the point. This guy wants to exact some kind of vengeance here, and by the time the FBI or the SFPD starts to piece together who he is, I'll be buried 6 feet under the earth, if things go according to his plan, that is."

The man in the denim shifted his weight at the counter.

Dean watched the man intently and wondered if he was the one responsible for his current predicament.

"Dean," Sheila cooed. "*Easy*."

Dean took his focus off the man in denim and sipped his coffee.

Think.

Do like Wilson always tells you to do.

Use that big squirrelly brain of yours to figure this out.

"Okay," Dean said. "Let's think about what we know about the suspect, what we've learned about him at this point."

"You said he's got some kind of vendetta against couples," Sheila said, "something about him being impotent in that arena."

"The women weren't sexually assaulted. Have your people confirmed that?"

"Kits were run on the female victims. They were clean."

"It's possible he might have some kind of physical impairment."

Sheila wrinkled her brow. "Really?"

"It's a possibility, but don't bank on it. A physical impairment might line up with the profile of killers like him who have committed these kinds of attacks before."

"What kind of disability? I mean, if he does have one."

"Not sure." Dean narrowed his eyes. "But I'm currently scouring through a mental list of the people I've taken down who had one—or were given one by me."

Who do you know?

Who fits the profile?

Come on, man!

Someone has to stand out.

Dean's eyelids lowered slowly like stage curtains. "I don't know, She. But it's clear that this guy knows me—the way he spoke to me, how revved up he got when we talked on the phone. He knows how I operate. He knows all about me. I just can't figure out who he is."

"What about Bazz?" Sheila said. "Anything on his end?"

"I texted him right before we rolled in here. He said he needs a little more time to pinpoint the origin of that call."

"You think he can pull it off?"

The chime of the bell above the diner's door signaled

the arrival of a new customer. Eight construction workers stumbled into the diner, their cacophonous chatter revealing they were exchanging stories indicative of men who had pre-gamed before they walked in. In 2.5 seconds, the music on the jukebox was drowned out by their conversation as they sauntered up to the counter and started volleying their drink and dinner orders to the overwhelmed server who was doing her best to keep up.

Dean appraised each of the men, looking for anyone who looked out of place.

Just a gaggle of idiots.

Nothing to worry about save for the noise.

"Remember when they caught Bin Laden?" Dean said.

His sister nodded. "Yeah, the CIA located his courier through cell phone signals or something"

"Well, Bazz insinuated that he had *something* to do with that not that long ago. He's got a solid resume with this kind of work. I have no idea how he does what he does, but the results speak for themselves."

"I guess all we can do while we wait to hear back from him is go through the rogues' gallery you have stored away in that little mental vault of yours. Someone has to stick out."

Before Sheila was finished with her pitch, Dean produced his cell phone and slid out of the booth. "I'm gonna make a call back home really quick," he said. "I need to clear my head for a second." He nodded over his shoulder. "Keep an eye on me in case this nut job tries taking pot shots at me from the parking lot."

Sheila winked. "Tell Layla I said hi," she said as the server returned with two hot plates of food that she placed on the table.

Dean made his way through the front door of the diner.

Sheila picked up her fork and sifted through the shreds of chicken in her Caesar salad.

The short order cook in the kitchen started in on the orders for the construction workers.

At the rear entrance of the diner, the door opened, and a man who didn't work there quickly slipped inside.

In the parking lot, Dean plugged in Layla's number, waiting for three rings before he heard her voice on the other end of the line.

"Hello, Agent Blackwood."

A wry smile formed on Dean's lips. "Hey, you."

"How's it going?"

"It's going."

"You sound tired."

"Circle gets the square."

"Are you okay?"

"If I had a nickel for every time someone asked me that," Dean said, "we could have put a down payment on some seaside real estate in Cabo by now."

"Can you bring me up to speed?" Layla said. "I only got bits and pieces from you over text, *and* from what I saw on the news."

"So, you know."

"Do I need to worry?"

She does.

But there's no point in worrying her.

"It's nothing," Dean said. "Honestly, I—"

"Dean."

"Yeah?"

"I've been hitched to your wagon for a minute," Layla said. "You're a magnet for the bad things in this world. Also, I'm a journalist, so I think I have a pretty solid rundown of what's going on out there based on what I've heard in the rumor mill. Something's going on. I was just hoping you'd fess up to it and not keep me in the dark."

She's right.

Give the woman a little bit more credit, man.

"The guy doing this might have his sights set on me, Lay," he said. "I don't know who he is or what he wants. The only thing I do know is that he's itching to go toe to toe with me over it."

"Wait." Layla took a beat. "The guy who's doing this, he's after *you*?"

"Yeah." The fingers on Dean's hand clutching the phone secured a tighter grip. "That's the running theory."

Silence settled over the line. The lack of response from Layla triggered Dean's heart to pump to the point that it felt like it could keep the semi-truck on his left running.

There's only so much a partner can take.

You sign on for the Dean Blackwood roller coaster, it's a ride that never stops.

"I'm sorry," Dean said.

"Why are you apologizing?"

"This is a lot to handle. From the moment we met, my life has been nothing but a series of a non-stop—"

"*Babe*," Layla cut in, "don't think about that. You're focusing on all the wrong things right now. I don't need you to worry about me jumping ship. I *know* you, so I know that's what you're worried about right now."

Relief wrapped around Dean's chest like a warm compress.

She called me "babe."

He smirked.

She's never called me that before.

"I knew what I signed onto when I linked up with you," Layla went on. "To be honest," she chuckled, "there's a bit of a thrill in being with someone who lives his life the way you do. It keeps things interesting."

"Still," Dean said, "the two of us need to embrace some semblance of a normal life."

"And we will," she said, "but right now, you need to focus on what's in front of you. Figure it out. Get ahead of it. Knowing your track record, well, I think this guy that's got his sights set on you picked the wrong person to mess with."

"See, laddie?" Woody chimed in. "She's a great stand-up lady, this one. Why are you trying so hard to dick this up?"

"Shut up," Dean said.

Layla huffed. "Pardon me?"

Dean winced. "Sorry, I wasn't talking to you. I was clapping back to the unreasonable part of my brain that likes to chime in with his opinions every once in a while."

"Woody."

"Yep."

"Does it ever bother you?" Dean winced. "Me having little side conversations with that prick, I mean."

"Of course not," Layla said. "You work things out in your own way. Again, I *know* you. You're a tough nut to crack, but once I broke through that shell, I found a soft little nougat in the center."

"I don't know how I feel about being called a nougat."

"It's a term of endearment, smartass. Take the compliments where you can get them."

"Noted."

"I have every bit of confidence that you'll come through this intact, especially with another member of the Blackwood dynasty at your side. I just want you to be upfront with me from here on out. If something is wrong, don't hide it from me. I can handle it. We're in this together."

Dean's heart swelled with pride. "Understood."

"Call me soon. Willy and I will be right here waiting for you."

"I'll be back before you know it."

"We miss you."

"I miss you too."

"Tell her, laddie!" Woody barked. "Tell her how you *feel*."

Dean's mouth opened, three little words on the tip of his tongue on the cusp of rolling off—but then his cell phone buzzed. Dean spotted Claire's name on the display, which pulled him out of his train of thought. "Claire's calling me," he said to Layla. "I gotta hop off real quick."

"Go be a dad," Layla said warmly. "I'm not going anywhere."

"Talk soon."

"You know it."

Dean switched to the other call, greeted his ex-wife, and waited for a response.

"Someone wants to talk to you," Claire said. "Hold on one second."

The sound of the phone changing hands held sway over the line as Dean waited for several moments before he heard his son Jeremy say, "Hey, Dad" with a flat, monotone inflection.

"Pally!" Dean said, his heart swelling as he heard his son's voice. "How are you?"

"I'm okay."

"What are you doing?"

"Nothing really."

God almighty.

The kid sounds like he just ran a marathon.

"How are you feeling?" Dean said. "You doing all right?"

"I guess," Jeremy replied wearily. "I don't feel so good."

"What do you mean?"

"I'm tired. All the time. All day."

"You're having a rough time, Pally. You've had to deal with a lot."

His son said nothing.

"I, uh..." Dean furrowed his brow, "I heard what happened at school."

Jeremy held the line.

"You want to talk about it?" Dean said.

His son sighed. "Kids were picking on me," he said. "They were making fun of me. I just...I just got really angry."

"It's okay to be angry, kiddo. You just can't hit people. You know that, right?"

"I know."

Your son is a mess.

Get in front of this.

You can't let him turn out like you did.

"Buddy," Dean said, "I know you're going through a lot right now. It's going to take some time. Things aren't going to make sense for a while, but I promise you that everything is going to turn out okay."

"It doesn't feel that way," Jeremy said. "Everything is cloudy, like my head or something."

"Jeremy," Dean said, "do you trust me?"

"Yeah."

"Then I need you to hear my words. I need you to believe me when I tell you that we're going to work this out. You're the strongest kid in the world, and whatever is going on with you, all of us are going to figure it out. You, me, Geoff, your mom—all of us are going to make sure everything turns out okay." Tears welled in Dean's eyes. "Do you hear me?"

"I do," Jeremy said. "I believe you, Dad."

"I love you, Pally. Just rest up, and take it easy. I'll be back home before you know it. When I am, we'll get this all figured out. You have my word."

"I miss you, Dad."

"I miss you too."

"I'll see you soon?"

"Absolutely, buddy."

Dean signed off with his son, his ex-wife's voice coming over the line a moment later.

"Thank you," Claire said. "I think he just needed a bit of a pep talk from his dad."

"I'll get back as soon as I can."

"We'll be waiting."

"Take care."

"You too."

Dean pocketed his cell and drew a deep breath. "Figure this damn thing out," he whispered as the faces of Layla, Jeremy, Claire, Willy, and all the people he held close to his heart flashed in his mind. "Figure it out, and get your ass back home."

Dean headed back into the diner and stopped at his table. He got Sheila up to speed with what happened. She gave him her own little pep talk before Dean gestured to his uneaten burger and stated that he needed to use the head before he dived in.

Sheila told Dean to take his time.

Then Dean padded his way toward the hallway at the back of the diner that led to the restroom.

He walked through the door.

He headed toward one of the urinals.

Then Dean saw the booted feet of the man in the stall.

35

Dean positioned himself in front of the urinal. The truckers had walked in moments before he managed to get the server to turn up the volume on Robert Palmer's "Simply Irresistible," the noise reverberating throughout the diner to the point that it vibrated the walls of the bathroom.

The truckers in the diner laughed in unison.

One of them stomped their boots on the ground in sync to the beat.

"Good God," Dean grumbled. "I hope these guys aren't driving."

The toilet in the stall beside him flushed.

Dean started to unzip his fly.

The door to the stall opened with a creak.

Hold up.

Booted feet shuffled on the chipped tiles of the bathroom behind him.

This doesn't feel right.

Dean spun around.

His hand drifted toward his weapon.

Then his heart skipped a beat when he saw a 6-foot tall man wearing a black wool ski mask and leather gloves standing in front of him.

36

Dean made a move for his holstered SIG, his fingers wrapping around the weapon as the masked man thrust out his left hand, secured a grip on Dean's neck, and squeezed.

Christ.

Dean pawed at the tight grip the assailant had around his neck.

This guy is a beast.

A deep red hue tinted Dean's complexion as he drew out his SIG. His thumb fumbled for the safety. The masked man swiped his right hand and snatched the weapon away before he brought up his knee and planted it into Dean's nuptials.

A sickly sensation spread across Dean's lower body.

He crumpled to the floor tiles.

He struggled to find his footing as the masked man quickly stripped the SIG and tossed it across the floor in 3.2 seconds.

Dean got to his feet and charged his attacker. Spread his arms. Wrapped them around the man's waist, his hands grazing what he tallied as 190 pounds of ripped muscle under the man's shirt.

The attacker struck a fist against Dean's bum knee. The impact sent a signal to Dean's brain that triggered him to go limp. Dean fell face-first onto the tiles as his attacker gripped the back of his shirt collar, picked him up, and then threw him with ease into a wall.

Dean's head struck the wall, and for a moment, his world turned to a deep shade of black. No one outside the bathroom, it appeared, could make out the ruckus, thanks to the music, the boisterous construction workers, and the clanking of the short order cook's utensils.

Stars enveloped Dean's vision as he got to his feet. As he shook off his daze, he felt his attacker coil his arm around his neck. Dean tried to howl, but nothing came out other than a pitiful wheeze as his attacker hauled him into the stall.

The masked man kicked at the back of Dean's right leg and dropped him to his knees. Dean clawed at his attacker's face, fighting with every bit of energy he had in reserve as he felt a hand flatten against the back of his head.

Dean shot out his right hand to brace against the stall. On his knees, he eyed the toilet bowl a few inches in front of him. He attempted to plant his feet on the slick floor tiles, but his boots found no traction as he felt his attacker push his face slowly toward the toilet bowl.

I'm not dying in this greasy slop house.

Fury boiled inside of Dean.

No way in hell.

"You got no choice," Woody insisted. "This guy's got your number."

"Fuck you," Dean grumbled before he felt himself thrust face-first into the toilet.

Urine-tainted water seeped into Dean's nostrils and eyes as his attacker pressed his face deeper into the bowl. Dean thrashed his arms wildly, his neck muscles searing as he tried to push back against the pressure the attacker had against his head.

Seconds that felt like minutes ticked by as every part of Dean's body told him to succumb. His sinews slackened, and his mind signaled that he was about to give in as he felt his body lurch backward. Dean was thrown onto his back, blinking the toilet water out of his eyes as he fixed his gaze to the ceiling.

As his vision corrected, Dean made out the masked attacker standing over him, the man raising a fist before he brought it down for a strike against Dean's solar plexus that knocked the wind clean out of him.

Dean cradled his gut.

His attacker cocked his head to the side.

Then the assailant brought his mouth next to Dean's ear, and whispered, "I'll see you soon" before he threw a punch against Dean's temple that knocked him into a slumber.

37

Welts peppered Dean's head, torso, and arms as he sat on the hood of Sheila's sedan. On his left was a sheriff's deputy, a notepad clutched in one of the man's hands and a pen in the other that he used to gesture at the eight construction workers corralled together near the front of the diner.

"I spoke to a few of the guys over there," the deputy said. "I still need to talk to a couple of them, but all of them said they were sitting at the counter in there when you were assaulted."

Dean dabbed off the blood seeping out of the laceration on his forehead. "None of them did this. All those gentlemen over there are too liquored up to stand, much less kick my ass."

A pinched-faced Sheila paced the parking lot. "Whoever did this slipped in and out with no one noticing, Dean. He was watching you. When it got busy, he saw that as an opportunity to make his move."

"There's a rear entrance to the diner," Dean said. "Whoever did this came in that way. The cook and the server were too busy to see him walk in. By the time the guy was done tossing me around like a rag doll, he just left the same way he came in. I was out for at least 2 minutes after he threw that final jab at me, so he had plenty of time to make a run for it."

Every person in the diner—the cook, server, and construction workers—were questioned for close to 30 minutes. "I didn't see anybody come inside," one of them said. "Me either," said another. "I'm not sure what happened," a third one claimed.

"He's 6-foot-1," Dean told the deputy, "190 pounds, give or take. He got lucky that the music in the diner was playing as loud as it was. He used that to his advantage." He thought about the blow his attacker took to his knee. "And he knew I had a bum knee too. Son of a bitch knows every goddamn thing about me."

"Well," the deputy stuffed his thumbs into his belt, "we'll get you to the hospital and get you checked out. After that, we'll get you down to the station and—"

Dean pushed off the sedan and grimaced. The tax that his body had taken from the beating caused him to limp and swell all over, his bum knee searing and feeling the most strained of all the other injuries. "I'm not going to your station," he said. "It's a waste of time. This piece of shit is long gone by now."

"We should still take you in for a talk."

"Is that an order?"

""No," the deputy said. "I can *insist*, but—"

"Then we're done here," Dean said as he put his focus on Sheila. "No one here did this, and whoever did is having a good chuckle about it far away from here."

"I'll put the call out to some of my guys," the deputy said as Sheila and Dean piled into the sedan. "I'll get the units out there on the road to try to see if there's anyone driving through who might match your description."

"Good luck with that, deputy." Dean shook his head. "You guys aren't going to find him."

"You okay?" Sheila asked.

"It was *him*, She," Dean said as he took out a toothpick and clamped down. "This guy was waiting in the wings. He saw a perfect chance to strike, and he took it."

"Why didn't he kill you?"

"Because he's not ready yet. Because he just wanted to fuck with me." Dean closed his eyes. "Fucking hell. This guy whipped me without even trying. Whoever this is has been training to get to this point. He's a damn savage."

Sheila gazed at the windshield, her hands trembling as she gripped the steering wheel. "This is my fault."

"It's not your fault."

"We were supposed to stick together."

"We can't take trips to the bathroom with one another, She. I got lazy. This is my fault. I should have been more mindful." Dean sighed. "I was too preoccupied thinking about other things, so it diverted my focus."

Sheila did a scan of the road. Other than the muted glow of street lamps, the rest of the terrain was blanketed by the black of night. "This is too risky, being out on the road on our own like this," she said. "Maybe we should go back to the city."

"Maybe that's what he wants," Dean said. "This guy is good. He's composed a little symphony here. He's the conductor, and we're the string section following every little wave of his baton."

Dean's cell phone rang. Pain shot through his right arm as he reached into his pocket and pulled it out. He breathed a sigh of welcomed relief as he saw Bazz's name on the display.

"Hey, buddy," Bazz said. "Is this a bad time?"

Don't tell him you just got tuned-up.

I'm not in the mood to listen to his jokes.

"Not at all," Dean said. "Talk to me."

"Well, I worked my magic for you. I had to hit up some lowlives I used to know back at the Agency to try to trace where this call was made. I can't tell you how I did it, but we managed to find where your suspect rang you up from."

Dean's eyes widened. "Where?"

"San Francisco," Bazz said. "This degenerate whack job called you from an apartment about two blocks from the Robbery Homicide Department."

38

E ven though Dean pleaded his case to take the lead, Greer was the one who kicked in the door of the apartment where Bazz had traced the call. The door slammed against the wall after Greer booted it. Greer then moved aside as four HRT members flooded into the residence and cleared the foyer. Dean—sporting bandages on his arm and a fresh row of stitches on his head—lingered in the background with Sheila, watching as the HRT team scoured the residence with all the machismo in the world on display.

"Clear!" one of them yelled.

Dean and Sheila made their way into the residence, a two-bedroom, derelict dwelling replete with peeled wallpaper, water-stained floors, and fogged windows that overlooked San Francisco's financial district. A sunken mattress was in the living room. Day-old food containers were scattered about beside it. The bathroom was covered in a thin layer of grime. The entire layout—in Dean's mind—toted an aesthetic from something out of a David Fincher film.

"Agent Greer," an HRT member said. "Take a look at this."

Dean perked up as he followed Greer into the kitchen area. Beside the one window was a long table, and on top of it was a decades-old Apple Macbook and several stacks of used DVDs. Dean's eyes narrowed as he perused the selections—copies of *The Fog*, *Se7en*, *Apocalypse Now*, *Speed*, *The Manchurian Candidate*, and *Blue Steel*, among what he tallied as close to twenty-five films in total.

"Son of a bitch," Greer mumbled. "How did you guys find this place?"

Sheila shot her brother a look.

Dean lied through his teeth to Greer. "Someone phoned me with an anonymous tip."

Greer and his partner Dewitt slipped on gloves. Dewitt then began photographing the evidence on the table, fielding phone calls between shots from her superiors to inform them of the update.

"This is big," Greer said. "We needed this." He swung his focus around and put it on Dean. "You're telling me that you two were just taking some time to yourself and someone just happened to call you up and tell you this was all here?"

"Yep." Dean flashed a shit-eating grin. "That's what I said, Aden."

"What about you?"

"What about me?"

"You look like someone beat you senseless."

"I tripped down some stairs," Dean said. "I'm a clumsy son of a gun. Just ask my sister. I couldn't walk in a straight line until my teens."

"I'm supposed to buy that bullshit?"

"With what you throw down on hair care products, I don't think you could afford it."

"This true?" A stone-faced Greer shot his chin at Sheila. "I'm supposed to believe your brother over there pulled a Mr. Magoo?"

"Magoo never tripped," Sheila explained. "The guy always managed to stay on his feet."

Dean squinted. "What was his dog's name?"

"McBarker."

"That's it."

"Good dog name."

"I know, right?" Dean smirked. "Pretty killer."

Greer shook his head.

Dean shrugged.

Sheila tamped down the urge to laugh.

Then Dean tried to take out a toothpick, but his sister batted it out of his grip.

Thirty minutes went by as Dewitt and Greer worked the scene. A pair of techs showed up at one point to assist them. As the agents sifted through everything at the crime scene, Greer, his face glazed with irritation, walked up to Dean and came an inch shy of being nose to nose with him.

"Level with me," Greer said. "What the hell is going on here?"

"Your guess is as good as mine, Aden," Dean replied. "Someone called in the tip, we let you guys know, and now we're here trying to figure out what's going on."

"You've been working on this case, haven't you? You talked to someone. This whole thing didn't just float across your radar." Greer pointed to the wound on Dean's forehead. "That's why you got that nifty little cut on your head. Something tells me you've been doing what you do best— stirring things up until you draw someone out of hiding."

"And you're doing what *you* do best, Aden," Dean said. "You strut around with your Brooks Brothers suit acting like you're the cock of the walk when really you're just an over-hyped errand boy riding the coattails of people like your partner there."

As she snapped a picture of the Macbook, Dewitt said, "Keep me out of it" and then turned her attention to the DVDs.

"I'm going to make some calls here in a minute, Blackwood," Greer said. "I don't know what you're up to or how the hell you stumbled across this, but rest assured, you'll be working cold cases in Anchorage by the time all is said and done."

"Good God, man." Dean sighed. "Do you just sit at home all day watching police procedurals and jotting down quippy one-liners?"

"Get off my crime scene," Greer said. "And don't go too far. I'm not done with you by a long shot."

Sheila grabbed her brother's arm and pulled him out of earshot. "Okay," she said. "Maybe now is the time we tell them about what happened at the diner."

Dean shook his head. "The hell with that. We need to look at the stuff inside that room over there."

"These people are about to bag all that stuff up and take it out of here," Sheila said. "Maybe we need to bring your people into the loop here."

"Maybe that's what this guy *wants*. He's been miles ahead of us at any given moment, so maybe we need to start being unpredictable to throw him off our trail."

"He doesn't know about Bazz," Sheila said. "He doesn't know we're here."

"I'm not going to bet on any of that." Dean cut a glance at Greer conferring with one of the HRT members. "What we need to do is continue to work this from our own angle. If we spook this guy too soon, we might lose him. He might go into hiding, hibernate for a while, and then come back with a vengeance."

Sheila let out a deep sigh. "Okay," she said. "Let's work the scene."

The two reentered the apartment, hovering near the table with the Macbook and the DVDs while Greer and Dewitt worked their way through the other rooms. Sheila pulled out her cell phone and took a series of photos, filling her storage with enough pictures that she could have reconstructed the entire apartment from the ground up.

"Why DVDs?" Sheila said. "What does that mean?"

Dean shrugged. "Best guess? Maybe he's using analog methods of watching movies. It's better for him than streaming. Streaming requires a computer, an account, something we would be able to trace more easily."

But why?

What is the MO?

Why the obsession with movies?

Dean fixated on the DVDs. His eyelids tapered when he saw what looked like the remnants of a sticker that had been torn off from the front of a copy of *The Fog*.

I know who I can call.

"Hey, Aden," Dean said. "Who are you going to send this stuff to?"

Greer poked his head out through the doorway that led into the kitchen. "Our people at Quantico. We're going to put a rush on it to see if we can pull anything."

"Didn't Baumgardner transfer back not that long ago?"

"Yeah, so what?"

Perfect.

"Okay," Dean said. "We're headed out now. Need to get some chow. I'll link up with you guys later, all right?"

Greer crooked his finger at Dean. "You're not leaving."

"Really?" Dean moved to the door. "Because my feet would indicate otherwise."

"Blackwood, don't you walk out that door."

Dean grabbed Sheila by the arm. "Hey, Greer," he said. "What has two thumbs and thinks you're a top-shelf dickhead?" He pointed at himself with both of his thumbs. "*This* guy."

"*Blackwood.*"

"Later!"

Dean hustled out of the apartment with Sheila in tow. Her eyes were wide, her mouth agape and a bewildered expression on her face.

"Dean," Sheila said, "what the hell are we doing?"

"We're leaving."

"We need to stick around here. Greer and his people need to work the scene. We need to hang close by in case they get a hit on something. This is the first time we've been allowed back into the fold on this whole thing."

"Greer won't find any prints," he said. "This suspect of ours is too smart to leave anything in the way of prints. He didn't leave them at the crime scenes, so he's sure as hell not going to leave them in that apartment." He pulled out his cell phone. "I know what we need to do."

"For crying out loud," Sheila said. "Why does everything have to be so complicated with you?"

"I don't make things complicated." Dean's eyes shimmered. "That's just how they get all by themselves."

"You stole that line."

"No, I didn't."

"Yes, you did." Sheila rolled her eyes. "That was from *Lethal Weapon*, the first one."

"You're right," Dean said. "I guess all this movie trivia bullshit is starting to rub off on me."

The muscles in Sheila's jaw tensed. "I don't know where Mom and Dad went wrong with you. Seriously, did you get hit on the head or something as a kid?"

"Once or twice. Why?"

"Be a normal human man for a second, okay? What are you trying to do? Clue me in here, please."

Dean pulled out his cell. "I've got a friend over at Quantico that we're going to hit up. We go back a little ways." He plugged in a number, hit call, and then held it to his ear. "And he owes me one," he laughed. "He just doesn't know it yet."

39

Baumgardner had the Twinkie halfway into his mouth when the phone on his desk started to chirp. The portly tech gnashed his teeth as he gawked at the device. Odds were high that it was his eighty-three-year-old grandmother who called three or four times a day to complain about her shoulder pain, the leaky water faucet, or the neighbor's dog.

"Damn it," Baumgardner mumbled as he picked up the receiver and held it to his ear. "This is Baumgardner."

"*Heyyyy*, buddy."

The timbre of Dean Blackwood's voice stirred up nausea in Baumgardner's guts. He hunched over his desk, shaking his head and preparing himself mentally to shoot down whatever off-the-books request Blackwood was inevitably going to make.

"Whatever it is," Baumgardner said, "whatever you want, Dean, I don't have time for this."

"Let me guess," Dean said. "You're ogling a Snowball or a Hostess cupcake right now."

"It's a Twinkie."

"No kidding."

The heavyset tech shot a look over his shoulder at a pair of his colleagues examining a pair of blood-slicked slacks through a microscope. "Just ask whatever you're going to ask," he said to Blackwood. "We're a bit busy over here at the moment."

"You're about to get busier," Dean said. "You know Agents Greer and Dewitt?"

"Dewitt's nice enough." Baumgardner rolled his eyes. "Greer's about as soft as a mattress made out of gravel."

"You should be a writer."

"Quit mucking around, Dean."

"Greer and Dewitt are running point on a multi-homicide investigation in the Bay Area," Dean said. "They're about to overnight a slew of evidence your way—a Macbook and a series of used DVDs."

Baumgardner cupped his meaty palm over the phone and whistled to the pair of techs picking at the bloodied slacks. "Are we expecting something from the San Francisco field office?"

The tech with the Buddy Holly glasses nodded. "Yeah, it should be here around noon."

Baumgardner ripped his hand off the receiver. "It's on its way," he said to Dean. "Satisfied?"

"Never," Dean said. "Look, I need you to do me a favor."

"No way."

"Zachary."

"Please, don't call me that."

"Look, buddy," Dean said, "I'm not asking you to do anything other than the job the Bureau pays you so handsomely to do."

Baumgardner switched the phone to his other ear, eyeballing the Twinkie as he calculated how long the chemically produced confection could sit out before it went stale. "It's never straightforward with you, Blackwood," he said. "So please, for the love of Newton, tell me what it is you want me to do."

"Your job," Dean said. "You're going to examine the evidence that's being sent to you. You're going to sift through the data on that hard drive along with those DVDs."

"And?"

"*And* I want you to take a hard look at the DVDs that are being sent to you. They belong to the prime suspect that the Bureau is looking at. There's stickers that have been ripped off the covers of several of them. My guess is that a thorough examination of them will point you to the source of where they were purchased or stolen from."

Baumgardner's eyes constricted. "What's the ask here?"

"The ask," Dean said, "is simple. I want you to call me before you call anyone else once you pinpoint where the DVDs came from."

The lines in the tech's face slackened. "For the love of God—"

"It's not that big of a deal, slick."

"They log every single call and key stroke from this office."

"So?"

"So," Baumgardner huffed, "what am I supposed to say when someone from OPR comes knocking on my door asking why I'm calling you? I assume you've been pulled from this case and are now operating in an unofficial capacity."

"You know me too well, buddy."

"I'm not doing it."

"Yes, you are."

"What's my motivation?"

"Because," Dean said, "you don't want anyone in your desk clump over there knowing that you took sick leave eight weeks ago to go to a Comic Con convention."

Hairs on the back of Baumgardner's neck prickled as he lowered his voice to a whisper. "How the heck do you know about that?"

"We're best friends, buddy," Dean said. "Friends stay up to date with each other's comings and goings."

"We're not friends," Baumgardner said. "You're like some kind of funhouse version of Nostradamus, except you're not fun at all. You're a nightmare."

"Just call me when you get something of value, all right? All I'm asking is for a courtesy call before you ring up anyone else, that's all."

"I'm gonna get fired."

"No, you're not. Just do your job. Call me when you get something."

The click through the earpiece signaled that the call was terminated.

Baumgardner huffed out the air in his lungs as he placed the receiver back in its cradle.

"How the hell does he do that?"

40

Dean pocketed his cell and approached Sheila's sedan. His sister was fishing out her keys as she asked her brother what he thought was so damn funny.

"A buddy of mine at the Hoover Building," Dean explained, "is going to give us a shout once he gets a hit on that evidence Greer and Dewitt just bagged up."

Sheila piled into the sedan and slipped the key into the ignition. "Sean Wallace."

"The kid who used to live on our old street?"

"Yeah."

"What about him?"

Sheila turned the engine over. "You and Tommy convinced him one time to get on a skateboard and tether a rope to his dog's collar. The kid wiped out and got road rash all over his palms."

"Point being?"

"You had that same squirrelly smile on your face after it happened," Sheila said. "Mom called you Devious Dean when Sean's mother knocked on the front door and started raising hell."

The sedan pulled away from the curb and linked up with the traffic. Dean's gaze was at the top floor of the apartment building where the killer's crash pad had been found, his eyes scanning the adjacent units and wondering if the killer was pulling a Lee Harvey Oswald and watching him and Sheila at that very moment.

"Where are you?" Dean whispered. "Why don't you just come out and look me in the eye?" He raised two fingers and gingerly grazed the bandage on his head. A sharp pain discharged across his forehead and triggered him to wince.

"What?" Sheila said.

"I don't like this," Dean replied. "I don't like being toyed with. I don't like that this guy has some kind of vendetta with me but sees fit to kill innocent people in the process."

"He told you he wanted to get you all riled up."

"Well, it's working."

Sheila glanced at the clock on the radio and saw that the 2:00 p.m. hour was creeping in. "What now?" she said. "We've got time to chew up before your friend over in Washington calls back," she huffed. "And knowing *you*, I don't think he's comfortable calling you a 'friend.'"

You need to dig into your past, Blackwood.

You need to get a solid list of suspects going.

And you're going to need some help.

Dean pulled out his phone and punched in Bazz's number, the line ringing twice before Bazz answered.

"What do you need now?" Bazz said, sounding more amused than annoyed based on the hint of laughter that glazed his tone.

"How hard would it be," Dean said, "to rummage through all my old case files?"

"You mean accessing the FBI database, so to speak?"

"I didn't say that." Dean shrugged. "Well, not *explicitly*."

"My friend," Bazz said, "you are in a unique position to have a friend with the kind of resources I have. I could get you a live satellite feed to a Saudi prince sitting on his crapper if I was so inclined."

"I don't want or need that, thankfully."

"Well, what *do* you need?"

"Here's the short version of what's playing out, Bazzy," Dean said. "We've got a killer with a hard-on for me. My gut, coupled with the writing on the wall, tells me that this guy is someone from my past, someone I've slighted, and based on our previous calls, it looks like whoever it is might have been on the armed services payroll at some point, maybe a cop."

"I can do that," Bazz said. "The only problem is—"

"I've pissed off plenty of people."

"Correct," Bazz said. "Look, are there any keywords I should plug in as I do this? If this guy has some kind of MO, that'll help narrow down the searches."

"Domestic violence charges," Dean said. "Anything along those lines. Look for arrests, convictions, or even instances where the individual was merely questioned. You also need to check for anyone with significant or noteworthy physical impairments."

"Copy that."

"How long will it take? I hate the idea of rushing you, but this guy just whooped my rear end in a bathroom stall, which kind of has me worked up at the moment."

"You're kidding."

"Afraid not."

"Wish I could have seen that."

"I'll tell you all about it when I see you," Dean said. "For now, just help me try to figure out who this guy might be.

We're on a timetable here, and this guy is going to rear his head again sooner rather than later."

"Give me a few hours," Bazz said. "I mean, I *was* planning on fishing today, but how could I say no to a friend in need?"

"I owe you one."

"You owe me *more* than one, skippy. I'll be in touch."

Dean slipped his cell into his jacket pocket and rested back in his seat. He dished out the details of the call with Bazz to Sheila, his sister nodding her head and feeling like each second that passed drew them closer to a finale that both of them knew would be more lively than a 4th of July fireworks display.

"We should stay on the move until Bazz calls back," Sheila said. "I don't like the idea of staying in one place for too long if this guy is tailing us."

Dean glanced at his rearview mirror. All the cars in the reflection were suspect in his mind. Every person he and his sister crossed paths with until the situation reached its conclusion was untrustworthy and—in his mind—out to get him.

"He's out there, Sheila," Dean said. "This guy is out there somewhere."

41

The only option Sheila and Dean settled on until Bazz or Baumgardner got back to them was to keep driving. They had to *literally* stay on the move until they had something to work with. After they filled up the sedan with gas, they proceeded to drive up the coast, never moving in a straight line and making sure they lingered close enough to San Francisco that they could double back and be in the city limits within an hour.

Slivers of the sun retreated into the west as they drove. Dean, who was in the driver's seat, fiddled with the car radio. He threw a quick look at Sheila in the passenger seat. Her eyes were closed, and her head rested against the window. She shuddered and then tensed her body, the fingers on both her hands arching into a fist.

Dean shook his head.

The Blackwood way of life.

Always on the defensive.

Always on the move.

A few seconds of scrolling through the radio waves

brought Dean to a soft rock hits station, Chicago's "Baby, What a Big Surprise" thumping through the car's speakers at a low volume. Dean made a move to turn down the volume for his sister's sake, and as his fingertips brushed the dial, she said, "Keep it there."

"You can sleep with the music playing?"

"I need music to sleep," Sheila said. "It's like those trickling water fountains in a therapist's office." She peeled open her eyes. "But I *can't* sleep," she said as she sat up straight. "I was just closing my eyes for a second."

Dean scanned the highway in front of them, a two-lane road with a view of the Pacific Ocean off to his left and a cliffside on his right. He batted his eyelids that felt like they were painted with lead, his blinking triggering the memory of the beating he took in the diner bathroom to run back at high speed. Dean squinted, trying to focus on the mental snapshot he had in his brain of the masked man's face, in a bid to make out something he could use to his advantage.

"What are you thinking about?" Sheila said.

"The beating I took in the bathroom," Dean said. "I was playing it back in my head. I was hoping I'd be able to recall something physical about the guy."

"Anything?"

"He wore a mask. By the time I was on my back, right before he knocked me out, my vision was shot. It was all blurry."

"The guy could have killed you if he wanted to."

"But he didn't."

"Who did you tick off to the point that they would go through this whole rigamarole?" Sheila said. "Someone has to stand out. You've got a memory like a steel vault."

"There's no point in asking the same questions a million

times over," Dean said. "Let's just wait until Bazz comes up with something."

"Wager a guess."

Dean shook his head. "You don't get it, She. I spent a solid few years of my life rubbing shoulders with a variety of bottom-dwelling scum for the Bureau—drug dealers, neo-Nazis, the kind of people who'd eat their young if it benefited them to some extent."

His sister arched her eyebrow curiously. "I've never heard any of the stories."

"You don't want to. Believe me."

"It was undercover work, though, right?"

"Three years."

Sheila whistled. "That's a lot."

"More than any other agent in the FBI's history," Dean said. "I don't say that with an air of pride. Going undercover is like rolling the dice. It's an odds game."

"There's gotta be a playbook you stick to though."

"A loose one," Dean said. "But I tended to throw the rulebook by the wayside more often than not."

"Well," Sheila said, "*that* I could have guessed. This isn't the first time you've heard someone say this, but I am surprised the Bureau didn't put a pink slip in your stocking when you take into account your tenacity for bending the rules."

Dean's eyes shimmered. "They need guys like me. It's a tale as old as time. When you can't get things done via the regular rules, procedures, or standards, you call in a ringer." He shot his sister a look. "And I'm the ringer."

Sheila winced. "But if things go south—"

"They can throw me under the bus."

"Because of your personality, your profile."

"Ed Zachary."

Sheila furrowed her brow. "What?"

Dean said, "Say it out loud." After Sheila did, she proceeded to roll her eyes.

"How do you not lose sleep over that?" Sheila said. "Being the dirty work guy, I mean?"

"I have."

"It sounds like they treat you like an expendable asset, little brother. Like you said before, you're running a numbers game, toying with the odds. You don't think that those odds will catch up to you sooner or later?"

"I think about that all the time. There's only one problem though."

"What?"

Dean threw up his hands. "I don't know how to do anything else. Maybe I'm hooked on it just like I was with booze."

"Well," Sheila said, "as crazy as it sounds, you're more likely to get killed partaking in these rogue missions for the Bureau than you are the bottle, if you catch my drift."

"Are you implying I should take up a different field of work?"

"Maybe. I guess I'm just giving you food for thought."

Dean tightened his grip on the steering wheel as he marinated on the conversation he just had with Sheila.

What if I don't live through this bullshit contract with the Bureau?

I've got a kid.

A good thing going with Layla.

And how much longer will it be before the next grade-A psycho comes after me with a death wish?

"Hey, laddie," Woody cooed. "How's it going?"

Dean squinted his eyes.

What the hell do you want?

"You can't feel that?"

Feel what?

"That same feeling you had at the lighthouse," Woody said. "Don't you feel like you're being *watched*?"

42

Nerves stirred inside of Dean like water in a boiling kettle. He shook the sensation off, convinced that it was nothing more than paranoid delusions creeping out of the unreasonable part of his mind trying to get the better of him.

Sheila checked her watch: 8:10 p.m. "We should find somewhere to eat," she said. "I'm starving. Maybe we should head back toward the city."

"Good idea." Dean flicked a glance toward his mirrors. "The sign 2 miles back said there's an exit coming up ahead. I'll turn off there and do a U-turn."

A pair of headlamps 100 yards behind the sedan lit up the rearview mirror.

Dean squinted as he tried to get a look at the approaching vehicle, but all he could make out were its lights.

Another weary traveler.

Dean's neck muscles constricted as he eased down on the accelerator.

All we're doing is driving, ambling toward an unknown destination until something happens.

This is what this son of a bitch wants.

He wants to bring me to the point of exhaustion until I'm ready to tap out.

The outro of the song over the radio played out and cross-faded into "Don't Stop the Dance" by Bryan Ferry. Dean felt the fatigue from the road, the beating he took, and the stress of the situation settle throughout his body.

Get some coffee.

Get some chow.

Try to turn your brain off until you need *it.*

The highway curved slightly to the right. Dean eased the steering wheel and tapped the brakes, riding the curve as he spotted the off-ramp a half-mile off in the distance.

"Dean," Sheila said as she angled her body toward the rear window.

"What?"

"It's getting closer."

"What is?"

"The vehicle behind us." Sheila's hand drifted toward the service piece nestled into her holster. "It's speeding up."

43

As soon as Dean spotted the vehicle approaching him swiftly from the rear, he cursed under his breath. He tightened his grip on the steering wheel, all thoughts of weariness gone, replaced with a high dose of adrenaline.

"*See*?" Woody said. "I told you something was up."

Knock it off.

"You knock it off." Woody jeered. "Where would you be if I wasn't here?"

Dean's foot jammed down on the gas pedal. The motor under the hood of the sedan perked up, and the needle on the speedometer jumped from 60 to 65 miles per hour.

A couple seconds later, Dean felt his body wrench forward. The vehicle behind him smashed into the rear of the sedan and caused the back end to fishtail.

"*Damn it*," Sheila grumbled as she whipped out her service weapon. "It's him."

"Yeah," Dean said as he threw a quick look into the rearview mirror and made out the outline of a pickup truck. "No shit."

Dean jerked the steering wheel hard to the left and dashed into the opposite lane. The truck followed suit. The driver behind the wheel—neither Dean nor Sheila could make out his face—gunned the pickup and kept up the pace like its front bumper was tethered by cables to the rear of the sedan.

How did he find us?

How is he doing this?

How the hell is this guy always one step ahead?

Ahead, Dean could make out the exit on his right. He quickly sifted through his options, glancing at Sheila as the rage inside of him reached a boiling point. "She," he said, "do me a favor and shoot this guy's tires, will you?"

Sheila rolled down her window.

She thumbed the safety on the Glock in her right hand.

Then she poked her head out the window and squinted at the wind that struck her in the face.

Two shots rang out from behind the sedan. Dean registered a pair of muzzle flashes from the driver's side of the pickup truck. Sheila ducked back into the sedan as a bullet whizzed past and took out the side mirror. She crouched down behind her headrest, patting herself over and widening her eyes upon realizing the bullet had missed her by just a couple of inches.

"Okay," Dean grumbled as his face turned a shade of beet red. "This guy just gave you the green light to take him out."

Sheila gripped her weapon with both hands and took aim through the rear window. "On it," she said before she squeezed the trigger and shot off two rounds that shattered their rear window.

The pickup swerved out of the way as the bullets from Sheila's glock drilled into its windshield. The driver of the pickup then fired two rounds of his own, the first bullet clipping the sedan's center rearview mirror and shattering it to pieces, the second one striking Dean's headrest, which caused a flurry of stuffing to pepper his right cheek.

Sheila fired a shot in reply.

The driver of the pickup followed suit.

Both of them volleyed gunfire for a collective total of six rounds before the driver of the pickup squeezed off a shot that punctured the left rear tire of the sedan.

Dean's heart felt like it was lodged in his throat as the rear end of the sedan bobbed and weaved from side to side. He turned the steering wheel to the right and then to the left, his eyes widening as he realized the vehicle was ready to go into a spin.

"Dean!" Sheila hollered as she braced herself in her seat, using her left hand to buckle her seatbelt as the scent of burnt rubber filtered in through the air conditioning units.

The motor of the truck growled as it closed in on the left side of the sedan. The driver behind the wheel revved the engine before the pickup shot forward, the front bumper kissing the left back side of the sedan, sending it into a 360-degree spin.

Dean's vision became a kaleidoscope blur of colors and shapes as he tried to turn out of the spin. He heard his sister scream something to him, but her words were drowned out by the combined racket of the truck's engine and the squeal of the sedan's tires. A few moments later, Dean felt his body become weightless as he stared through the windshield, the landscape outside the car turning upside-down and bringing Dean to the quick realization that the sedan was flipping over.

"Sheila," Dean said. "Hang on!"

The pickup slammed into the sedan once more. The ear-piercing metal-on-metal thwack of the cars impacting one another prickled Dean's ears.

Dean held his breath.

The sedan flipped over.

Then he saw the sign for the off-ramp closing in.

Dean shot a look at his sister.

She closed her eyes and braced.

The last thing Dean saw was the pickup zipping down the road before his world—for the second time in two days—cut to black.

44

A steady, soft *beep-beep-beep* stirred Dean out of his slumber. He opened his eyes and shuddered, a harsh white light blinding his vision that forced him to snap his eyes back shut.

"Hey," a voice whispered. "Look at me."

Dean parted his chapped lips, his words raspy and clinging to his parched throat as they stammered out of him. "Am I dead?"

"Far from it, babe," Layla whispered. "*Far* from it."

A few moments went by as Dean rallied his senses. The sinews in his body stirred and twitched and allowed him to flex his fingers and toes, pinpoints of pain shooting through a few areas of his body as he wiggled around and realized he was lying on a bed. Dean then slowly opened his eyes once again, the same bright light greeting him and triggering a pulsating headache to settle in the back of his head.

He blinked his eyes. His blurred vision now calibrated, he gazed upon the face of Layla Edith Adrian.

"Are you sure," Dean groaned, "that this isn't heaven?"

Layla nodded to the IV drip beside her tethered to his

body. "If you're about to say 'because I'm looking at an angel,'" she replied, "I'll pull the cord right now."

Dean laughed and felt a searing pain in his ribs. He did an appraisal of his body and saw the line tethered to the IV beside his bed, the wires and pads on his torso jacked into the heart rate monitor next to his headboard. "How long have I been out?"

"About 4 hours," Layla said. "You've been in and out for a little while."

"Where's Sheila?"

"She's awake."

"Is she hurt?"

"She has a small fracture in her wrist, but she's fine." Layla flexed her brow. "You actually took the worst of it. The doctors told me you have a mild concussion and some bruised ribs." She cocked her head to the side. "They also said you have some cuts and bruises that *aren't* from the accident, so I'm curious to hear about that once you're back on your feet."

Dean, with Layla's assistance, propped up his head on the pillow. "How did you know I was here?"

"Sheila called me not long after you guys were brought here," Layla said. "I came up as soon as I could."

"You drove all the way up here from LA?"

"No, I flew."

"God," Dean groaned. "That must've cost you an arm and a leg."

"Make me dinner, and we'll call it even," Layla said. "Also, your neighbors across the street are looking after Willy until I get back."

"You're the best."

"Feel free to put me as your emergency contact. Next

time you wind up getting knocked into a coma, they can just call me directly."

"Is this your way of telling me you want to go steady?"

Planting a kiss on his cheek, Layla replied in the same comforting tone she always tended to have. "Yeah, something like that."

"So," Dean said as he propped himself up on his elbows, "how long are you sticking around?"

"As long as you'll let me, I suppose."

"If I had it my way, it would be forever. Unfortunately, being that there's a lunatic hot on our heels, it's probably not a wise move to have you hanging around."

"If this guy is stalking you like you say he is," Layla said, "then it's possible that he's already seen me."

She's right.

And she shouldn't be here.

It's bad enough that Sheila's already caught in this guy's crosshairs.

"Do you have your gun on you?" Dean asked.

"It's in the car," Layla said.

"Keep it on you at all times. I need to know that you're safe, and I can't be with you twenty-four hours a day."

Drawing a deep breath, Layla nodded and agreed. "Okay," she said as a pair of sheriff's deputies entered the room.

One was named Larson.

The other announced himself as Daylami.

The two then proceeded to take Dean's statement regarding the "road rage" incident—their words—over the course of 30 minutes. Once they finished, they told Dean they'd "be in touch" and then dawdled their way out of the room.

"They'll never find the truck," Dean said to Layla. "I

wouldn't be surprised if the guy has torched the thing by now."

"What's he waiting for?" Layla asked. "If this guy wants a showdown with you, what's holding him off?"

Shivers tickled the base of Dean's neck. "He wants to make a show of it," he said. "He wants to make a full-on friggin' production of this thing."

A moment later, Sheila poked her head in the room. Dean breathed a sigh of relief as he took in his sister's appearance, one replete with a few tiny scratches on her face and the jewel in the crown that came in the form of the cast on her left wrist.

"It's too bad you're on the wagon," Sheila said as she showed off her cast. "These painkillers they gave me are a godsend."

"I bet," Dean said. "Did you talk to the police?"

"Not long after they brought us in."

"How's the sedan?"

"Wrecked."

"Figures. Any updates from your colleagues at SFPD?"

"They haven't turned up a thing," Sheila said. "Neither has anyone from the Bureau. As for the deputies and the CHP officials I talked to who are covering our little fender bender, they're working on trying to find the truck that ran us off the road."

Dean shook his head. "They won't find it."

"He's probably torched the car."

"That's what I said."

"So," Sheila sighed, "then we're right back where we started."

"You know," Layla said to Dean as she cut a glance at Sheila, "I had a long chat with your sister here while you were sleeping."

The lines in Dean's face screwed into a wince. "What was the topic of conversation?"

"Oh, I told her everything about you that you've been withholding from her," Sheila said, "including the incident where you mooned a kid on the track back in the ninth grade."

"I'm all for our two families coming closer together," Dean said, "but not at the expense of my reputation."

"Was it true?" Layla said. "About the time Sheila put you in a dress when you were four and locked you in the back-yard?" She laughed. "The neighbors across the way thought you were a girl cousin of the family they didn't know about or something?"

The ringing cell phone on the cabinet beside Dean prompted him to turn his head. "Thanks, She," he said as he scooped up the cell. "You're a real gem."

As Sheila and Layla whispered secrets to one another, Dean saw Bazz's name flashing on the phone's display—the display cracked as a result of the crash—and answered.

"Go ahead."

Bazz chuckled. "I think I found someone who might be your guy."

45

Hearing that Bazz had—possibly—pinpointed the man who used Dean's head as a mop in the diner restroom triggered Dean to shoot up in his bed. "Who did you find?"

"I've got two people here. The first is a guy you had a pretty bad run-in with back in the day, *and* he fits the profile you gave me."

"Who is it?"

"Former Special Agent Adam Pafchek," Bazz said. "Does that ring a bell?"

A litany of movies from Dean's cerebral vault played back at high speed. "Pafchek," he said. "I worked on an internal case on behalf of the Office of Professional Responsibility."

"According to what I've got in front of me, you busted him for taking bribes from a guy named Leonard Contrell. Pafchek was looking into a statewide gambling racket that Contrell was running in Washington. Contrell ended up putting Pafchek on his payroll so Pafchek would turn a blind eye on his operations."

Dean nodded. "Pafchek fudged paperwork and ended up lying on reports for close to twelve months. The two of us ended up getting into," he rolled his eyes, "well, a bit of a sparring match when I tried to bring him in."

Bazz laughed. "You broke his arm in three places. The guy ended up doing three months of rehab while he was in prison because of it."

"Where's Pafchek now?"

"He got out in 2018 and ended up starting his life over. Then in 2020, he ended up getting pulled in by Oregon State Police for a domestic assault charge. He beat his wife until she went into a coma."

Dean's eyes widened. "You're shitting me."

"Pafchek's wife was cheating on him," Bazz said. "He ended up beating her to the point that she had to have her jaw reconstructed. Pafchek cut a deal with the DA's office and ended up investing what he had left in savings to hire this slimeball criminal defense attorney named Gibbons. He ended up only doing six months before he got sprung."

"Where is he now?"

"San Francisco, my boy."

Dean pulled up the information he still had on Pafchek logged away in his mental files.

He does fit the profile.

He was in the Army for six years before he became an agent, so he has the training.

"Tell me you've got an address," Dean said.

Bazz replied, "I'm sending it to you now. I'm going to do a little more digging in the meantime, but I have a good feeling this guy Pafchek is your best lead at the moment. If it doesn't pan out, contact me about the second guy, Devon McNeil. He lives in the Bay Area, too, so he might be someone you want to check out."

"You're the king."

"That's what they say."

After Dean terminated the call, he threw the bed covers off his legs and moved toward his clothes draped over a chair. "We've got a person of interest," he told Layla and his sister. "He's in San Francisco, and he fits the profile."

Layla gripped Dean's arms. "You need to talk to the doctor first before you go anywhere."

"Tell him to give me a scrip and send me on my way."

"You don't take drugs."

"Well, then get me my jeans, and we'll call it even," Dean said. "We gotta move." He locked eyes with Layla. "And I want you to go back to LA after I leave here. Take Willy and go somewhere until this blows over. Maybe Big Bear. You told me you've got a cousin up there. That town also leans to the right with its politics, so I'm sure your family up there has a gun or two in their closets."

Sheila inched toward her brother. "Dean, slow down. What did Bazz say?"

Details of the phone call spilled out of Dean faster than he could draw the breath he needed to tell the story. When he finished, he was dressed and slipping on the last piece of his ensemble, the chestnut-colored leather jacket that once belonged to his grandfather.

"Okay," Sheila said. "We'll head back to San Francisco and check this guy out."

"We'll need a car."

"I'll get a rental. In the meantime, let me get everything squared away with the doctor. He wanted you to stay overnight for observation." A chuckle trickled out of Sheila's mouth as she headed through the door. "Obviously, that's not gonna happen."

Dean clipped his FBI shield to his belt. Layla was

positioned in front of him with her arms crossed and a look of fatigue spliced with defeat seeping out of her pores.

"You know I hate leaving you," Dean said, "but I need to find whoever's doing this."

Layla's eyebrows smashed together. "There's one thing I want to ask you before you go, something I've brought up on more than one occasion."

"What is it?"

Layla extended her hand, her fingertips brushing along the sleeve of his leather jacket. She secured a gentle grip on Dean's arm, a pleading look glossing her eyes as she said to him, "Remember when we talked about going on a vacation?"

"Of course." Dean nodded. "That still stands."

"The more I think about it," Layla said, "the more I'm led to believe that this," she flinched, "*job* is taking a toll on you more than it should, this way of life that you've been sticking to for so long."

"Sheila shares a similar sentiment."

"She's right."

"I agree."

"So," Layla said, "what do you think about the prospect of … stepping away, so to speak? I'm not asking you to resign your duties or make a major life choice right here and now. It would just be nice to know what your thoughts are in terms of the future."

"That we have to have one in order to plan anything," Dean said. "That living this way is not healthy for me. For you. For *us*." He hung his head. "But I've got a contract. If I break it—"

"There has to be a way."

"There's not, Lay." Dean swallowed the lump in his

throat. "I'm in this for the duration. Once it's done, though, *I'm* done. You have my word."

But will I ever be done?

Will I survive it?

Christ, I can't even take a vacation without some lunatic trying to kill me.

The belief that he may have been cursed, that his life was preordained by fate or God or the universe long before he was born became Dean's monomania as he gazed upon Layla's face.

Tommy's demise.

Jeremy's predicament.

All the events in his existence that paved the way toward the man he was today—a paranoid, pent-up, teeth-grinding ball of anxiety who couldn't break free of the pandemonium that plodded behind him every step of the way like a shadow.

"Sometimes I wonder," Dean said as he took Layla's hand, "if all I am is the guy who stands in the way."

Layla shrugged. "In the way of what?"

"The bad things in this world. Some guys are born to guard the gates. They like it. They want to be warriors, but I never did. I only joined the Rangers because I needed"—images of Tommy's lifeless body resurfaced in Dean's mind—"I needed to get something out. I wanted to purge, to take my anger out on something. When I joined the Bureau, it was for the same reason. Once I got out, once I cleared my head, I just wanted a normal life. No matter how hard I try, I can't seem to have it."

Layla coiled her arms around Dean's waist. "You will." She tightened her embrace. "*We* will."

"When?"

"Soon." Layla flickered her gaze up to Dean and hooked a finger under his chin. "*God*, I hate seeing you like this."

"Some guys I know," Dean summoned a mental list of names from his old unit, several of whom now had podcasts, books, and programs dedicated to showing guys how to be tough and unwavering, "would call me weak for feeling like this."

"Screw them. You're allowed to be upset. With everything you've been through, most people would have thrown in the towel by now." Layla shook her head. "But not you. You're still here, and I plan on keeping it that way. I just need you to be safe. I need you to do what you do best. I don't want to wake up to an empty bed one day."

His heart swelling with a mixture of pride, fear, regret, and uncertainty, Dean whispered, "That's not going to happen."

Layla reached up and touched Dean's lips. "Find this guy," she said. "Find him, and come home."

"I will." A fiery look shimmered in Dean's eyes. "I promise."

The two held each other close as Dean thought of Layla, Sheila, his father, his son Jeremy, and all the people in his life that he held closest to his heart. As all their faces danced collectively in his mind, Dean became more deadset than he ever had been to find the guy who beat him to a pulp, ran him off the road, and savagely murdered the young couples back in San Francisco.

You're going to pay, asshole.

I'm coming for you with everything I've got.

46

The moment Dean saw Adam Pafchek's house, he was itching to grab the guy by his throat. The one-story, bungalow-style home was nestled between a gallery of other rundown homes on a residential street well off the beaten path from the more upscale dwellings Dean had seen when he first arrived in San Francisco. To him, the entire block felt like a series of rotted teeth. The dead lawns, chipped facades and busted-up bits of concrete on the sidewalk made the block look something akin to a cancerous tumor, one that Dean wanted to send into remission by lighting the entire street on fire, starting with the residence of his prime suspect.

Please, let this be our guy, Dean thought as Sheila parked the rental car two doors down from Pafchek's place. *Please.*

Sheila, seated behind the wheel, said to her brother, "What if he starts shooting? I mean, if this is our guy, he's not going to go down easy."

"If he does," Dean said, "we'll just have to put him down first."

"Solid plan, Dean."

"I'm picking up on your sarcasm."

"Good, 'cause I'm laying it on pretty thick."

Dean pulled out his SIG, did a thumb check, and stuffed it back into his holster. "We'll just ask the guy a few questions. After that, we'll go from there."

"I'm not big on improv, Dean," Sheila said. "I tried doing that in drama class once in high school, and I hated it."

Dean shot an inquisitive gaze at his sister. "You took drama in high school?"

"Yeah, for about 5 minutes. I was crushing on a girl named Sadie in my class at the time. That's the only reason I took it."

Dean flexed his eyebrows twice. "Did you get a date with her?"

The question elicited a frown from Sheila. She pulled out her Glock, did a thumb check of the rounds, and said, "Let's go" before she piled out of the car and slammed the door.

Dean walked side by side with his sister. "Was she cute?"

Sheila flexed her jaw muscles. "Don't."

"How tall was she? Did she have a volleyball build or more of a point guard thing going on?"

"*Can it.*"

The two approached the sagging, rusted gate at the front of Adam Pafchek's house, their hands resting on the grips of their holstered weapons as they did a scan of their surroundings.

Dean placed his foot on the first step that led up to the porch.

A moment later, the door burst open, and a man who towered at 6-foot-2 and sported a solid 200 pounds of bulk stood in the doorway gripping a Smith & Wesson M&P9 in his hand.

47

I t felt like 10 whole minutes went by as Dean, Sheila, and Adam Pafchek stared each other down. Only the sound of the wind rustling the branches of a nearby tree could be heard. Pafchek flexed his grip on the Smith & Wesson clutched in his hand and flicked angry eyes from Sheila to Dean.

"Long time, Blackwood," Pafchek said as he motioned to Dean's welts and scrapes. "It's good to see you still walking around with a shiner or two."

"It's an iron deficiency thing," Dean said. "Don't hold it against me."

"I take it the Bureau is still making you do its dirty work."

"What can I say?" Dean narrowed his eyes. "I get a kick out of smacking around deadbeats."

"Was that supposed to be a slight on me?" Pafchek sneered.

"No, I just meant in general. If I was trying to throw shade at *you*, I would have come up with some quippy one-liner about wife beaters."

"You got a big mouth."

"And you've still got a bit of a welt from where I clocked you on yours, Paffers."

A deep red hue came into Pafchek's face as he crept toward the porch steps. "If you're looking for a problem," he said with a hiss coating his words, "you came to the right place."

"Whatever, Eastwood." Dean gestured with the hand not molded around the grip of his SIG to the weapon in Pafchek's mitt. "And convicted felons aren't allowed to have guns, by the way. That's a big no-no right there."

"Tell that to every dipshit walking around this city."

"They're not my problem," Dean said. "*You* are."

Pafchek shifted his weight, sucking air through his teeth as he narrowed his eyes into fine slits. "You better cut to the punchline, Blackwood. I'm well within my rights to defend myself if the two of you are planning on raising hell."

Dean held his head high like he was sniffing the air. "You hear about the murders that have happened around here?"

"Who hasn't?"

"Then you'll understand why I decided to pop in to ask a convicted spouse abuser about it."

Pafchek huffed. "Oh, I get it. You think *I* had something to do with it."

Dean nodded. "It crossed my mind."

"You're digging in the wrong spot, Blackwood. I had nothing to do with any of that."

"If I had a nickel for every time I heard that—"

"Let me guess," Pafchek said. "You'd have enough to retire or something?"

Dean shook his head. "No, I'd have about 35 to 40 cents, something like that."

"That's cute." Pafchek pointed a finger toward the street.

"Now get off my lawn. Unless you got a warrant or something along those lines, start moving."

Sheila edged toward the porch, her hands held high in the air. "We just want to ask you a few questions, Mr. Pafchek."

"Ask them somewhere else. I don't know anything about these murders. I've been sitting here in my house all day every day for the past three years."

"Ever since your wife ditched you for popping her across the mouth," Dean said. "Right?"

The lines in Pafchek's face tensed. "I've got a lawyer," he said. "He's pretty good too. Believe me when I tell you that he'd *love* to hear about this little exchange taking place right now. I'll be cashing in on a six-figure settlement paid out by the Bureau before Christmas."

"Cut the bullshit," Dean said. "I want to know what you've been up to the past few days. I've got six dead bodies and a nasty little concussion I'm trying to kick, and right now, I've got good reason to come around here asking what you've been up to."

"Again," Pafchek said, "you're hitting up the wrong guy."

"Prove it."

"I don't have to prove shit."

Dean flashed his badge, the gold shield catching the sunlight overhead. "Try me."

Pafchek smirked. "I'd like nothing more than to go a few rounds with you, Blackwood. You screwed up my life." He examined the Smith & Wesson in his hand and tossed it to the side. "I think you owe me something in the way of recompense after what you did to me."

The beating Dean took, the lack of consistent sleep he had, and the fact that he was staring at a man who saw fit to abuse his spouse stirred up a whirlwind of anger inside of him. He projected all his rage onto Pafchek, wanting nothing more than to beat the man senseless for the sake of relieving some of his tension.

There's a good chance this is the guy who killed those people.

The guy who's tried to turn my world upside down.

This is my chance to put this thing to bed for good.

Dean handed Sheila his badge.

Palmed her his gun.

Then he slipped off his jacket and stepped toward the porch, but he was stopped in his tracks when Sheila grabbed him by the arm.

"Dean," his sister grumbled, "*don't*."

"I'm not going to make the first move," Dean said. "But if this creep wants to come at me, I've got no choice but to defend myself."

The fingers on Pafchek's right hand arched into a claw. He took one step off the porch, moving toward Dean as he widened his eyes. "I've been waiting a long time for this, Blackwood."

Dean took on a boxer's stance and flexed the digits on both his hands. "Quit flapping your gums, and hop to it, Paffers."

Pafchek's nostrils flared as he charged toward Dean.

Dean gnashed his teeth as he raised back his fist and prepared to throw the first jab.

48

Dean threw a haymaker at Pafchek and caught him in the chin. The force of the strike was hard enough that it should have taken Pafchek off his feet, but it didn't. Pafchek's head jerked back after Dean struck him. Pafchek quickly cocked his head back as he planted his feet, swiveled his hips, and threw a jab into Dean's ribs.

Pulsating pain flashed across Dean's rib cage. The area was still tender thanks to the fiasco that played out on the roadway the night before. Dean doubled over, flicking a glance up at Pafchek as he attempted to bring down his fist across his cheek.

Dean shot his body up and threw a blow into Pafchek's chin. Pafchek stumbled and fell to one knee, shooting out his hand against the dead lawn to break his fall before he quickly got back on two feet.

"Come on," Dean said. "Let's get this over with."

Pafchek spit on the ground and closed the distance. He faked a jab with his left hand and prompted Dean to take a step back. Pafchek then followed up by faking another jab with his right hand. Dean ducked away from it only to move right into the punch Pafchek shot out with his left hand.

Stars blanketed Dean's vision as Pafchek landed the strike. Dean was unable to stave off the thought.

Christ, I'm going to need a CT scan after all of these beatings.

Channeling all the energy he could rally into his right arm, Dean threw a rabbit punch into Pafchek's cheek, letting out a primal growl as his fist struck Pafchek's face with a gut-churning, flesh-on-bone smack.

Pafchek stumbled over his feet, waving his arms like a windmill to stabilize himself. Dean then planted his feet on the ground, spreading out his arms as he dashed toward his opponent, wrapped his arms around him, and tackled him to the ground.

The two men barrel-rolled over one another, Dean catching a glimpse of Sheila playing witness to the bout with a mixture of panic, horror, and irritation plastered on her face. Dean, on top of Pafchek, pinned his opponent's left arm to the ground with his knee as Pafchek threw a punch with his right hand. Dean defended himself by securing a grip on Pafchek's arm before he twisted it. Pafchek's face turned a shade of crimson as Dean raised back his head and then slammed the thick part of his forehead into Pafchek's nose. The nauseating crack of Pafchek's nose breaking drew a wince from Dean as he turned the man onto his stomach, fished the handcuffs from his pocket, and then slapped them on him.

"That was too easy, Deano," Woody said. "The guy who came after you in that bathroom whooped you a lot easier than this."

Yeah, Dean nodded. *I know.*

49

Dean turned Pafchek on his back and patted him on the chest. A pair of crimson ribbons flowed freely out of Pafchek's nose and glazed his teeth. Pafchek shook his head and went limp as Dean massaged the swollen areas of his face where he had been hit.

"So what now?" Pafchek said. "You going to take me in for assaulting a federal agent?"

"No," Dean replied, "but I'm taking you in for questioning about these murders, you prick. I want to know for sure what your level of involvement is."

"You made my life miserable that day you busted me, you know that?"

"Well, if I find out you're the one responsible for killing all these people and making my life a living hell, it's about to get a lot worse for you."

"I'm a lot of things," Pafchek said, "but a killer ain't one of them."

"Stop talking."

Pafchek closed his eyes, his vocal chords tensing as he spoke to Dean like he was in a confessional booth. "You fucked up my life, Blackwood. You're the reason things turned out for me the way they did."

"Tell it to a therapist," Dean said. "*You're* the one who took the bribe money. *You're* the one who raised his hand to his wife. Don't try to act like your world of hurt was brought on by anyone else other than yourself."

A cross between a wheeze and a chuckle shot out of Pafchek. "You know, you talk about me living in a world of hurt, Blackwood," his eyes widened, "but you know who's really cursed around here? It's *you*. Yeah, this whole hit 'em hard and heavy bullshit of yours is catching up to you quick, isn't it? How long do you think you can keep going like this, huh? I mean, I'm doing away with this whole shooting you bit I had my sights set on a moment ago, but you gotta ask yourself when the day will come that you'll cross paths with the guy who *will* shoot you. Will it be tomorrow? Maybe the day after that? Whatever the case, rest assured, my friend," Pafchek winked. "It's coming."

As Dean weighed what his next move would be, he heard Sheila's phone ring. He kept his sights glued to Pafchek as she answered the call, his index finger caressing the trigger guard of his SIG and part of him hoping that Pafchek would try to do something stupid.

"Dean," Sheila said as she let the phone drop from her ear. "Cut this guy loose."

"Why?"

His sister held out her cell. "Because the guy who's really doing this is on the phone right now."

50

The synapses in Dean's brain sparked to life like a million little fuses being lit as he took Sheila's phone. He turned his back on Pafchek, gritting his teeth as he held the cell to his ear.

"Hello?"

"You're looking at the wrong guy, Blackwood," greeted the same equalized voice that taunted Dean so many times before. "How's your head, by the way?"

Dean spun around and put his focus on Pafchek to make sure some silly little trick wasn't being pulled on him.

It's no trick.

He ogled Pafchek from head to toe.

I've got the wrong guy.

"Enough already," Dean said into the phone. "Let's cut to this finale of yours and meet face to face."

"We're getting close."

"You plan on killing a few people before that happens? Something like that?"

"Maybe your sister," the voice said. "Maybe a few other people. I'm not sure yet. Rest assured, we're about to reach the climax here. It's gonna be a real Hollywood showdown, believe me."

"Hop to it, ace," Dean said, not surprised at all that the killer knew Sheila was his kin. "I'm getting tired of this shit."

"That's the idea. I told you before, I want you to endure as difficult a time as possible before I kill you. I knew you'd have to hit up the people from the past that you fucked over in order to find me, and that was the point."

"He's right," Woody chimed in. "He's making you come face to face with all the people you've had conflicts with before."

Son of a bitch.

Dean shook his head.

The Irish prick is right.

"Don't worry, Dean," the caller said. "It's almost over. I promise. Until then, enjoy your last sunset or two. It's the least I can give you."

The line clicked off, and Dean tossed Sheila her phone before he pulled out his own. "Cut Pafchek loose," he told his sister. "We're getting out of here."

Sheila threw up her hands. "What if this guy calls his attorney? You do realize you just reenacted a scene from *Fight Club* with him with God only knows how many witnesses."

Plugging in Bazz's number, Dean, already on his way back to the rental car, brushed his sister's comment aside with a swipe of his hand. "He's not calling anyone. He knows if he does, I'll violate his ass so quickly for that Smith & Wesson he's carrying that he'll be sitting in a cell by sundown."

A moment later, Sheila took the cuffs off of Pafchek and then hightailed it after Dean as he slipped behind the wheel of the rental car.

Dean was fuming as he cranked the key in the ignition, his cell on speaker and ringing as he rolled down the window and said to Pafchek, "*Pray* you never see me again."

Pafchek flashed a crooked smile, saluted to Dean with two fingers, and then hauled his blood and grass-slicked body back into his house.

Seconds later, Dean was pulling a hard U-turn on the street. He drove with one hand, his cell in his lap and waiting for Bazz to answer the call.

Dean flexed his jaw muscles. He was past the point of being more than slightly lost, certain that he'd suffer from something akin to that of an aneurism if he kept up the pace he was at.

I want this guy.

I want him so bad I can taste it.

"Any luck?" Bazz answered.

"It's a bust," Dean said. "It's not Pafchek."

"You're sure?"

"The real guy called me right after I got into a fisticuffs match with Pafchek. I'm going to forward Sheila's cell number to you. I don't know how the guy did it, but he called her phone this time. Maybe you can try to run a trace on it. I don't want to leave any stone unturned."

Bazz hissed. "This guy is good, man. This level of encryption he has with these little phone tag games is on the level with the kind of stuff the Agency pulled back in Baghdad."

"Write a dissertation about it later, Bazzy," Dean said. "This freak show is still running around playing games with me, and I've had my fill." He looked in the rearview mirror and appraised the fresh welts Pafchek had gifted him. "You said there was a second guy I should look into. Devon McNeil."

"Right," Bazz said. "Do you remember him?"

"Yeah." Dean dwelled on the memory of the time he was put on another case for OPR. "McNeil was commissioning sex workers for, well, *free rides* by using his badge. It was a case I was tasked with back in 2017. McNeil was never brought up on charges, but he was dismissed from the Bureau. He threw a rage-fit at me when we crossed paths in a hallway during his dismissal when we both testified on the same day."

"I assumed the two of you had some words."

Dean's memory of Devon McNeil coming nose to nose with him in the hallways of the Hoover Building flashed through his mind. Dean could still see the three-piece suit McNeil was wearing at the time, the sweat on his brow, the smell of booze on his breath as McNeil got in his face and gave him a piece of his mind.

"You'll get yours, boy scout," McNeil had grumbled. "You can't keep screwing guys over and think it won't catch up."

Just like Pafchek.

Just like so many other guys who wanted a piece of me.

Dean tightened his grip on the steering wheel.

How many demons have I created?

How many enemies do I have?

Whoever's doing this is right.

I'm being tormented by the sins of the past.

Dean blinked his eyes and walked out of the pity party he was throwing for himself. "Where do I find McNeil?" he asked Bazz as he spotted a sign that pointed him toward the freeway.

"McNeil lives about an hour outside San Francisco," Bazz said. "I just forwarded you the address. Considering his financial situation right now, I'm shocked the guy can afford such a nice place."

"Interesting." Dean arched his brow. "Well, give me the rundown. Tell me what's been occupying McNeil after the Bureau canned him."

"McNeil, after he took his leave from the FBI, ended up going to work in Hollywood."

"Doing what?"

"A paid consultant for film and TV. McNeil worked for a few shows that filmed in LA. He had a residence there for a while, but in 2020, he was kicked off the Paramount lot in the middle of filming."

"For what?"

"It turns out," Bazz explained, "that McNeil's taste for ladies of the night didn't diminish once he left the Bureau. Apparently, the LAPD had an open case against him. Three sex workers reported McNeil over the span of six months. Apparently, McNiel paid for their services and proceeded to assault them during the course of the act."

"What about his relationships?" Dean said. "Was McNeil ever married?"

"He was engaged a year after he left the FBI. This was right before his run-in with the LAPD and the cases by the three women that were filed against him. A woman by the name of Shannon Sell called the police twice on McNeil. Apparently, the two of them got into a shouting match, and McNeil's ex claimed he hit her. She eventually dropped the charges. From what I'm reading here, it looks like McNeil used his old connections during his time at the Bureau to intimidate her into dropping the charges. McNeil shelled out close to six figures to remedy the situation. So again, I'm surprised he's living in a four-bedroom house valued at close to a million."

A former fed turned Hollywood consultant.

A history of sexual and domestic violence.

It fits the profile.

Dean sighed.

Or maybe I'm just hoping *that he will.*

"I'll check him out," Dean said to Bazz. "I've got nothing else to go off of."

"Dean," Bazz said, "be careful, all right? Even if McNeil isn't your guy, I can't help but feel like you're reaching some kind of finish line here, and part of me worries that there's a negative connotation attached to that statement."

"You and me both, buddy."

"Stay frosty."

"Will do."

Dean eased the rental car onto the freeway, plugged in the address Bazz forwarded him to Devon McNeil's place, and then gave Sheila the update.

"If we find this guy," his sister said, "if we bring him in—"

"We *will* bring him in," Dean replied. "No matter what it takes."

"You can't go cowboy on this, little brother. We have to do this the right way. Don't forget that."

The conversation Dean had with Layla popped into his mind. He felt a sense of euphoria overcome him, perhaps the first bit of relief—other than when Layla came to his aid in the hospital—in the past few days.

You know what you need to do.

You always did.

"I've spent my life chasing guys like Pafchek and McNeil," Dean said. "And they weren't even the worst of them. This guy killed six people, She. He's tormented and toyed with us and is doing it for no other reason than to satisfy his sick little urges. I want him. I want him so I can be done with this and go home."

Sheila reached out and rested her hand on his shoulder. "We will, Dean," she said. "We'll get him."

Dean locked eyes briefly with Sheila.

He put his eyes on the map application on his phone.

He noted that they were fifty-two minutes away from Devon McNeil's home in Vacaville, California. He jammed down on the gas in hopes he could cut down on that time.

51

When Dean pulled up to the outskirts of the city of Vacaville, he felt like the town's aesthetic was more on par with something out of the Pacific Northwest. Rich greenery canvassed the landscape. A majority of the homes stood two stories with manicured lawns and American flags and—Dean counted them—three guys trimming their grass in checkered shorts. Neighbors waved to one another. Dogs were being walked. Happy families threaded through a town square that looked like something Dean had seen in one of those Hallmark Christmas movies that Layla had a penchant for, even in the offseason.

I'll watch all of them once we're done with this.

I'll watch Hallmark movies for the rest of my life, grow a potbelly, and really lean into the whole Dad-bod thing once this contract is up.

"If that happens," Woody said. "Who knows what the next couple of years have in store for us, laddie."

Woody...

Dean cracked the knuckles on his left hand.

...please shut the hell up.

After cruising through the town for close to fifteen minutes, Dean drove the rental car on Adobe Drive, his sights on the sky-blue house at the end of the block—Devon McNeil's house. Dean slowed the rental two doors down from McNeil's place, all of his senses perking up and making him feel like he was a hawk on the lookout for the animal above him on the pecking order.

"Same as last time," Dean said to his sister. "We'll knock on the door and have a chat with the guy."

"No fistfights this time," Sheila said. "I'm surprised your brain isn't scrambled from the amount of beatings you've taken."

"My brain was scrambled a long time ago, She."

After doing a check of their weapons, Dean and his sister stepped out of the rental, noted their surroundings, and proceeded to make their way toward the front door of Devon McNeil's home.

Nice place, Dean thought as he glanced at the manicured lawns and the surrounding houses with Mercedes, BMWs, and other high-ticket vehicles parked in the driveways. *Way nicer than a guy like him should be able to afford.*

Dean's hand crept toward his SIG.

Sheila followed suit with her Glock.

Then when the pair were 6 feet shy from arriving on the porch, a gunshot registered from inside of the house.

52

Dean ducked low and dashed to his left just beside the front door. Sheila did the same on her right as she pulled her cell and punched in 9-1-1.

"Shots fired," Sheila said to the operator before giving the address, her name, and then stating that she was a fellow police officer.

Another gunshot bellowed from inside the home.

Dean stood back.

Then he booted the door, moved inside, and cleared the corners.

Sheila followed behind her brother, her gun raised as she trailed Dean through the vestibule to another door that had already been kicked in.

Someone broke in.

Dean trained his SIG on the staircase ahead of them.

Someone came in here before we did.

An aroma of cordite teased Dean's nostrils as he approached the staircase. "FBI!" he shouted as he swept the SIG across the room. "If I see you with a weapon, I *will* shoot you."

Something clamored at the top of the staircase.

Dean spun around.

He saw a man at the top of the steps, his arm bloodied and face soaked with perspiration, his eyes rolling back white as he tumbled head over heels down the stairs.

That's McNeil, Dean thought as he rushed to the man's aid, yelling at Sheila to cover him as he helped break McNeil's fall halfway down the stairs and then whisked him away. Dean cradled McNeil in his arms. McNeil was panting and heaving as Dean placed him on his back.

"Son of a bitch," McNeil grumbled as he locked eyes with Dean. "What the hell are you doing here?"

"Talk to me," Dean said as he shot a glance at Sheila. "What the hell's going on?"

"A guy broke in here," McNeil replied. "He pointed a gun at me. He tried to—"

"Where is he?"

McNeil crooked his finger toward the staircase. "He's up there, in my bedroom. He came at me, so I started shooting."

"Where are you hit?"

"My arm," McNeil grimaced in pain. "It went in and out."

The inharmonious racket of glass shattering tickled Dean's ears.

A window.

Fucker is making a break for it.

Dean dashed toward the staircase, hollering at Sheila, "He's moving!" He skipped every third step, toggled the safety switch on his weapon to "fire" and readied himself for the inevitable pursuit.

53

Dean poked his head into McNeil's bedroom Six feet off to his left was the broken window he heard being busted when he was downstairs. Dean swung his SIG toward the window, broken glass jutting out of the frame like shark's teeth. Just beyond it were a pair of legs and booted feet dashing across the rooftop.

"Stop!" Dean yelled through the broken window. "*Freeze!*"

After he cleared the busted bits of glass jutting out of the window frame, Dean climbed out onto the rooftop that slanted down to the left, raised his weapon, and took aim at a figure 10 feet away. The figure was dressed in jeans, boots, and an olive Army jacket draped over a black T-shirt. He was sporting what Dean figured was the same black woolen mask he saw before, and the man had a Glock 19 in his hand pointed directly at Dean.

Dean's eyes widened as the figure beat him to the punch and squeezed off six rounds. Even though Dean knew the guy had him dead to rights, the man wielding the gun made it a point to shoot at Dean's feet, the rounds punching through the roof shingles and causing Dean to stumble.

In the blink of an eye, Dean lost his footing. His bunk knee that he received as a parting gift from his time with the Rangers bawled in pain as it twisted 10 degrees in the wrong direction. Dean, for the second time in several days, saw his vision gyrate as he tumbled head over heels down the slanted rooftop, his heart beating feverishly when he realized he was sliding head-first toward the lawnmower, rakes, tools, and shovels that jutted out like jagged headstones on the lawn.

The SIG in Dean's hand left his grip and skipped like a stone off the rooftop before it landed on the lawn. A few seconds shy of falling off the roof and becoming impaled by the lawn equipment below, Dean shot out his hand, felt his fingertips brush against the rain gutter, secured a grip, came to a stop, and breathed easy once he managed to terminate his fall.

"Okay," Dean said with a trembling voice. "Just take it nice and slow."

Dean pulled himself up.

The rain gutter snapped in half.

Dean oscillated on the busted limb of the gutter like he was Tarzan swinging through the jungle. He shot a look down toward the lawn, saw that the lawn equipment was no longer underneath him, and then made out a patch of grass he was swaying over.

Dean released his grip on the rain gutter.

He dropped rear-end first toward the lawn.

Two seconds felt to him like two minutes before he landed on his back.

All the air in Dean's lungs was pushed out the moment his body made impact with the lawn. He struggled to rally his senses, seconds feeling like minutes as he turned onto his belly, sucked in a breath, and then pushed off the grass. Once Dean spotted his SIG laying several feet away, he scooped it up, shot a glance to his left toward the fence on the side of the house, and saw the figure fleeing across the front lawn.

No quippy one-liners, Dean.

Just get him.

Dean, still the record holder for the Pasadena High School track team's mile, dashed through the gate and passed the side entrance of the home. He spilled out onto the lawn and saw that the figure was moving toward the driver's side door of a green pickup truck. Dean planted his feet, raised his SIG, and lined up the figure's back between his sights.

"Freeze, motherfucker!" Dean screamed. "*Now!*"

The figure spun around just as he reached the handle of the pickup truck's door. As he turned, he fired off three rounds at Dean. The first two bullets drilled into the lawn by Dean's feet before the third punched its way through the front door.

Dean sidestepped to his left and returned fire, making sure not to fire blind for sake of the rounds ricocheting and hitting someone other than his target. He squeezed off two rounds. The first one took out the windshield of the pickup, and the second one shattered the rearview mirror.

The figure abandoned his attempt to get into the pickup and rattled off two more rounds at Dean before he took cover on the opposite side of the truck. Once he was concealed, the figure fired two more bullets that missed hitting Dean by just a couple of inches.

Dean ducked and dived for cover behind the Audi parked in the driveway six paces off to his left. He rested his left shoulder against the grill of the Audi, peeking out quickly and seeing that the figure's legs were scurrying around underneath the pickup he was hiding behind.

No shot at hitting his legs.

You're too far away.

Dean glanced over his shoulder toward the house. "She," he yelled. "I could use some help here!"

There was no response from Sheila, no movement, nothing from the house that indicated she was on her way.

Maybe she's dealing with McNeil, Dean figured as a round from his opponent's gun pinged off the trunk of the Audi.

Oh, hell.

I don't have time to think.

Just fucking shoot *this prick.*

Dean peeked around the hood of the Audi. He caught a glimpse of the suspect peering over the rear of the pickup. He raised his SIG and fired until he heard the weapon rack back empty.

He went back into cover.

Mag-flipped his depleted magazine like John Wick.

Slapped a fresh one as he heard the truck door slam shut.

The squealing of tires out on the street indicated one thing to Dean—the suspect was on the move. Dean peeked around the Audi and saw the rear tires of the pickup churning up smoke as it tore down the street. Moving out of cover in an all-out sprint, Dean dashed down the driveway, ran into the street, and took aim at the back of the pickup. He proceeded to empty another magazine into the back of the vehicle, the rear windows shattering as the figure took a hard left down the street and disappeared from sight.

Not again, damn it, Dean's brain screamed as he pulled

out his cell phone and punched in 9-1-1. *I can't believe the son of a bitch is getting away.*

Dean rushed through his spiel with the operator. He gave her the details of the car he had just shot out, a description of the suspect, the area the pickup had fled in, and the fact that he and Sheila were on the scene. After the operator relayed that emergency services were on their way, Dean heard McNeil shout, "Get in here!" at a volume loud enough that it sounded like he was only a few feet away.

A sickly feeling washed over Dean as he rushed toward the house.

He sprinted inside.

Then his eyes widened to silver dollars as he saw McNeil tending to the blood seeping out of the hole in Sheila's neck.

54

"One of the bullets the suspect fired at me whizzed past me," Dean explained to Wilson, "went through the front door, and hit Sheila as she was tending to McNeil."

Wilson stood beside Dean outside of Sheila's hospital room, his eyes fixed to Dean's unconscious sister lying in a bed and tethered to a series of machines.

A sheet-white Dean crossed his arms, pure uncurbed rage pumping through his veins as he checked his watch and saw that twelve hours had gone by since he brought Sheila to the hospital.

"The doctors," Wilson said. "What did they have to say?"

"The surgery went well," Dean said, "but it's still touch and go. She has to go back in for another round in a few hours. The bullet grazed her carotid artery. The doctor I spoke to said if it had been half a centimeter closer, she would have been dead. She's in a medically induced coma for the time being."

A handful of seconds ticked by. Only the sounds of the

beeping machines in Sheila's room were audible. "I'm so sorry, kid," Wilson said. "I just—"

"I don't want to hear it, Willy." Dean took a seat beside the door. "I want to know what local PD and our people are doing to find this guy. What about the pickup I shot at? What are they doing to find it?"

"Everyone's following the playbook and canvassing the area. The pickup was found 6 miles from the neighborhood where you shot it out with this guy. It was burnt to a crisp."

"What about traffic cams? Doorbell cams? We have to track this guy."

"We're working on it. It's going to take time, but after what happened at McNeil's place, the net is closing in on him. We'll find him sooner rather than later."

"What about the evidence from the crime scenes?" Dean said. "Our people have been working on it, and I've been kept out of the loop. Tell me you've made progress. Throw me a bone here."

A deep sigh trickled out of Wilson. "We're certain that the knife this guy used is an M3 trench knife."

Dean's stomach knotted. "That's a Ranger weapon." His eyes flickered up to his boss. "That's the exact same knife that guys in my old unit used to use."

"Well, we're working with Army CID right now to pull up their open investigations as well as cold cases to see if someone stands out."

"That'll take days. That's time we don't have." *And what little of it we do have is running out.* "What about McNeil? What did he have to say?"

"We questioned McNeil for four hours straight," Wilson said. "He's not your guy. He's a dirtbag, but he's got an alibi for the time of the murders. We've also got a comprehensive list of cell phone records as well as security footage from a bar that places him far away from you and Sheila when the two of you got run off the road that night."

"What story is he telling? Sheila and I rolled in right in the middle of the scuffle."

"McNeil said someone knocked on the door," Wilson said. "When he answered, a guy pointed a gun at his face and ordered him to go upstairs. The guy told McNeil to turn around and then laid down a bag on McNeil's bed. He tried to get McNeil to go into the bathroom, and that's when McNeil made a move for the piece he had stuffed in his pillow. Shots were fired. McNeil took a slug to the arm. Not long after that, you and Sheila rolled in."

Dean furrowed his brow. "The guy had a bag on him?"

His boss nodded. "We recovered it at the scene. The thing had a bunch of used DVDs in it, DNA samples that were being kept in tubes," his eyes widened, "*and* an M3 trench knife. We sent the thing to the lab for analysis. The thing looked clean, but I'm hoping we'll find some residuals on it. What we do know is that preliminary findings indicate that the wounds we found on the victim are consistent with the knife we recovered at McNeil's place."

"*Christ.*" Dean closed his eyes. "This guy was trying to set McNeil up. He was gonna kill him, make it look like a suicide, and then doctor the scene to make it look like McNeil was our killer."

"The guy you're chasing knew you were closing in on him," Wilson said. "He knew you were rummaging through your old case files trying to find a hit on someone who matched the profile you were looking into."

"But how did he know about McNeil? How the *fuck* would this guy have access to those kind of files?"

"I'm not sure. There could be a variety of reasons that he was able to get access to FBI case files. The Cyber Division is doing a sweep right now of our network to see if this guy was able to get backdoor access to our files. How the hell he could have pulled that off," Wilson shrugged, "I'm not sure."

"The chances of that are slim," Dean said. "Have you thought about the more likely scenario here?"

"And that would be?"

"What about a mole? Maybe this guy made contact with someone in our ranks and paid him off to slip him information."

Wilson nodded. "It's a theory I'm entertaining. The only issue is that looking into that is going to require a multi-field office investigation. Sussing out a potential mole is going to take months, if not years."

Something's not right.

McNeil is a former fed. He's a creep, but he's not stupid.

He just opens the door?

He doesn't check through the peephole first?

He came to the door unarmed, and no one *in the neighborhood saw anything suspicious?*

Horse.

Fucking.

SHIT.

"When you pulled McNeil in," Dean said, "you ran his file, yes?"

"We did."

"What's his current employment situation?"

"He's managed to collect disability from the state."

"What's his excuse?"

"Clinical depression," Wilson said. "He got a clinical psychologist to sign off on it."

Dean rummaged through the files in his mental vault. "He couldn't collect enough to pay for that lofty spread of his in Vacaville," he said. "No way in hell. The guy should be living in a one-bedroom apartment if all he's collecting is disability."

"All right, kid." Wilson crossed his arms. "What are you trying to get at?"

Dean shot Wilson a look. "I want to talk to McNeil."

"What for?"

"So I can hear from his mouth what went down. I need to know, boss. I need to look into his eyes and hear the story from him. Something's up, and I guarantee if I get five minutes with the guy," Dean narrowed his eyes, "I'm going to dig up something he's not spilling."

55

Ten minutes after leaving the hospital, Dean and Wilson walked into the Vacaville Police Department off Merchant Street. They were led to an interrogation room where McNeil, his arm in a sling, sat at a metal desk and hacked on a cigarette as he threw the occasional glance toward the beat cop guarding him.

"Just the two of us," Dean said to Wilson as they walked toward the interrogation room. "No one else."

"Kid," Wilson replied, "I think it's better if—"

"I'm not planning on putting my hands on this guy. I've had my fill of throwing fists in the past seventy-two hours." Dean locked his eyes on Wilson's. "I just want to talk to him."

Wilson nodded.

Dean approached the door.

Then he stepped into the room, closed the door, pulled out a chair, and sat down in front of McNeil.

McNeil took a long drag of his cigarette, his eyelids tapered sluggishly as he blew the carcinogens out of his nostrils. "Never thought I'd live to see the day where I was happy you showed up on my doorstep."

Dean brushed the tobacco ash off the table. "Repeat the story you told the FBI and Vacaville PD."

"I figured you'd be in the know already."

"I want to hear it from you."

"Well," McNeil reclined back in his chair, "it's pretty simple. Someone knocked on my door, I answered it, and then some hooded creep pulled a gun on me. He told me to keep quiet, and then he took me upstairs. He told me to turn around, placed a bag on the bed, and then told me to go into the bathroom. Halfway through the walk, I chucked a lamp shade at the guy, went for the gun stuffed under my pillow, and then the two of us shot it out."

"He's *lying*," Woody whispered.

Yeah.

The fingers on Dean's right hand contorted into a claw.

I know.

Every part of Dean tensed. Part of him wanted to go old school on McNeil, to just vault over the table, pin him up against the wall, and squeeze the truth out of him.

"I guess you were lucky my sister and I showed up when we did, huh?"

"I heard about that," McNeil huffed. "Didn't know this whole thing was a family affair."

"How much do you know about this case in San Francisco?" Dean said. "This guy that's been carving up couples?"

"I know my fair share. Unfortunately, in this day and age, it's hard to not stay in the loop with everything going on in the world, even when you don't want to. Every time I open my cell, I gotta read about a flood in Nantucket or some sexual deviant snuffing out women in New York."

"Sounds like a plot line to one of those shows you worked on in LA."

McNeil flexed his brow and took a pull of his cancer stick. "You heard about that, huh?"

Dean nodded. "I also heard about you rousting hookers and beating them up for kicks while you were out there. I gotta tell you, I've crossed paths lately with one too many disgraced feds with a proclivity for hitting women. I feel like I'm going to have to take ten hot showers in a row to wash the stink off of me."

McNeil shook his head. "That's old news, Blackwood. I'm a reformed citizen."

"*Horse shit*," Dean said. "The minute guys like you turn to the dark side, you stay there. The only thing that stops someone like you is the day you get caught or fitted for a toe tag."

"I feel like you're trying to imply something here."

"Oh, I am." Dean interlaced his fingers, rested his hands behind his head, and then leaned back. "I know you're full of shit, and I know that this story you're spinning to everyone about a home invasion is about as cookie-cutter a plot as every Marvel movie in their canon."

A few seconds ticked by as McNeil ashed his cigarette in the tray in front of him. "You've been doing this too long, Blackwood," he said. "Maybe it's time you take a sojourn to the beach for a while. You should clear your head."

"It's on my bucket list," Dean said. "But before that happens," he leaned forward and fixed his unblinking eyes on McNeil, "I want you to tell me the truth. Whoever this guy is that I'm chasing has somehow managed to get his hands on FBI case files. He's got a deep and comprehensive history of me, my cases, and all the people I've had run-ins with, and there's only two ways he could have pulled that off." Dean held up one finger. "He somehow hacked into the FBI's database, which is about as easy to pull off as playing a guitar with no arms." He shot up another finger. "Or he paid someone off to dish him information."

Laugher shot out of McNeil like it was packed with gunpowder. "You've lost it, my friend. You really have gone off the deep end, haven't you?"

"You'd be a great source for someone like the guy I'm chasing," Dean said. "You were working at the highest levels of the Bureau before they busted your ass and sent you packing. Maybe someone approached you one night to make a deal."

"You got a knack for fiction, brother. Maybe you should consider a career in the literary arts when the Bureau inevitably dishes you a pink slip."

Dean rose from his chair. "Funny you should mention that." He paced. "You see, the second you got kicked out of Hollywood after the LAPD dragged you in for beating up sex workers, your choice of employment was slim. I know a guy like you probably drank away what little he had of his pension, and based on the house you're living in, there's no way you're making the mortgage payments without some kind of income." He walked over to McNeil, stooped down, and leaned in close to the point that his nose nearly brushed against McNeil's cheek. "I know you're collecting disability, but the going rate for the kind of house you're living in is just shy of a million."

McNeil huffed. "So what? I saved what I got from the work I did out in LA."

"Get fucked," Dean hissed. "You were living the high life out in LA. Even if you weren't using what you were making to buy drugs, booze, and nice suits, you would've pissed it away on whatever lofty rental you procured for yourself in the hills. Even if you were being modest, which we know you weren't, you wouldn't have accrued enough scratch to pay for that Audi you got or that monstrosity of a house where it's parked."

A sweat-glazed McNeil shot a look toward the door. "I want a lawyer."

Dean circled McNeil like a vulture closing in on a dying animal. "Now we're getting somewhere."

"I'm done talking to you."

"Well, I'm not done talking to you, *shithead*." Dean kicked the table and caused McNeil to shudder. "You see, I got this aching feeling right now. Something is screaming at me that you might be the one dishing out secrets to the guy I'm looking for."

"Enough," McNeil shouted as he fixed his gaze on the door. "I'm done talking, all right? I've got nothing to say to you."

Dean moved toward the door. "This son of a bitch could have contacted you and started paying you off for information," he said. "He could've used any number of methods to make sure you guys never met face to face to make that happen. He also could have paid you off via any number of crypto apps that would take some deep digging to uncover."

A red-faced McNeil shot up out of his chair. "I can't wait to sic my attorney on you, Blackwood. By the time he's finished, you're going to be babysitting parking lots for the rest of your natural freakin' life!"

Dean raised his foot, kicked the door closed, and locked it.

Fists pounded on the door.

Wilson hollered for Dean to stop.

Then Dean grabbed a chair, wedged it under the door handle, and charged toward a trembling McNeil with a pair of claw-like hands.

56

Dean grabbed McNeil by his shirt, hauled him over the table, picked him up, and then slammed him down on the desk. Even Dean was surprised by his display of strength, the whole mothers-being-able-to-lift-a-car-to-save-their infant bit floating through his mind as he pressed his face against McNeil's and widened his eyes to a point that he looked like a crazed maniac.

"This guy paid you off," Dean grumbled. "Then he came after you in the hopes that he'd doctor the scene and make it look like *you* were the killer to buy himself some time."

McNeil pawed fruitlessly at Dean's hands, his lips quivering and eyes darting back and forth in his skull. "Let me go!"

Dean shot out his hand and secured a grip on McNeil's throat. "I'm fine catching a case after I'm done with you here, Devon. After what I've been through, being tossed in a cell sounds like a *reprieve*. Now, there are two ways that this ends. Either you tell me the truth," he tightened his grip on McNeil's throat, "or I choke you to death before that door behind me gets kicked in."

"Get off of—"

"*Talk!*" Dean screamed as he pulled out his SIG and buried the business end into McNeil's sternum. "You've got five fucking seconds."

A puddle of urine spread across the front of McNeil's jeans. He shook to the point that he appeared epileptic, looking at Dean as though he were death incarnate. "*Please*," he whimpered. "Blackwood, I—"

Dean disengaged the safety on his SIG with a cringe-inducing click and looked deep into McNeil's eyes. "Last chance," he whispered as he coiled his finger around the trigger.

The door to the interrogation room shook, the handle jiggling as fists rapped on the door and Dean made out the sound of clanking keys.

"Three seconds," Dean said. "Let's count them down. One."

McNeil shook his head. "Dean, please—"

"Two."

"I swear to God, I—"

"*Three.*"

"I never saw his face!" McNeil shouted toward the heavens. "He contacted me through a burner. I never saw him in person until he showed up to kill me!"

Dean pulled the gun out of McNeil's gut.

Then the door behind him busted in followed by the sensation of several hands ripping him off of McNeil.

57

Night had fallen as Dean sat on the hood of Wilson's sedan outside the police station, still rubbing his wrists where one of the Vacaville beat boys had secured them with handcuffs.

Wilson stood in front of Dean, the expression on his face composed of disgust, exhaustion, and anger. "Well," he said, "I'm not sure what we're supposed to do now."

"We pegged Devon McNeil as this killer's source," Dean said. "McNeil was the one who provided our suspect with information. All you gotta do now is start using what McNeil tells you to piece together a roadmap to our suspect."

"You understand that McNeil's counsel is going to get him the deal of the century after you put your hands on him."

Dean averted his gaze. "Fuck him. It would've taken days to try and sniff out that McNeil was the rat, and it would have taken you even longer to pull that information out of him that I did. Then you guys would've tiptoed around interrogating him and wasting God knows how much time trying to reel a confession out of him."

"But we would have gotten in the right way," Wilson said. "The *legal* way. Everything you pulled in there, all the stuff McNeil spilled, would have been inadmissible in court. Luckily for us, the guy is so scared of you coming back in for a second round that he's agreed to tell us everything we need to know."

"You know who I am, Willy," Dean said. "You know how I do things. Don't act surprised that everything happened the way that it did." He hopped off of the hood. "And you're welcome, by the way."

A red-faced Wilson turned his back on Dean. "I bought you maybe a couple of days before you get pulled in for this. You'll avoid any time or charges by the time I'm done working my magic on this, but you need to anticipate something in the way of a suspension, termination, or reassignment to God only knows whatever depths of hell OPR will recommend that you be sent to."

"I'll worry about that later," Dean said. "In the meantime, I need to find this guy before anyone else gets killed."

His boss spun around and looked at him like he had just conjured up Jesus Christ in the flesh. "Tell me you're not that dense," he said. "You don't really think you're going to have any level of involvement in this thing anymore, do you?"

Dean shrugged. "I'll do it with or without you guys, Willy. And I'm pretty sure it's going to be the latter."

"You're off of this, Dean. Hell, you weren't even on it officially to begin with! We're doing this *our* way now, not yours."

The muscles in the back of Dean's neck twisted into a knot and triggered a headache at the base of his neck. "More people will get hurt by the time you finish doing things your way, boss. Let's be clear about that. And this guy almost killed my sister." His temper flared. "I'm not going to give that a pass."

"All right." Wilson crooked a finger. "Enough is enough. This whole thing has gone completely off of the rails. You should have stayed off the playing field when you and Sheila had the chance."

"I was worried he'd go after other people if I disappeared. You have no idea the type of things this guy knows. He has access to all my information thanks to McNeil, and it was a legitimate concern to me that he'd go after someone in my family as a way to draw me out." Dean hung his head. "I thought if I played his little game, that would be my best shot at trying to get him."

"And look at the cost of that decision." Wilson's eyes widened. "We've got six dead people on our hands, and now your own sister is holding on for dear life. I'm sorry to say it, kid, but your way of doing things really screwed things up on this one."

Dean unclipped his FBI shield, held it up, and tossed it over to Wilson. His boss caught it one-handed and gawked at the badge as though it was the code for the nuclear football.

"I'm cashing out," Dean said, "before you or anyone else hauls me in for a sit down. Consider this my two week notice."

Wilson tapped the badge on his palm. "That's not how this works."

"I don't care."

"I need you to breathe, Dean," Wilson said. "I need you to rally and maintain your focus here, but more importantly, I need you to come in and debrief."

"I need to stay with my sister. I have to call my brother, my father, my ex." Dean waved Wilson off. "I have a long list of shit I gotta do in the interim. The last thing I need is to have a chat with my superiors about my thoughts and feelings at the moment. As for my contract, tell Sloane and whoever else is involved to shove it as far up their ass as possible."

Not a word passed between the two men for several moments. Dean used the time to slow his breathing in a bid to tick down his heart rate.

"You know what gets me?" Dean said to his boss, his tone more level and his nerves on the cusp of subsiding. "The notion of my sister losing her life over this bullshit line of work. Of her going to an early grave because of this," he winced, "*career* that she and I chose to take part in. It's more losses than wins, more questions without answers at the end of every single assignment that floats across our radar." He looked at Wilson. "Why do we do this, Willy?"

Wilson took on a more relaxed comportment and spoke to Dean like he was his high school football coach. "You can cry in your beer when this is finished, Dean. I need you to screw your head on straight and follow the procedures here. Let us handle this. We'll find this guy."

Dean shook his head. "No way. This guy is mine. I'm his endgame, the reason all of this is happening, and if he wants a showdown with me, he's going to get it."

His boss's eyes narrowed. "If you see fit to ignore a direct order or fail to follow everything I tell you from here on out, I can't protect you. I can't run interference for you."

"Well, it wouldn't be the first time I've been in that position."

"This time the repercussions for you will be far more dire than you could ever imagine, kid. Be smart here. Listen to what I'm saying." Wilson moved toward the driver's side of his sedan. "Just stay with your sister." He held out Dean's FBI shield. "And keep your phone on you. Consider this the first and last warning I'm going to give you. Don't leave that hospital unless you're going somewhere to crash. Clear?"

Saying nothing, Dean snagged the badge from his boss and stuffed it into the pocket of his leather jacket. He placed calls to his brother and his father on the way to the hospital, and twenty minutes later, Dean was back at the hospital, threading his way down the hallway toward Sheila's room.

The sight of a pale, weak, unconscious Sheila triggered Dean's eyes to mist. He reached out and laid his hand delicately on top of Sheila's. The sensation of the tape, the tube, and the needle in her hand tethered to the IV and machines triggered him to flinch.

"I'm so sorry, She," Dean whispered, "for everything. But I'll find this guy. I'll take him down. He'll pay. I swear to you." He tightened his grip on her hand. "I swear to *God*, he's going to pay."

After spending a few minutes by his sister's side, Dean left the room and sat in the chair just outside the door. He held his head in his hands as the countless memories of his life, all the decisions he had made—both good and bad—played back like a sizzle reel.

"You know what you gotta do, laddie," Woody said. "You gotta listen to me. That's always why I've been here. You may hate me, you may *despise* me, but I'm the part of you that's saved your life more times than you'd like to admit."

I can't keep living like this, you asshole.

I need some peace in my life.

"Then find this guy and take him out."

I will.

As God is my witness, if it's the last thing I ever do, I will.

———

An hour went by as Dean sat outside his sister's room. He fielded phone calls and texts from his family, updating them on Sheila's situation. Dean also checked on updates online about the case in San Francisco, perturbed upon finding that Greer, Dewitt, and the SFPD were at a dead end with the investigation and that the families of the six victims were demanding answers no one could give them.

I'll bring them justice.

I don't know how, and I don't know when, but rest assured, these people will not have died in vain.

I'll put this son of a bitch's head on a stake and spike it into the front lawn of City Hall by the time I'm finished.

The ringing of Dean's cell pulled him out of his vengeful train of thought. He saw that it was Bazz calling, and after waiting several rings as he debated to pick up, he finally caved, thumbed the answer button, and greeted his friend with a grunt.

"What's the news?" Bazz said.

Dean told him the whole story—the shootout, choking McNeil, learning that McNeil was the source, every nitty-gritty detail.

"My God," Bazz said. "Are you all right?"

"That's a silly question."

"Is there anything I can do to help?"

"I don't know what more you can do," Dean said. "I don't know who this guy is, and the only leads you were able to find turned up nothing."

"Hope isn't lost," Bazz said. "There's still a solution out there."

"Don't give me that, Bazzy. You worked for the Agency. You of all people should know that life doesn't play out like a police procedural. Sometimes things have no resolution. Sometimes there are no answers."

"Are you saying you're going to give up?"

"That's the rub, my friend," Dean said. "Even though I've got nothing to go on, I'm not giving up. I'm not going to let this guy win."

Bazz chuckled. "That's the spirit. Listen, I've gotta go. If you need anything, call me. I'm sorry I couldn't help you out more, bub."

"Thanks for being there, Bazzy."

"Don't get all sentimental on me. You're not the type."

With that, the line clicked off, and Dean put away his phone. He started pacing the floors of the hallway again, watching the nurses and other staff move through the hallway as he tried to think of what his next move would be when his cell phone rang again. Dean figured it was probably Layla or his old man or someone else who had a vested interest in the situation, but when he laid his eyes on the display and saw it was a number from the Hoover Building, he flexed his brow, thumbed the answer button, and held it to his ear.

"Blackwood."

"It's Baumgardner."

"What do you got?"

"I just finished running a series of analyses on the DVDs that were sent over," Baumgardner said. "I think I found something that might help you."

Dean's heartbeat sped up as he heard the news. "What did you find?"

"I examined the labels that were torn off the DVDs through a few different series of—"

"Don't tell me the process, Baumgardner," Dean cut in. "Tell me what you *found*."

The pudgy tech sighed. "There was partial printing on labels of the DVDs that I managed to piece together. Long story short, I found that the DVDs were purchased or taken from a rental shop that has long-since closed out in LA, a place called West Coast Cinema House."

I know that place.

Dean's eyes widened.

I know exactly *where that is.*

59

Silence settled over the line as Dean recalled the location of the West Coast Cinema House back in his home turf of LA.

It's near Cedars Sinai, about one block away from the hospital.

I never went there, but I remember seeing it every time we went to visit Mom in the hospital.

He closed his eyes.

What does that mean?

Damn it, Blackwood.

Think!

"Dean," Baumgardner said. "Are you there?"

Dean snapped open his eyes. "Yeah, I'm still here."

"Did you get the name of that rental place?"

"Yeah, I got it."

"Well," Baumgardner said, "I gotta call Dewitt and Greer and some other people to give them the heads up, unless you need something else."

"When was the rental place closed down?" Dean said. "Do you remember?"

"Last year, from what it says here on the screen. The place has been boarded up ever since."

Greer and Dewitt and whoever else is working this case are going to spend weeks tracking down the owner and whatever logs were kept for sales and rentals.

By then, it'll be too late.

"Thanks, Baumy," Dean said. "I might call you back if I need more info."

"Try not to," Baumgardner said. "Knowing you, you've probably pissed off enough people that someone's going to come around here asking if I talked to you. I'd like to refrain from having to lie."

With that, the line clicked off, and Dean sat back and tried to think through what relevance the information had that Baumgardner had given him.

West Coast Cinema House.

Near the hospital.

But what does it mean?

Does the hospital have any relevance?

Or am I just grasping at straws?

Dean stood up and strolled down the hallway. A litany of memories were pulled up from his home movie collection. Dean fixated on the proximity of the West Coast Cinema House to the hospital. He couldn't pinpoint the reason why he was so fixated on that fact, but the way his mind processed things, he knew it wasn't for reasons unknown.

"It's not nonsense," Dean whispered to himself. "This is how your brain works. You know this killer that you're chasing likes movies. This guy has made it a point to flex that fact. The fact that the DVDs were traced from that location isn't a one-off," Dean winced, "so what does it mean? Your gut is speaking to you, man." He drew a deep breath. "What is it trying to say?"

Recollections of the time Dean spent at Cedars Sinai were not few and far between. His father had a check-up there for his heart when he was forty, a by-product of the taxing his ticker took from the stress of working with the LAPD. His brother Tommy had his arm put in a cast there when they were ten, and then there was the "big one" when his mother passed away there in what felt like a lifetime ago.

"There's more," Dean mumbled. "You're missing something. You went there not long ago. Why? Who was it? Who were you going to see?"

More memories played back at high speed for Dean.

You were never in a bed at Cedars, but you did *visit someone else who was.*

You know the answer is there, Blackwood.

It's right in front of your nose!

Dean breathed deeply and allowed his mind to go blank, knowing that if he just left everything vacant, the right memory would pop into his mind.

"You know," Woody said. "You *know* who you visited in that hospital."

One second ticked by.

Then two.

Then Dean's eyes snapped open, and he whispered the name "Tyler Adams" out loud. He felt all the pieces of the puzzle slipping into place.

60

"Tyler *who*?" Bazz said.

"Adams," Dean told his buddy as he walked through the doors that spilled into the hospital's parking lot. "He was a part of that SMASH case I worked on."

"How does Adams factor in?"

"He was in the SMASH unit," Dean said. "He was a rookie. He wasn't on the take like the rest of the cops I was looking into. Adams ended up serving as an informant for me at one point, but things went south. The kid took a spill down some stairs and ended up in Cedars in a coma."

"Yeah," Bazz groaned. "That's right."

"Adams' captain sniffed out that I was using him as an informant and ended up pushing Adams down a flight of stairs when he found out." Dean winced. "It was my fault. That kid getting hurt was on me."

"And you're thinking that Adams might be holding that against you?"

"Maybe," Dean said. "But I'm sure there's a huge section of Tyler's life story I don't know about, one that triggered him to turn into a homicidal maniac who decided to murder couples in an effort to rectify something. I visited him a few times after he got put in the hospital, but I lost touch with the kid. I'm not sure what happened to him."

Dean gave Bazz the full rundown—the fact that Tyler Adams used to be a cop *and* former Army Ranger. He told his buddy how it lined up with the killer's profile and how Adams would be the kind of guy who would not only know how to curate a crime scene to throw the cops off his scent but also execute his victims in a militaristic fashion.

"And the feds," Dean went on, "found an M3 trench knife, the same kind that guys in my unit used to use. They'll spend days trying to work with CID pulling case files and sifting through them."

"Forward this to your people," Bazz said. "As stoked as I am to hear that you've made some headway, I think you should have called them first."

Blood rushed into Dean's complexion. "I think I might've pissed them off for the last time after everything that happened with McNeil." He strode back to his rental car outside the hospital, eager to get behind the wheel and drive and find out where Adams was, but the only problem was that he had nothing in the way of a compass to point him in Adams' direction.

"Adams is our guy," Dean said. "All signs point to him being the asshole here, and I want this thing closed down as soon as humanly possible."

Bazz sighed. "I've known you a long time, Dean. God knows that trying to talk you down when you've got your sights set on something is about as easy as wrestling a grizzly with your bare hands."

"Then work with me here, Bazzy," Dean said. "I need to get a line on Adams. There's a solid chance that he knows

I'm getting close to figuring out who he is, so he might try to pull something drastic if that's the case."

"Okay," Bazz said. "What do you need from me?"

"Well, there's only one person I know who might be able to tell me where he is."

"Who?"

"He had a girlfriend the last time I saw him. Adams was about two seconds shy of getting down on one knee and proposing to her."

"What's her name?"

The image of a blonde woman, roughly 5 foot 6 inches flashed through Dean's mind. "Mayer," he said. "Kelly Erin Mayer."

61

It took Dean a moment to process Kelly Mayer's new look over their FaceTime call, one that was brought to fruition thanks to Bazz's knack for tracking people down. As Dean took in Kelly's appearance, he noticed that she seemed a few years older than when he last saw her. The wrinkles in the corners of her eyes were indicative of someone who went through a condensed period of stress that forced her to mature ten years in the span of one. The last time Dean had been in the woman's presence, her hair was blonde, but now she sported a chestnut wave of locks that brushed the shoulders of her aquamarine scrubs.

"Kelly," Dean said. "Thank you for taking my call."

"Agent Blackwood," the woman replied, her tone sounding more like she was uttering a curse than exchanging formalities. "How are you?"

"I don't know if you remember me, but—"

"I do. I saw you, in passing, back when Tyler was in the hospital."

"That's actually why I called. I hate to get right to the

point with you, but unfortunately, this is one of those situations where time is of the essence."

Kelly's skin turned ashen. "It's been a long time since his name has been brought up."

"I take it that the two of you don't keep in touch?"

"No." Kelly flickered her gaze toward the floor. "Things ended with him not long after he got discharged from Cedars."

Okay, Dean.

Hop to it.

Ask what you need to ask.

"Listen," Dean said, "I'm going to have to ask you a lot of personal questions about you and Tyler and your relationship. That's why I'm calling. To be frank with you, I have reason to believe that Tyler might be, well, in trouble."

Kelly blinked her eyelids slowly like they were leaded curtains, her expression chock full of dismay. "I'm not surprised. After everything that fell apart between us, I had a feeling this would happen sooner rather than later."

"What makes you say that?"

Kelly puffed her chest and rested her back against a wall. "At first, the doctors thought Tyler had suffered a mild concussion. He was in a coma for eight weeks. When he woke up, it took him a while to get oriented, but eventually he was back to who he was, or at least I thought as much. I took him back to the home we were renting, and we tried to pick up the pieces after everything that happened with that case you were working on, but—"

Dean could see her gaze drifting. "But what?"

"It started out small," Kelly said. "Tyler was agitated most days. I wrote that off as stress from what happened, maybe him needing time to process everything he went through.

The doctors said something like that would happen and that Tyler just needed some time to adjust. But then..." Kelly shook her head. "I don't know, things got weird."

"Weird how?"

Kelly played with the curled end of her hair, distraught. "He was up most nights just staring out the window in the kitchen. I can't tell you how many times I had to get up and bring him back to bed. During the daytime, since he was on department-mandated medical leave, he spent most of his time watching movies or sitting in our garage fiddling with his old Army gear."

"What do you mean?"

"It's hard to explain," Kelly said. "Tyler would just sit there sharpening his knives and cleaning his guns. Anytime I tried to get him to help out with chores, laundry, groceries, or any of the day-to-day stuff, he would," her voice trembled, "he would freak out."

The more the story unfolded, the more Dean felt like he was padding slowly down a hallway toward a door marked "THE TRUTH LIES HERE."

"We tried for months to make it work," Kelly said. "Well, at least *I* tried. Three months in, I just felt like I was reaching a breaking point with Tyler. He was distant. Moody. Prone to bouts of anger."

A personality change.

It happens in certain cases when people take a hit on the head too hard.

Aaron Hernandez.

Hell, maybe even OJ, had they ever had the chance to crack open his skull and take a glimmer inside.

"I can only imagine how hard that was," Dean said. "Especially with Tyler not working. You must have had to pick up a lot more of the slack than anyone should."

"Well," Kelly said, "it helped that Tyler got a $1.2 million settlement from the city after everything that happened to him."

"You're kidding."

She shook her head. "No, not at all. Tyler was living off of that. He didn't really spend any of it. He just sort of sat on it." Kelly kneaded the muscles in the back of her neck, the strain on her face palpable to Dean even on a phone screen. "Tyler's biggest focus was trying to get his job back with the department, but they wouldn't clear him. After he failed his medical and psych evaluation, they sent him packing. We tried to get Tyler something in the way of employment after that just to keep him busy, but he wasn't having it. When the LAPD told him he was unfit for duty, I think that's what finally did him in."

"Did him in?" Dean said, asking a question he knew he already could guess the answer to.

"He would disappear for hours at a time," Kelly said as tears glazed her eyes. "Then days at a time. I have no idea what the hell he was doing, and I tried everything to help him get back to a good place. I tried getting him into therapy, going back to the doctors, but Tyler refused anything I threw his way. Finally, after talking with my friends and my family, I knew it was time to leave. It broke my heart, but..." a single tear rolled down the woman's cheek, "I just couldn't live like that anymore."

She gave him everything.

She fought her hardest, but none of it could bring him back.

"How did Tyler handle it?" Dean said.

A deep gust of air shot out of Kelly like a cannonball. "Not well. He broke down pretty hard. He tried to find a way to get me to stay. He was saying anything he could, but I knew I couldn't give in. I think once Tyler realized I wasn't going to go back on my decision, he got pretty angry with me. At one point, he grabbed me by my arms and slammed me against the refrigerator. For a moment, I thought he was going to kill me. You should have seen his eyes." Kelly shuddered. "I've never seen that look on a man's face before. He let me go, but then he told me something I'll never forget."

Dean's stomach did a somersault.

"Tyler told me, 'They'll see. Everyone will see.' After that, he grabbed his bags and left. I came back with a friend the next day to get my stuff, but Tyler wasn't there. That night at our house when I left him was the last time I ever saw him, at least face to face."

Dean perked up. "What do you mean?"

"I'm pretty sure Tyler was following me for a little while. I felt like he was watching me from a distance. I'm pretty sure I saw his pickup outside the nursing home where I was working. Between what happened in LA, the breakup, and him, well, *stalking* me, I decided it was time for a change. I ended up moving back with my parents in Enid, Oklahoma, until I got a job in Kansas City. I've been here ever since."

"And you never saw Tyler again?" Dean said. "You never heard from him?"

"I've gotten a few prank calls a handful of times, heavy breathing, things like that, but eventually, the calls stopped."

"Do you remember when this last happened?"

"About a week ago, actually."

My God.

That was right before the murders started.

"Kelly," Dean said, "does the name West Coast Cinema House mean anything to you?"

She nodded. "Definitely. When Tyler woke up in Cedars, they kept him for observation about two weeks. He was going a little stir crazy, so I got him a bunch of DVDs from the West Coast Cinema House. It was close by, so I was able to just walk down the street and pick them up."

The pounding of Dean's heart intensified to the point that he could hear it in his ears. "Why DVDs?" he said. "Couldn't you have just watched them on a streaming platform?"

Kelly huffed. "Tyler was a big cinema freak. Remember that time you watched us when we were at Universal Studios? Tyler told me you approached him that day while my back was turned. He said you talked to him about being an informant."

The day was one Dean remembered well, as he did countless others. The memory blazed through his mind, sped up like it was playing back at ten times the speed.

Dean saw himself walking up to Tyler and offering him the chance to rat on the corrupt unit of officers he was embedded in.

Tyler agreed.

Then his captain tried to kill him.

Then Tyler went into a coma.

And then the kid woke up and apparently lost his mind.

"I remember," Dean said with a profound sadness coating his tone. "I remember it well."

"It was Tyler's favorite place," Kelly replied. "He loved the tram ride. He loved seeing the movie posters and looking at all the places where the classics were shot—his words, by the way." She fixed a stern pair of eyes on Dean, a gaze so heated that Dean could feel it pierce him through the phone's screen. "He always blamed you, Agent Blackwood. He always said if he had never agreed to be your informant, things might have been different. To be honest, for a while I thought the same."

Dean's heart dropped into his stomach. "You might be

right, Kelly. And not that it's worth anything, but I can't tell you how sorry I am."

Kelly pulled her eyes off of Dean, anchored her attention to the floor, and then wiped away the tear on her cheek.

"What about the DVDs I mentioned?" Dean said, "the ones you said you got for him."

"Tyler said that DVDs were the only real way to watch movies anymore if you had to do it from home," she said. "He told me a bunch of times that the picture quality dropped a lot when you watched it on a streaming app. He wouldn't stop talking about it. That's why I got him the DVDs. He took them home with him after he was discharged and kept watching a bunch of them on a loop."

You're there, Dean.

You're at the door, your palm is on the handle, and you're about to open it to reveal that Tyler Adams is waiting on the other side.

"I don't suppose," Dean said, "that you happen to recall any of the titles you rented for him, do you?"

Kelly squinted. "*Apocalypse Now* was definitely one of them. I remember *The Fog*. He watched those more than a handful of times."

The same movies we found in Tyler's crash pad.

It's him.

Holy Christ.

Adams is the killer.

62

Dean stood in front of Wilson in the interrogation room of the Vacaville Police station,; the same room where he had thrown McNeil onto a table and pressed a gun into his belly, his hands clasped in front of him and hunching his shoulders like a child who had been scolded. It took Dean a total of two minutes to tell his boss what he had uncovered, and once he finished, he tagged it with, "I think I know how to bring him in" and then proceeded to tighten his lips into a fine line.

A few seconds went by as Wilson drew slow, rhythmic breaths. His focus was on the wall behind Dean, not looking his subordinate directly in the eye as Dean watched him process the news.

"For all your faults," Wilson finally said, "you sure do have a knack for turning over the right stones."

"It's Tyler Adams, Willy," Dean said. "It has to be. You can sift through all the evidence you want until Jesus makes his second appearance, but it's him."

"You're sure?"

"It's him. He wants revenge against me for what

happened during the SMASH case." Dean paced. "This whole sideshow of his with the clues and all that other shit —me confronting guys from my past—has been designed by Tyler in a way that only *I* can play it, that only *I* can figure out that it's been him this whole time."

Dean's boss held up his hand like a crossing guard. "I have no doubt," he said. "But I'm still dealing with the blowback from that bullshit you pulled with McNeil. Word has already been passed up the chain of command about what you did, and they want you back in Washington for a full debrief."

Dean held out hands in a submissive pose, every part of his posture slackening like he was about to throw himself at Wilson's feet. "Buy me some time, boss. We just need one day, maybe two at the most to get Adams. I'm the one he wants. It's clear from the call I had with Kelly Mayer that Tyler Adams is blaming everything that's happened to him on *me*, and the only way we can draw him out of hiding is to use me as bait."

Wilson pointed at Dean. "Let's just entertain the hypothetical that we abide by whatever playbook you're drafting right now. Tell me what that would look like."

"Let's break this down," Dean said as he paced the room. "Tyler was pissed at Kelly for leaving him, but he couldn't bring himself to lay his hands on her. He just couldn't. He loved her too much. There was too much admiration for her, but the fact that she left him drove him *mad* nevertheless. Coupled with whatever mental affliction Tyler has that was never diagnosed as a result of his head injuries, he ended up developing a kind of psychosis that drove him to plan a series of murders aimed at taking out people who were living the life he had lost, just like our profile predicted."

"And you're the progenitor of all this in Adams' mind, so

to speak," Wilson said. "After Tyler commits the murders, he pins his sights on you, the man he believes is responsible for his predicament."

Dean snapped his fingers. "*Exactly*. He kills the couples, then he goes after me. He tortures me and my sister until he's ready to commit the final act of killing me."

"And he used McNeil as his source," Wilson said, "something we've confirmed through McNeil's ten-hour testimony with us. McNeill was contacted through an email that was sent via a VPN network and some other layers of encryption that we're still working on unfurling."

Dean furrowed his brow, slipped a toothpick in his mouth, and chomped down. "My only question is how Adams knew McNeil had beef with me. I get that Adams was able to recruit McNeil into being his source and that Adams was able to cover his tracks as they were keeping in touch, but how *did* Adams track down McNeil in the first place?"

"We're pretty sure," Wilson said, "that McNeil flagged himself down by writing *you* into one of the episodes of *FBI: Los Angeles.*"

"The CBS show?"

"McNeil got a writing credit for an episode titled 'Backstabbers.' There was a character McNeil wrote that was based on him, a character who got fired from the FBI after a rogue agent named Sean Darkwood ratted him out on the job."

Dean huffed. "'Sean Darkwood'?"

"Yeah," his boss said. "No points for creativity. Anyway, McNeil got a writing credit and a consulting credit for that episode, but it was one of the last shows McNeil worked on before he was fired after LAPD brought him in for those sexual assault charges."

"Still," Dean said, "how does Adams make the connection that Darkwood was based on the run-ins I had with McNeil? It's a bit of a leap."

"McNeil got contacted through social media one day. He used to be active on Twitter."

"It's called X now."

"*Whatever* it was called," Wilson continued, "McNeil was using the app when he was still working in the industry. McNeil used to tweet photos and updates from the set of *FBI: Los Angeles*, and one day, a user named DarkPassenger sent him a message about the episode titled 'Backstabbers.' The user told McNeil he was a big fan of the show." Wilson flexed his brow. "And then McNeil apparently told this user that the character Darkwood and the plot of the episode 'Backstabbers' was based on you."

Dean closed his eyes.

Unreal.

McNeil could have given the fictional version of me a better name though.

"After DarkPassenger hit up McNeil on Twitter about this 'Backstabbers' episode," Wilson went on, "McNeil then told the user the full story behind the inspiration of the episode, your real name, and everything else in between. He told the user who contacted him everything without leaving out any details. According to McNeil, he was pissed off and liquored up enough at the time that he had no filter."

Dean's eyes widened. "And we can assume that this user who called himself DarkPassenger is Adams."

"Possibly," Wilson said. "And not long after this initial exchange these two had, McNeil gets contacted again from the same user who claimed he was a journalist doing a piece on corruption in the FBI, and this individual also said he was willing to pay McNeil for his time. The two of them then took their chat to a secured message board the user made, and after a bit of time, the user persuaded McNeil to give him information on *you*. McNeil was paid close to $300k for the effort."

"Adams got a million from his settlement with the LAPD," Dean said. "He had enough to pay off McNeil *and* fund his little extracurricular activities."

"A guy like him," Wilson said, "had the means to purchase the kind of tech he needed for the job, and he had the police and, if it's Adams, the Rangers training to do it."

"So Adams is the killer," Dean said, "and McNeil is his source. Then when Adams knew I was getting close to finding him via McNeil, he tried to set up McNeil to look like the killer to buy him some time. The only problem was that I got to McNeil the same time Adams did. McNeil said the user wanted to meet him in person, that he had some more information he needed and was willing to pay McNeil another $50,000 for the meeting. The meeting was a ruse. It was Adams trying to kill McNeil and then set him up." Dean traced his fingers through his hair. "Christ, this is nuts."

"That it is. But we have the facts. We have the story." Wilson crossed his arms. "Now I want to know what plan you've been brewing up. If it's Adams, which I'm inclined to believe it is, what do you propose we do about it?"

The plan in Dean's brain pieced together like the Lego set he worked on with his son two years before. "After Kelly Mayer left Tyler Adams," he said, "Tyler was despondent. He was already on edge after the LAPD wouldn't take him back, and the fact that he never went back in for check-ups or therapy assisted him greatly in not getting flagged down. If Adams had gone in and been diagnosed with something, we might've caught onto this sooner."

"Tell me what you're thinking."

"You used to be married, Willy, correct?"

"And?"

"Well, all animosity aside with your ex-wife, if you knew she was in trouble, if she was in *real* danger and was caught up in something that put her in a bad situation, what would you do?"

"My ex wiped me out, Dean," Wilson said. "I'm forking over half my pay monthly for alimony."

"Stick with me here, boss," Dean said. "Entertain the scenario. If your ex-wife was in trouble, *deep trouble*, what would you do?"

"Are you asking if I still love my wife?"

"You still care about her. I still care about mine too. So," Dean held out his hands, "what would you do if someone you cared about was faced with a life or death situation?"

A contemplative countenance overcame Wilson. "I wouldn't leave her out to dry," he said with an air of defeat. "I'd want to help her. If she was in *real* danger, like you said."

"Then if Tyler Adams knew that Kelly Mayer—the *one* woman he could never lay his hands on, the person who left him and, in turn, indirectly sent him down the path he was on—was in trouble, what would Tyler do?"

Wilson held his head high, squinting like he was working through a trig equation. "It's possible that he would come out of hiding, that he'd be riled up enough to do something about it, depending on what kind of circumstances Kelly had landed herself in."

"Deep shit," Dean said, "the kind of trouble Tyler would know—if he's keeping track of the news, which, based on the profile, he is—that it's something *we* caused. That *I* caused, the one man he holds responsible for his life falling apart."

The hum of the fluorescent lights overhead were the

only sounds in the room as Wilson stroked his chin and thought through the proposal. He shook his head. Dean sensed that his boss was aging a year in five minutes from the stress of the situation, along with everything Dean had put him through during their time together.

"If we did this," Wilson said, "if we could arrange a ruse to lure Adams out, what happens next?"

"He'll come after me," Dean said. "I'll use Kelly as a bargaining chip."

"And you're fine with that? With putting yourself directly in this guy's warpath? With putting Kelly through this whole rigamarole?"

"It'll be a fabricated situation. Kelly won't be in any real trouble. She's already agreed to play ball after everything I told her. In terms of the first part about being caught in Adams' crosshairs," Dean squinted, "well, I've been in that position before."

Wilson approached the table and sat down. He picked at the callous on his palm, his shoulders slack and making him appear more wizened than the age stated on his birth certificate. "In a perfect world, we get Adams," he said. "We throw the cuffs on him and end this thing, and you get a pat on the back for a job well done, but we can't look at this situation with rose-colored lenses. Even if we do get our hands on Adams, everything you've done, all that shit with McNeil and operating off your own set of rules is something you're going to answer for, even if you are the one who collars Adams."

Dean tamped down his anxieties. "I'll face the repercussions with my head held high after all of this is said and done, Willy. I have no qualms with that." He sat beside his boss on the table. "You told me one time that I operate like a gambler, that whatever lucky streak I have will eventually come to an end."

"And this might be that time, Deano," Wilson said as he met his subordinate's gaze. "I think we've come to the end of the run of me putting in a few phone calls to save your ass."

"All I'm asking," Dean said as he squeezed his hands to stave off the shakes, "is to let me roll the dice one more time. Let me bring in Adams. Sheila deserves that much. So do the people Adams killed. They deserve to be more than just trivia facts in this case."

Wilson nodded, pulled air deep into his lungs, and then clapped his hand on Dean's shoulder. "I'll get the ball rolling. We just need to hope that once this thing is in motion, Adams will be able to find you."

The tension in Dean constricted the muscles in his chest. "Don't worry about that, Willy," he said. "He'll find me."

63

Becoming another one of the victims of the guy the news had dubbed "The San Francisco Reaper" was a numbers game to Morgan. *He killed couples*, she thought. *Rich people*, and she was a single white female with $200 in her checking account, a landlord breathing down her neck, and the DWP one late payment away from shutting off her power. All those elements combined put Morgan in a bracket that, as far as she figured, was one the killer who struck fear into the hearts of the citizenry *wouldn't* be inclined to target.

Morgan peeled the Starbucks employee ball cap off her head and stuffed it into her tote bag, eyeing the broken glass a few paces ahead of her on the sidewalk as she glanced at her shoddy apartment building one block away, backlit by the setting sun.

Call Dad tomorrow.

Maybe I should *go back home.*

I could live with him for a while, patch things up, and find a place where they don't charge you $1,800 for a piece of shit studio apartment.

The booze-saturated grunt that belched out from the corner on Morgan's left triggered a shudder up her neck. She shot a look toward it, eyeing the vagrant man with tattered clothes clutching onto a beer bottle and standing right in the middle of the walkway that led up to her front gate.

"*Shit*," Morgan whispered as she terminated her walk. The guy was lingering right by the front gate, and Morgan knew that if she doubled back and decided to go through the rear gate at the back of the complex, it would take her ten more minutes to circle the block to evade the second unhoused citizen in two weeks.

Morgan scanned the block, checking over both of her shoulders in the hopes of spotting someone she knew. She needed an escort, someone like Josh from apartment 2B or the maintenance guy Ronaldo who was always on the property, but no one was around. Most everyone had confined themselves to their homes because of the Reaper or had left the city altogether just to be safe.

You're going the long way, Morgan signaled her defeat with a hefty exhale. *Start walking, girl.*

Morgan turned on her heel and began her journey back down the sidewalk, shaking her head, squinting her eyelids, and cursing under her breath. As she rounded the corner at the end of the block and prepared to take the long route, her heart swelled enthusiastically when she spotted a tall, sinewy guy with a Giants cap on his head pushing a stroller with a blanket draped over the canopy.

"Excuse me?" Morgan said as she upped her voice an octave. "I'm so sorry to bother you."

The young father furrowed his brow and slowed the stroller he was pushing. "Yes?"

Morgan gestured over her shoulder. "I'm so sorry, but I

was," the words spilled out of her like a ruptured water line, "I was hoping you might be able to walk me to my apartment building. It's right around the corner. There's a homeless guy out in front of my gate. I know this is so out of left field, but between the stuff on the news and—"

The young father nodded knowingly. "No worries. I totally get it. I'd be happy to walk with you."

Relief washed over Morgan. Her posture slackened as a bit of red came into her complexion. "*Thank you.* Seriously, I know this is so weird of me to ask, it's just..." She shrugged.

"All good." The young father started pushing the stroller. "I was headed back home already, so it's not out of my way."

Now that Morgan had her temporary bodyguard, her panic and paranoia were replaced by an awkwardness on par with taking a long ride in an elevator with a stranger. She wasn't sure what to say or how to walk, taking each step as though the ground beneath her was made of thin ice.

"I'm Morgan," she said. "It's nice to meet you."

"I'm Nick." The young father gently tapped the top of the stroller. "The little one passed out underneath the blanket here is Miss Gracie."

Morgan softened her tone for fear of waking the child. "How old is she?"

"Sixteen weeks. She's fussy around this time of night. Walks calm her down."

Morgan strolled alongside Nick down the sidewalk and stared at the vagrant *still* camped out in front of her building. "Walking alone like this at night is becoming too much of a chore. Last week, some guy spit on me."

The lines in Nick's face screwed into a scowl. "You're kidding."

"My dad thinks I should leave the city."

"My wife is thinking the same, especially after this whole, well..." Nick dawdled his lips. "You know."

"Especially with a new baby." Morgan gestured to the stroller. "I mean, I'm not a parent, but I can only imagine how stressful that can make stuff feel, if that makes any sense."

"They'll catch this guy sooner rather than later."

"You really think so?"

"They always do."

"Not that guy from back in the day. It took them like, what, forty years to find him?"

"Which guy?"

"The Golden State Killer," Morgan said. "There was a book and a show about him. Michelle McNamara wrote the book." Her lips turned down into a frown. "She practically caught the guy herself, but she passed away from the stress it put on her. I mean, that was part of the reason, but..." Morgan's voice trailed off.

"That's terrible," Nick said. "But it just goes to show that guys like him and the Reaper always end up getting caught."

Morgan's eyes narrowed, the gears in her brain turning. "This Reaper guy is weird though. The cops say they haven't found any forensic evidence or DNA or any of that stuff. He's also killed a lot faster than most serial killers do." She recalled something that a CNN anchor had spoken about and recited it verbatim. "The timeline of the murders and the fact that they've come to an abrupt stop is something that hasn't been seen in over thirty years. He's methodical, but he's not patient, but even though he's not patient, he's not sloppy."

A snicker shot out of Nick. "You must be one of those true-crime junkies."

"I'm a single white female." Morgan shrugged. "We tend to have a penchant for that stuff."

"Because it makes you feel safer. Watching that stuff makes you feel like it could never happen to you."

An icy sensation spread across the back of Morgan's neck. "I guess so," she said, trying to hide the fact that she was both offended, curious, and disquieted all at the same time.

Nick winced. "I'm sorry, that sounded weird. It's just something my wife said one time."

A bit of tension slipped off of Morgan's shoulders. "Yeah, I get it."

"When my wife was still pregnant," Nick said as he dug into the front pocket of his jeans, "she was actually watching." He terminated his walk. "Oh, *hell.*"

Morgan winced. "What?"

"I think I left my phone in my truck." Nick huffed. "*Damn it.* I keep doing that." He pointed to the Ford F-350 ten paces away hugging the sidewalk. "It's right up there." He took out his keys. "I'm just going to check really quickly if that's okay before I walk you to your gate."

"All good," Morgan said as she tailed Nick to his truck. "I've locked myself out of my apartment like three times this past year."

"Hopefully, my wife didn't call. She checks in three times an hour when I'm out strolling with Gracie at night."

The two arrived at the pickup as Nick thumbed his clicker. The lights on the vehicle flashed to signal that it had been unlocked. He opened the passenger door, informing Morgan that he needed "just one second" as he dug around in the front of the cab.

Morgan tapped her foot nervously as she clung to her bag, her eyes ping-ponging between Nick and the stroller.

Several seconds ticked by as Nick grumbled and searched for his keys, a cocktail of uneasiness and irritation mixing in her gut as she wanted to get into her apartment, kick off her shoes, and call it a night.

Morgan fixed her gaze on the stroller. She was curious to lay her eyes on little Gracie and figured that Nick wouldn't get too worked up if she peeled back the blanket to catch a little glimpse.

She stuck her index finger under the flap.

She pulled it half an inch so she could take in little Gracie, but Morgan saw nothing.

Morgan's heart shot into her throat. Her knees felt like they had turned into rubber when she looked up at Nick and saw that the young father was aiming a steel-blue pistol at her waist.

"Get in the car," Nick said, his voice pitched deeper, a more menacing ice-like octave. "*Now!*"

64

Dean's focus was on the television screen in the corner of the bar as he thumbed the rim of the cranberry juice in his glass. He took one last bite of the cheeseburger in front of him, pushed away the plate, and dismissed the nerves that tensed his stomach into a knot.

"You think it'll work?" Woody said.

"I think so," Dean replied.

"You *think*?"

"Like I told Wilson, I'm a gambler. I've always got one last lucky roll of the dice in me."

"God bless you, laddie," Woody groaned. "It's amazing you can operate with such a seat-of-your-pants rationale and survive this long."

"Yep." Dean scooped up his glass and took a swig. "The feeling's mutual."

"So," Woody said, "if it works, what then? You're gonna put the cuffs on Adams? Put him in a cell? Go home and live a regular Joe life?"

"That's the idea."

"You *can't* live a normal life, Deano. That's not who you are."

"If I don't, I'll get shot or drop dead of a heart attack by the time I'm fifty."

"*Or* turn into your old man, withered and broken with life clinging onto you like cancer."

"Leave the old man out of this," Dean said. "I mean it."

"Hey, I'm just the voice in your head," Woody replied. "You're not having a real conversation right now. This is all in your mind. You're the one pulling the strings here."

"Then kindly piss off and let me think."

"Not until you admit a few things, laddie. You're smart. You know why I'm here."

Dean closed his eyes.

I do.

This is my mind trying to work something out, just like how dreams are the mind's subconscious way of solving an internal dilemma.

"You know why I'm here," Woody said again, his tone less menacing and on brand as some Irish version of the demon from *The Exorcist.* In many ways to Dean, the more he thought about it, the more he realized the voice of his internal monologue sounded a lot like the voice of his late brother Tommy.

"I know," Dean muttered softly. "I need to be a father. I need to be present like I've said so many times before but never actually did."

"Right," Woody said. "And what else?"

The words were on the tip of Dean's tongue, burning with an acidic quality like he had just swigged on some OJ after brushing his teeth. "I need to tell Layla I love her," he whispered. "I need to accept the good things in my life."

"Well done, laddie. I think we're done here."

"Good."

"I'll see you around."

"Hopefully not."

A weight felt like it had been lifted off of Dean's shoulder as he downed the last of his cranberry juice.

Look at that.

I didn't even need to shell out $200 an hour to a therapist to work that one out.

Vibrant colors danced on the television screen above the bar. A title placard that read "BREAKING NEWS" triggered Dean to sit up straight in his seat. A moment later, the image faded into a shot of a glossed-up reporter standing in front of a stucco building with the words Federal Bureau of Investigation behind her.

"This is Lydia Cho reporting from the FBI field office here in Dallas, Texas," the reporter said. "Federal authorities today have released an update to the press in regard to a recent series of slayings in San Francisco. Special Agent in Charge of the Dallas field office, Michael Landy, has stated that agents have arrested a suspect with supposed connections to the murders, and in a startling turn of events have *even* released her name to the general public."

Here we go.

Dean stood and padded his way slowly toward the television.

Make it happen, Willy.

A mugshot of Kelly Mayer unfurled across the television screen in dramatic fashion like a map being rolled out on a table, her hair disheveled, her eyes cracked and red as she stared into the camera with a petrified expression.

Dean smirked.

Well done, boss.

You really hammed it up good.

"Kelly Mayer," Cho said as Kelly's image stayed on the screen, "is believed to be involved with the murders that took place in San Francisco. As of now, authorities are currently questioning her, and it is expected that formal charges will be brought against her in the coming days."

Dean took out his cell, tapped in Wilson's number, and heard the line ring twice before his superior picked up.

"How'd it look?" Wilson answered.

"You got a flair for the theatrics, Willy." Dean motioned with his chin toward the television. "I just hope Kelly's employers are in the know with what's going on. I want to make sure her reputation is intact once this is done."

"They know," his boss said. "And once we get Adams and bring him in, we'll follow up with a news conference stating that Kelly was in on the whole thing. We'll make sure the media knows that everything was a ruse. In the meantime, Kelly is safe and sound in a suite at the Hilton in Dallas."

"News outlets will be chomping at the bit to get her on camera afterward," Dean said. "Kelly could make six figures in interviews if she decides to go that route."

"I told her the same thing. She appears quite adamant about going back to life as it was when it's over. Now, down to brass tacks."

"I wait for Adams to call," Dean said. "Make sure this story is circulating through all the major networks so he sees it."

"That's already happening," Wilson replied. "Fox News and CNN are all over it."

"Then it's just a matter of time before I hear from Adams."

"Then you lie low in the meantime. Have you checked into the motel?"

"I have," Dean said. "It's a few blocks from here.

Crummy little place with crappy sheets and water stains on the walls. No one can find me."

"Understood," Wilson said. "Don't go anywhere else. Once Adam gets in touch with you, you let me know ASAP."

"Copy that."

"And Dean?"

A long pause settled over the line for a few moments. Finally, Wilson broke the silence, and said, "Stay sharp."

Dean hung up the call and kept his eyes glued to the television, listening in as Kelly Mayer's name and face were shown and mentioned over and over again. Satisfied that word had been put out in the ether, he paid his bill, walked back to his hotel room two blocks away, and locked the door.

Dean sat on the edge of the bed, his belly full from the meal and the anticipation as he took out his SIG and placed it on the bedspread beside him.

One hour ticked by.

Then two.

At the two-hour-and-thirty-two-minute mark, Dean's cell chirped, and he saw an unknown number flashing on the screen as he put the phone on speaker.

"Hello?"

A few seconds passed.

Then the undoctored voice of Tyler Adams said, "It's me," with all the hate in the world glazing his tone.

65

A surge of adrenaline shot through Dean like he had been struck by a bolt of lightning. He shot up from the bed, a half-smile, half-scowl on his face as he tightened his grip on the phone.

"Adams?" Dean said. "Is that you?"

Heavy breathing came over the line—canine-like panting—and what felt like an entire minute passed before Adams replied, "You fucked up. You fucked up *royally*, Blackwood."

"So, it is you."

"You shouldn't have brought her into this, you son of a bitch. You had no right."

He's worked up.

Good.

"So," Dean smirked. "I take it that pisses you off?"

Thrashing came over the line, the ruckus thundering enough that it made Dean palpitate. It sounded like Adams was chucking over a table, a cacophonous blend of glass, wood, and metal being thrashed about. After a moment, the sound settled, and Adams' breathing came back over the line.

"Well," Dean said, "if you want Kelly to—"

"Don't you ever say her name!" Adams screamed. "*Ever*."

"Listen, kid, I—"

"I'm not a kid anymore, Blackwood." Adams' voice was more tranquil now like he'd had been jabbed with a sedative. "After I woke up, I *evolved*. Whatever you think you know about me, the man you conned into your world is dead."

Dean's heart pulsated inside his chest, pinpricks rippling across the flesh of his arms. "I heard all about it. Sounds like that bonk you took on the noggin really did a number on your mental state there, slick."

"Even if that never happened, it wouldn't have changed the trajectory I'm on now. It's *you*, Blackwood. You're the one who's responsible for what's happened. For the death. The decay. For the way things are now."

The tensed muscles in the back of Dean's neck teased the start of a headache. "Don't put that shit on me, Tyler," the words seethed out of his mouth. "I'm not going to buy into this Dahmer-esque rhetoric. The devil didn't make you do this. Not being held by your mother or having your girl leave you isn't at the epicenter of all this. You made a choice. It had no fuck-all to do with me."

"She left me because of *you*," Adams said. "It's because of what you did to me that my life ended up getting flushed down the toilet. I had a life. I had a future. The second you barged into my world and forced me to do your bidding was the moment I lost everything."

The sinews in Dean's jaw tensed. "I'm done playing Sigmund Freud with you, bud. The net is closing in on you. The Bureau knows who you are. We got it all figured out, and now that McNeil is singing like a choir boy, it's only a matter of time until we get to you."

"You think I planned on steering clear of you and your people forever?" Adams huffed. "This wasn't a game that was meant to last all four quarters. I'm not one of those run-of-the-mill nutcases the Bureau gets their rocks off chasing. I'm not in this for the long haul. Sure, you getting the drop on me when I tried to do McNeil may have dicked with my timeline, but I still got what I wanted. I got to carve up six people, *and* I was able to watch that sister of yours get thrown into a permanent sleep." He laughed. "How's she doing, by the way?"

Dean tightened his grip on the phone. "I'm blowing the whistle here, Adams. Now you have one of two choices to make before we bring this game to an end."

"The cuffs or a bullet," Adams said. "Something like that, right?"

"Pick one or the other. I'm fine with either. But the longer you wait, the more we'll throw everything we can in the book at Kelly. She'll be sitting in a federal correctional facility until the ice caps melt."

"You had no right." Adams' voice trembled. "You should have left her alone."

"Enough," Dean said. "You want me? I'm right here. You want us to cut Kelly loose? You want the one thing you hold such an affinity for to be sprung from a fate like the one you're facing now? *Turn yourself in.*"

"This is about you and me, Blackwood. Killing those couples, toying with you and your sister, all that was fore-play, the buildup to the final release. I want what I want."

"Well, you're not going to get it. I've got your manhood tied to the rear end of a pickup, and I'm two seconds shy of stamping down on the gas pedal."

"You're still playing by my rules, Blackwood," Adams said. "Even though the last of the grains in the hourglass are trickling down, you don't really think I'm going to let you slip through my fingers, do you? I want a one on one with you, and I've made sure I'm going to get it."

"Is that a fact?"

"Give me some credit here." Adams laughed. "After all we've been through, after all I've shown you that I'm capable of, you *know* I had to have something in the way of insurance."

Nausea settled in the pit of Dean's stomach. He sat on the edge of the bed, fear creeping up behind him as though Adams was physically in the room and coiling his arms around his neck.

"What did you do?" Dean said.

"Why tell you," Adams said, "when I can show you?"

The sounds of the phone being shuffled came over the line. A moment later, a woman's voice, choked with trepidation and anxiety, whimpered, "Please, help me," which triggered thick beads of sweat to accumulate on Dean's brow.

66

Every inch of Dean's flesh prickled when he heard the desperate plea of the woman over the line. He shot up from the bed, his fingers curled into a fist. Dean debated punching a hole in the wall of his crappy hotel room just to have something in the way of a release.

"You listen," Dean said, "and you listen good."

"Save it," Adams cut in. "You've been faced with a hostage situation more than a handful of times, and the first lesson your instructors at Quantico taught you was that the guy with the gun holds all the cards at the start of the match."

Breathe, Dean.

Compose yourself.

Don't get emotional.

If you do, this woman is going to die.

Dean straightened his posture.

Closed his eyes.

Then he nodded his acceptance of the situation and adopted the same tone—ironically enough—that his hostage negotiation instructor back at Quantico told him to put on display.

"Okay," Dean said. "What do you want?"

"Like I said," Tyler told him, "I want *you*. Man versus man. You versus me. No one else. No backup, no lifelines, just a toe-to-toe match between the two of us. I hate to implement some cliché rhetoric into my spiel here, but I have to do it nonetheless. If you call for help, if you tell anyone where you are going, what you are doing, if you send anything in the way of a signal to anyone, I'll make sure this woman suffers the worst fate of anyone I've put my hands on yet."

Play his game.

Get him out in the open.

That's your only chance to bring this woman in alive.

"All right, I'm on board," Dean said. "Just tell me what you wanna do."

"The Redwoods," Adams said. "Jedediah Smith State Park. Don't be an asshole and start calling your superiors to tell them where you're going. I'll make sure this woman suffers if you do."

"Once I get to where I'm going," Dean shrugged, "what then?"

"Just start walking. We'll cross each other's paths sooner or later."

God damn right we will, Dean thought as he fought to tamp down the adrenaline pumping through his veins.

"When we're done with this phone call," Adams continued, "you'll hang up the cell you have on you and dismantle it. You're well aware by now that I have the ability to trace you better than any satellite orbiting the planet. I'll *know* if you call anyone or attempt to take your phone with you.

And I've got my eyes on you at all times, so if you deviate or try to flag anyone down, I swear—"

"You'll kill her," Dean said. "I get the picture."

"Then we're done talking," Adams replied. "You have two hours to get to your final destination. One minute over that, she dies."

"I hear you."

"Good." Tyler took a beat. "Then I'll see you soon."

The line clicked off. Dean, feeling like a fuse had been lit, took apart his cell, broke the sim card in half, and then dropped the phone to the floor. He raised his booted foot, brought it down on the phone, and smashed it into oblivion before he grabbed the keys to his rental car and headed out for the Redwoods.

67

When Morgan awoke, she registered the headache wrapped around her skull. It was faint and dull, throbbing like a giant Band-Aid was cinching her skull like a vice grip. The next thing she sensed was the lack of energy she had when she tried to flex her fingers or shuffle her legs, the sensation similar to the ones she had experienced during the mornings when she had one too many the night before. Morgan felt weak, lethargic, unable to move a single inch of her body.

Then there was the darkness.

The stuffiness when she tried to draw a breath.

That feeling that she couldn't see anything reminded her of the time her brother Matthew locked her in the linen closet as a goof.

Morgan parted her chapped lips and tried to groan, but when she stuck her tongue through her mouth and the tip grazed against a saliva-soaked rag, the reality of her situation struck her in the face like someone had whacked her upside the head with a two-by-four.

Her eyes widened.

Her heart skipped a beat.

In two blinks of her eyes, a surge of adrenaline shot through Morgan and jolted her awake like she had been shot up with 500 milligrams of caffeine.

Morgan suddenly realized she wasn't in her bed. She wasn't stirring from a hangover. She was confined to some kind of cramped space, duct tape over her mouth and another strip placed over her eyes, her lashes sticking to it each time she tried to blink. Her arms and legs had been secured with tape, and based on the faint smell of gasoline that lapped at her nostrils coupled with the dull rumble of a car motor, Morgan knew she was somewhere inside a vehicle.

Morgan hollered as loudly as she could, but the gag in her mouth and the duct tape that sealed her lips stifled her cries to the point that they registered as nothing more than whimpers.

Oh, God! Morgan thought, the synapses in her brain firing off like fireworks. *Where am I? Am I hurt? I can't feel a thing.*

The vehicle shifted on its axis and triggered Morgan to tense up. She held her breath, curling into a fetal position as she made out a faint scraping outside.

Footsteps.

Broken tree limbs.

Someone grunting like a trucker ten hours into his shift.

Morgan's ears tickled as she made out the jingling of keys. A moment later, she heard something open. Morgan tensed up, squeezing her eyes closed even harder and hoping she'd fall back into a slumber, that maybe—just *maybe*—if she squeezed her eyelids tight enough, she'd stir from her nightmare and be back in her bed in her shoddy apartment.

A gloved hand tightened around the back of Morgan's neck and caused her to squeal. She tensed up as she felt herself being pulled out of the back of the truck. Morgan hugged her chest with her chin as her body was thrown onto the ground.

She smelled dirt.

Wet leaves.

The lingering scent of motor oil and the hot rubber of tires.

Dampened grass.

Birds chirping.

Wind rustling the tree leaves.

Then the deep breathing of the monster who had placed her in her current predicament.

Morgan shuddered as someone—some*thing*—secured a grip on her shirt and hoisted her to her feet. She was frightened beyond measure, a nonplussed terror wracking her like nothing she had ever felt before—but God be damned if she was going to lose her dignity.

One second went by.

Two.

Then Morgan heard the voice of the man she knew as "Nick" whisper, "Be calm. Don't scream. You do as I say, you'll be home before you know it."

Bullshit, Morgan thought, recalling all the true crime shows she now regretted binge watching. *That's what they say.*

That's what they always *say before they rape or kill you or both.*

"Just sit still," Nick said as he peeled the tape off of Morgan's mouth. She spit the gag out. "I'm not going to hurt you. I need you to stay calm, Morgan. Don't scream. If you're not relaxed, if you budge a single inch, something bad will happen."

Morgan felt a hand brush past her waist and flinched, certain that "Nick" was about to disrobe her and have his way with her or God only knew what else, but that didn't happen. She heard "Nick" sifting around inside the truck like he did when he was looking for his "cell phone." Morgan heard what sounded like grocery bags being rifled through followed by the clanking of metal.

"Stand up straight," Nick said. "Hands at your sides. Again, don't move. Don't flinch. It's important that you remain as still as possible."

Morgan followed her captor's instructions to the letter as she sensed something heavy being draped over her neck, shoulders, and chest. The bulk of the unknown object weighed her down and made her conjure up the memory of those little vests she wore with Matthew back when they played laser tag when they were kids.

Morgan felt "Nick" tighten a series of straps around her ribcage and waist. The tips of shoes then brushed against hers, her captor standing toe to toe with her as he sighed and tapped on whatever had been placed over her chest.

Morgan then heard a series of beeps like someone plugging in a cell phone number. Then she heard another beeping noise, louder than the other. "Nick" clapped his hands together before he mumbled, "All set," and then instructed her to turn around.

"Please," Morgan said. "I can't see anything."

"You don't need to see."

"*Please...*"

A moment passed.

Then Morgan felt the tape over her eyes being gently stripped away.

She batted her eyelids open and looked straight at Nick's face.

She shuddered as she found herself standing face to face with the man who was about to do whatever it was he was going to do.

"It'll be okay," Nick said as he prepared to put the tape back over Morgan's eyes. "Don't worry."

"Can you leave the tape off?" Morgan pleaded. "I'm scared of being in the dark."

Nick narrowed his eyelids.

He took a beat.

Then he let the strip of tape flutter out of his hand.

"I'm sorry," he said. "I'm sorry I have to do this."

"Then *don't* do this," Morgan said as a single tear rolled down her cheek. "I'm *begging* you."

Nick shook his head. He straightened his back. Then he placed his hands gently on Morgan's shoulders and edged her back into the truck.

"Just relax," Nick said. "Close your eyes. Maybe try to go back to sleep. I pulled off the tape because I want to let you breathe, but don't scream. It might set the device off if you do."

Morgan felt herself being nudged back into the truck before she heard the door being slammed. Once everything around her fell silent, she heard a faint ticking sound emitting from the thing that had been strapped to her chest. It was similar to the timer her mother would set when she prepared the family's annual Thanksgiving feast.

68

Dean had to fight the urge to pull over, find a phone, and call for help, but he knew that Adams had eyes on him like he had for the past several days, his proverbial big brother, the eye in the sky watching him every single minute.

Keep your head down, Deano.

Keep your eyes open.

Play Adams' little game.

It's just you and him now, and he won't win.

You can't let him.

After Dean pulled into a gas station and filled up his rental car, he entered the convenience store and perused the handful of aisles supplied with the finest selections of junk food cuisine that the place had to offer—beef jerky, potato chips, sodas, candy bars—the four main food groups. Dean figured the guy behind the counter was chowing down on some of that food based on his portly, unkempt build.

Dean palmed a bag of beef jerky followed by a bottle of water, opting for the lesser of the four sustenance evils as he fished out his wallet.

Use your credit card.

If something goes wrong, if I end up in Adams' truck, the men and women at the Bureau will be able to trace my steps.

The guy behind the counter rang up the jerky and water by punching his fingers at the register, his mouth open to tell Dean the final price when the telephone next to the register chirped to life.

"Yeah?" the guy grunted, greeting whoever was calling with an unenthused timbre like the phone call was a giant inconvenience.

Dean's debit card was in his hand, pinched between two fingers, extending it out toward the clerk when the guy told him, "It's for you."

69

The look on Dean's face matched the clerk's—confused, bewildered, a little bit vexed. Grabbing the phone receiver from the clerk, Dean held it to his ear. His stomach knotted when he heard Adams say, "Pay in cash, Blackwood. Don't be stupid. When you're done, go into the bathroom. I left you something in there."

The line clicked off.

Dean handed the phone back to the clerk.

Then the clerk shrugged. "The hell was that?"

"My ex-wife," Dean said as he nestled his debit card back in his wallet, pulled out a $20 bill, and placed it on the counter.

"*Huh.*" The unconvinced clerk took the cash and handed Dean his change. Dean asked if there was a code to the bathroom in the back, and the clerk responded by grabbing a key looped to a ruler from underneath the countertop and tossing it next to the bag of beef jerky.

Dean scooped up the key, nodded thanks, and made a beeline for the restroom at the back of the store. He slipped inside and locked the door, his hand drifting toward his SIG as he played back the memory of Adams using his head to mop the floors of the diner restroom several days prior.

Dean saw the urinal on his left and then the stall on his right. He edged toward it, pushing the door open with two fingers before he zeroed in on the tank above the bowl. He sighed, inching toward the bowl and weighing the odds that Adams had rigged the thing with some kind of explosive.

Too boring a climax for Adams.

He wants this last showdown face to face.

Dean lifted the lid off of the tank, shaking his head as he made out a black object wrapped in plastic. He pinched the bag and removed it, weighing the thing in his hands before he ripped open the bag and located the prepaid, flip-style cellular phone inside. He stuffed the device in his jacket. He washed his hands. Then he exited the restroom, handed the clerk the key, scooped up his water and jerky, and headed toward his car. Once Dean was behind the wheel, he flipped open the phone and turned it on. Only a few seconds ticked by before it began to ring.

"Blackwood's toilet emporium," Dean greeted, ogling his rearview mirror for signs of a vehicle or pedestrian lingering nearby.

"That's funny," Adams said. "Now drive. And don't bother trying to shoot anyone a text from that phone. It won't work."

Dean obliged as he put the phone on speaker and linked up with the highway on his left.

"Good job," Adams said. "Feel free to eat, by the way, while we talk. You'll need your strength."

Dean ripped open the bag, took some of the jerky, and stuffed it into his mouth like it was some of the dip his old Ranger chums had a penchant for. "I take it that you'll know if I try to hang up and call someone else, right?"

Adams huffed. "Circle gets the square."

"Why'd you go to the effort of leaving that phone for me?"

"Figured we'd have one last conversation before the shots start firing."

"How the hell did you know that I'd stop at that gas station? I could have kept driving right past it."

"It's the last one until you get to the Redwoods," Adams said. "I knew you needed gas at some point, so I figured I had something in the way of a fifty-fifty shot of you stopping where I left the phone. I mean, I'm watching you pretty much all the time, so it's not that difficult."

"And if I didn't go there?" Dean said. "What then?"

"It would have been disappointing. I was hoping to have another chit-chat with you before we met up. Luckily, it worked out in my favor because, well, here we are."

Dean skimmed the road outside the windshield. "You're ahead of me then, aren't you?"

"Don't waste time trying to pinpoint my location."

"Well, I've got about an hour before I get to this little meeting spot of yours. Why'd you leave the phone? To toy with me some more? Something like that?"

"Yeah," Adams said. "Something like that."

Dean smirked. "You're good, brother. I gotta hand it to you. Everything you've managed to pull off from a technical standpoint would give intelligence agency spooks a run for their money. How'd you do it? I mean, like you said, we got the time."

"Honestly," Adams sighed, "having the cash on hand to pay for all these expenses took care of about half of it. The rest was just relying on all that know-how I learned back with the Rangers, something you could attest to."

"You probably used RAT devices," Dean said, recalling

some of the tech that Bazz told him about that the Agency used in the same part of the world he had spent two tours of his life in. "A VPN, maybe something along the lines of—"

"It doesn't matter," Adams cut in. "I don't want to sit here sifting through the items I picked up at Radio Shack."

"Then what do you want to talk about?"

"Life, maybe. How bad things can turn out when one simple mistake is made."

Nausea churned in Dean's bowels. "I think I'm done being a plus-one to your pity party, Adams. If you want to keep droning on about how hard things got for you, maybe we should put this off for a day so you can talk to a shrink or a priest."

"I tried all that," Adams said with a forlorn tone. "By the time I knew I was going mad, I thought maybe there'd be a way to bounce back from it. Maybe there'd be some hope. Maybe there was some kind of twelve-step program I could take up before things got worse, but that's not how things panned out."

He's less articulate. Dean noted that every word Adams spoke was done with less of a fever-pitch and more in line with a man uttering his last words from his deathbed. *A guy on a train in the dead of night knowing that he's about to arrive at his final stop.*

"Why kill those couples?" Dean said. "Why not just kill me? Why the games? The clues only I could figure out? You could've just walked up to me and shot me."

A few moments went by with only Adams' breathing audible over the line. Finally, he said, "I guess I needed a release. After Kelly left me, I..." He sighed. "Well, I remember taking a long walk down our street one day not long after she moved out. I was in a bad spot. I was toying with the idea of putting a gun in my mouth that very night."

Maybe you should have.

You could have spared us this entire thing.

"I saw this couple next door to me on my walk," Adams continued. "Andrew and Roxanne. Kelly had dinner with them a few times. I saw them sitting on their porch having coffee or tea or something. They waved at me. Both of them were grinning like they were getting paid for it, and..." He drew a deep breath. "I don't know, it was like a switch got turned on in my brain. It was almost like I was looking into the future that I had with Kelly, one that got taken from me. I resented it. I couldn't stand it."

"*So*," Dean said, "you gave yourself the green light to kill innocent people? You saw fit to obliterate the lives of others to rectify whatever inadequacies you felt you had with yours? Something like that?"

"Watch it."

"Fuck you, Adams. I'm done trying to build a psych profile on you. You've killed innocent people—"

"And I'm prepared to do it again," Adams said. "Don't forget that I've got one last innocent bystander in my custody, and I'm more than willing to cut her little head off and overnight it to your father's place in LA just for good measure."

"You sick *prick*." Dean punched his steering wheel. "When I find you, I swear to God—"

"Don't," Adams said. "Just don't. No one here is free of guilt, Blackwood. Not you, not your sister, not any one of these people I carved up, and definitely not this woman I've got with me right now. Everyone is a sinner. Whatever sterling facade people advertise to the world in an effort to show they're good people is nothing more than that. It's false advertising, a fugazi."

"So, that's the reasoning," Dean said. "You knew you

turned to the dark side so you tried to slap together this narrative that everyone around you is too."

"We're *all* evil. Every single one of us. I guess that was the point I was trying to express."

Dean shook his head. "You're fucked in the head, brother. You've tumbled so far down the rabbit hole that you're incapable of seeing things straight."

"There's only one person free of guilt in this scenario, Blackwood," Adams said, "and you and your cronies at the Bureau saw fit to bring her into this."

"And she'll stay that way," Dean said, "until you end this. Just hit the pause button, man. Let this woman go, and turn yourself in. You do that, it'll take just one phone call and Kelly will get sprung from her cell. You do that, maybe you got a shot at seeing her one last time before your execution."

A deep exhale came over the line. Adams' voice then cracked, rupturing, a reflection of his mindset, one that was in the throes of fracturing. "I don't want to see her again," he said. "She deserves better than that. I don't think I can stomach laying eyes on her again."

"Then you'll leave her to her fate?" Dean shrugged. "Is that it?"

"When the dust settles, everyone will know that all this was done by me. They'll find all the evidence they need to piece that together. When all is said and done, you guys will cut her loose. I'll take comfort in knowing that's how this will all pan out."

"What about us?" Dean said. "What about you and me? Do you really think that putting a bullet in me is going to bring you peace?"

"I do," Adams said. "It'll be my final reward before I turn the gun on myself."

"Unless I do it for you."

"That is a likelihood I have to accept. But I won't see it as a loss if that's how all this goes down. I *want* to die. I'm just resolved to make sure you go down with me."

That won't happen.

It can't.

I won't leave Layla behind.

I won't make Jeremy or Claire or Sheila or Pop or anyone else have to stand at my funeral.

"You can still put a stop to this, Tyler," Dean said as he embraced a less hostile tone. "You can turn around. You can let that woman go. Please, for your sake, for *Kelly's* sake, back off of this."

One second ticked by.

Two.

Then Adams said, "As tempting as that is, I've made my decision, Dean. And I think we're going jab for jab here. I'm going to hang up now. When I do, I want you to snap that phone in half and dump it. I'll know if you don't."

Dean's eyes widened. "Adams—"

The call was terminated.

Dean shook his head.

Then he snapped the phone in half, rolled down the window, and tossed the pieces onto the highway.

70

Dean rolled up the window and clamped down on a nicotine toothpick.

It's over.

The talking is through.

You can't get through to Adams.

All you can do now is bring him down and shut this whole thing down once and for all.

The sign for Redwood National Park was on Dean's left. He eyed the odometer, doing some quick math in his head, and figuring he'd arrived just before nightfall.

He wants it that way.

He wants to do this while it's dark out.

He wants to stalk me through the woods like a goddamn deer.

Slivers of autumn hues painted the front of the rental's hood, the first fragments of the setting sun indicating that the day was cresting and paving its way to the night. Dean considered if this would be his last day on earth, like he had several times before during the course of his life and career.

No, Dean thought as he flexed his grip on the steering

wheel. *You'll find Adams. You'll take him down. You'll go home to your family.*

Dean wanted to get word to the people he loved and the people who loved him back—his clan, his family, all the cherished humans he wasn't ready to leave behind—but he knew it was impossible. Even writing something on a scrap of paper and dumping it would likely be found by Adams, and if it was, the hostage he had taken, the innocent woman who probably had a gun to her head at that very moment, would die.

This is not the end of the line for you.

You're going to live.

You're going to end this and turn the page.

You're going to write a new book.

You're going to tell Layla you love her.

You're going to find happiness for the first time in your miserable life.

The onslaught of thoughts and personal musings cramped the muscles in the back of Dean's neck. Looking for a reprieve, he toggled the car radio's switch, scanned the stations, and landed on the first song he felt was suitable enough to drown the contemplations running amok in his mind, "Falling to Pieces" by Faith No More.

Sheila would approve, Dean thought as he tapped his finger to the beat, the heavy bass and throaty vocals harkening back to the times he would "jock up" with his fellow Rangers right before a mission.

"Use it," Dean whispered as he cranked up the volume, an image flashing through his mind of Sergeant Pages right before they took that village in Afghanistan's Ghazni province, his first true firefight. Someone in the unit saw fit to throw on heavy metal right before they loaded into Black

Hawks, Pages stooping down on one knee in front of Dean as Dean was securing the straps of his Kevlar.

"You good?" Pages said, his smooth voice and almond-shaped face still vivid in Dean's mind.

Dean, sporting a jarhead haircut at the time, nodded at his superior officer. "Good."

"Pre-show jitters?"

"Yes, sir."

Pages' eyes flickered. "You ever been shot at before?"

Dean shook his head. "Negative, Sergeant."

The sergeant clapped his hand on Dean's shoulder. "Use that fear; *channel it.* You've trained for this. You've got this, brother. Just focus on the man next to you. He'll do the same. We'll be back here before you know. Hooah?"

Holding his head high, Dean replied, "*Hooah,*" and slapped the magazine into his M4.

"Use it," Dean said as he flicked off the memory, stamped down on the accelerator, and gunned it for his final destination. "*Use it.*"

71

The dirt roadway Dean pulled the rental car onto cut through a vast expanse of forest, a thicketed dense of towering Coastal Redwoods and Douglas firs that scraped the night sky riddled with stars that twinkled with a coruscant luminosity thanks to the lack of big city obfuscation.

Dean put the rental into park, his SIG resting on his lap, his heart beating to the point that it felt like it was causing his shirt to ripple. He slid out of the car, the sweet aroma of rain-slicked shrubbery teasing his nostrils and causing them to flare.

Do not think about Jeremy.

Don't think about Layla, Sheila, or anyone else.

Focus on the task in front of you.

Tune the rest out.

Be critical.

Ruthless.

Switch that animal part of your brain on, and do what needs to be done.

Dean rounded the rental and stooped down behind the

bumper. He ejected the magazine from his SIG, checking that there were fifteen rounds in it before he proceeded to do a thumb check of the safety in the chamber. He slapped the magazine back into place, the nighttime chill lapping at the back of his neck as he took out the two spare magazines from his pocket—thirty collective rounds in total—caressed them with his thumb, and then slipped them back into his pocket.

Dean pulled in a breath.

Held it for four seconds.

Then he released it and repeated the process three more times, slowing his heart rate to just above sixty beats per minute as he peeked over the trunk of the rental and did a scan of his surroundings.

Not a soul was in sight—nothing, not even a woodland creature or a bug. All that surrounded Dean was a thick terrain of greenland. Dean took mental snapshots of what he tallied as ten solid acres of rolling terrain ripe with trees so tall and thick that their silhouettes looked like giants in the black of night.

He's here.

The hairs on the back of Dean's neck prickled like they did back when he knew Adams was watching him at the lighthouse.

He's here somewhere.

SIG clutched in both his hands, Dean rounded the rear of the rental, moved off the dirt path, and made his way into the forest. He slowed his breathing, making sure his breath didn't show and that each step he took was calculated and precise for fear of breaking a twig or crunching leaves— noise that would give away his position.

Dean padded his way through the woodlands for 30 yards, moving in a zigzag direction and making it a point not to walk in a straight line. Adams was a Ranger like he was. He knew the moves. Knew the plays. Knew how to flank an enemy and blitz them and shoot them dead in their tracks before the enemy's brain registered that it had even happened, same as Dean.

The treeline above Dean's head caught his eye.

Adams might be camped out in one of these suckers.

He might have a rifle.

He might be looking at me through a scope at this very moment.

Dean moved into cover behind a 60-foot tall redwood, his back hugging the tree as he slowly zipped up his jacket, using his thumb to muffle the sound and waiting for several moments for something to happen that would signal the start of the fight.

One second ticked by.

Two.

Three and then four.

Then, from about 40 yards away inside the abyss of the Redwoods, a brisk whistle cut through the silence—a *human*-produced hoot.

Dean tightened his grip on his SIG, casting a look over his right shoulder and then his left as he slowly disengaged the safety on his weapon.

Is that you, buddy boy?

Are you calling out to me?

Another second went by.

Several more followed.

Adams then whispered, "I see you," his voice echoing off the trees and sending a shudder up Dean's spine.

Thirty yards away.

Dean cut a glance to his right.

Move.

You can't stay here.

Dean dashed out of cover and looked at a cedar tree twelve paces to his right. He kept low, scanning the terrain with his SIG, certain that Adams was going to squeeze off a shot as he went into cover, but Adams didn't make a move.

Nothing happened.

Only the noise of Dean's booted feet crunching the terrain cut through the void.

Son of a bitch.

Dean shook his head and regretted his decision to pivot to another area of concealment.

He wanted you to move.

He's trying to get a fix on your location, and you just gave it to him.

Dean tapped his finger on the trigger guard.

You're getting rusty, old-timer.

"Blackwood," Adams hissed, his voice echoing off the trees like a pinball. Dean was unable to pinpoint the origin that had triggered him to gnash his teeth.

Enough.

Kick this thing off.

The son of a bitch is going to keep playing games until he gets the drop on you.

Make a move, Deano.

Take the first shot.

Dean slowly angled his body toward the cedar, his nose scraping against the bark as he drew a breath and held it.

He counted to three.

Coiled around the trigger.

Then Dean peeked out of cover, took aim with his SIG, and fired off one round that echoed through the redwoods like the blast of a cannon.

72

The shot Dean fired echoed through the woods like the trees were playing hot potato with the reverb. The crack rolled like thunder for several seconds before it dissipated completely. Right after Dean took the shot, he stepped back into cover, hoping that Adams would respond with a shot so Dean could use the muzzle flare to get a fix on his location.

Silence held sway.

An owl hooted off in the distance.

A second after that, a single gunshot discharged from 20 yards off to Dean's right. Dean registered the muzzle flash right as a bullet punched into the tree bark two inches from his face. Splinters of wood sprayed him in the mouth and eyes. Dean squeezed off two shots toward the direction of the muzzle flash before he darted to his right toward a Douglas fir six paces away.

Dean counted three rounds being fired from Adams' location—three shots lobbed off in rapid succession, the staccato drumbeat of the noise triggering a sensory memory to be pulled from the mental files of Dean's mind.

M4A1 Carbine.

A shudder snaked up his spine.

Christ, I'm outgunned here.

Dean arrived at the Douglas fir as he registered two more rounds being shot his way from Adams' location. The bullets clipped the tree a few inches from hitting Dean's torso. Dean squeezed off two more rounds in reply as he hugged the tree with his back.

Eleven rounds left in this mag.

Dean eyed the SIG in his hands.

Use them conservatively.

The echo from the gunshots evaporated into the wind after a few moments, the redwoods becoming silent once again, the greenery unfazed and silent in response to the firefight that was playing out in their midst. The eeriness sat like a rotten pot roast in Dean's stomach. Even if he were to bleed out in the middle of these redwoods, it would make no difference to the nature that surrounded him.

The sun would still rise.

The cedars and Douglas firs would continue to grow.

Life would go on, and the redwoods could consume his remains without skipping a beat.

"Blackwood," Adams shouted. "You gotta come out sometime, brother."

He's moving closer, Dean thought as he heard Adams' voice travel. *He's about 20 yards away on my left.*

He's moving in for the kill.

Dean waited for any kind of noise to flag down Adams' exact location. Several moments into waiting, he heard something brush against the shrubbery 15 yards away on his left. The noise stimulated his ears and fine-tuned his senses to the point that he felt like he was using sonar detection to get the drop on his opponent.

Dean planted his feet, turned around, and peeked out of cover, pointing the business end of his weapon toward the noise he heard just moments before. He fired off three rounds toward a silhouette staffing across the terrain, the shadow ducking down after Dean fired his first shot before doubling back in the direction it had come from.

He's right there!

Move! Move! Move!

Dean stepped out of cover, squeezed off another shot toward the retreating shadow, and closed in toward it, the specter scurrying away as Dean proceeded to empty his magazine. After Dean fired his fifth shot, he heard a sickly, flesh-on-flesh wallop emanating from the shadow's location. The shadow grunted. Dean knew, based on prior experience, that the shot had managed to hit his target.

Dean ditched his dry magazine and prepared to load up another.

As he slapped the magazine in, a burst of gunfire belched from the shadow's location.

The moment Dean saw the muzzle flash, he felt his body spin like a top, a searing pain radiating across his left shoulder as he tumbled toward the ground, followed by a warm sensation that sluiced his torso.

You're hit, Deano.

The son of bitch just shot you.

73

Lying on his side, Dean rolled toward his left toward a grouping of trees several feet away, moving away from a series of rounds that stitched the earth around him. The crack of the shots Adams was taking were just half inches away from turning Dean into Swiss cheese. Dean managed to roll into cover behind a Douglas fir. Adams took several more shots that splintered apart the trunk of the tree as Dean rested his back against it and then slowly rose to his feet.

The pain in Dean's left shoulder caused him to wince. He stuck his hand under his jacket and gingerly touched the area where he had been shot. His fingertips grazed the wound, and he deduced that it was nothing more than a flesh wound.

Stitches and some peroxide will fix that up quick.

A half-inch closer, your shoulder would've become useless.

Dean brought out his hand and examined it. His palm was coated with blood that appeared like black ooze, thanks to the lack of overhead light. He gritted his teeth through the pain, the rapid beat of his heart coupled with the adrenaline pulsating through his body and taking the edge off the pricking in his shoulder.

Dean thumb-checked his rounds in his SIG—fifteen in total. Dean patted the last and final spare magazine in his jacket pocket as he waited for Adams to make his next move.

"You got me," Adams shouted, his voice weaker now and sounding somewhat amused that he had been hit.

"Yeah, I figured." Dean puttered his lips. "You ready to pack it in now?"

"Negative, soldier. I could do this all day."

"Now you're stealing lines from Captain America, Tyler?" Dean rolled his eyes. "Based on your taste for top-tier cinema, I'm disappointed that you're quoting quips from shit my kid watches."

A flurry of bullets chewed up the Douglas fir Dean was posted up behind. Dean dropped into a seated position as the bark above his head splintered and rained down on him like confetti. After a moment, the shooting ceased, and once the reverb of the shots dissipated, Adams said, "I learned *that one* from the Rangers, brother."

Dean poked his head out, directed his SIG toward the origin of the muzzle flashes, and fired off two rounds. He ducked back into cover as Tyler opened fire. Six rounds stitched into the Douglas fir before Dean heard a soft metal *click* followed by a cease fire.

He's empty.

Go!

Dean darted out of cover and opened fire on Adams' location, side-stepping to his left toward another grouping of trees. He fired six rounds, the fifth one striking something in the distance, the sound like a ball-ping hammer being struck against a piece of sheet metal.

Tyler grunted.

Then Dean heard two gunshots pop off followed by a pair of muzzle flashes that haloed in the darkness as he arrived into cover.

He's using a sidearm now.

He ditched his rifle.

Three bullets drilled into the wood around Dean, the cedar tree throbbing like it had its own heartbeat as the rounds slapped into it. After the reverb of the shots died off, Dean heard footsteps patter away from Adams' position, followed by the crunching of leaves and the rustling of tree limbs.

Dean did a thumb-check of his rounds—seven were left.

Tyler's retreating.

I think I got him.

Several moments went by as Dean remained concealed behind the cedar. The seconds that ticked by felt more like minutes, and once an eerie silence had settled through the woodlands, Dean peeked out of cover.

No shots were taken.

The silhouette had vanished.

Pain throbbed in Dean's shoulder, the muscles tightening and registering a sensation like they had been lit on fire.

Don't think about it.

Tyler's on the run.

He's wounded.

Close in for the kill.

Dean stepped out of cover, got into a crouch, and moved in a zigzag pattern toward the shooting position Tyler had vacated. His head rotated on a swivel as he arrived at Tyler's prior position. Dean's eyes widened as he laid eyes on a discarded M4A1 carbine on the ground a few feet from the trunk of the Douglas fir.

Dean grabbed the rifle and pressed his back against the tree, checking over both shoulders before he stuffed his SIG in his waistband and proceeded to examine the M4A1.

Dean saw that blood was splattered along the weapon like a Pollock painting. He ejected the magazine, examined it, and discovered that twelve rounds remained. Dean was set on trading up his firearm game until he saw the hole that had been bored into the bolt catch.

Dean shook his head.

The thing is shot.

Out of commision.

He dropped the rifle and whipped out his SIG.

Back to basics.

Dean planted his feet.

Drew a shaky breath.

Then he stepped slowly out of cover, kept low, and descended farther into the woodlands to close in on his prey.

74

Dean, his SIG raised, stalked through the forest with slow, fluid strides, appraising every shadow, piece of shrubbery, and tree for signs of a threat. He threw a glance toward the ground. The hairs on the back of his neck prickled as he made out a series of crimson droplets snaking through the terrain.

He's losing blood fast.

I must've hit him where it counted.

Dean followed the blood trail for 10 yards until it came to a stop. His nostrils flared and his eyelids tapered as he set his sights on the treeline above his head and wondered if Adams had scaled one of the trees to get to an elevated position.

I would have heard the ruckus.

No, he's hiding out somewhere.

If the blood trail vanished, that means he wrapped the wound.

Dean took cover behind a grouping of cedars, adjusting his grip on his SIG as his back hugged the tree.

He waited for several moments.

Then he heard the crack of two gunshots that drilled their way into his cover on his right.

Dean fired blindly over his shoulder as he dived and rolled across the ground. He emptied his mag as he got to his feet, ditched it, darted toward another series of trees, and loaded the last magazine he had into his SIG.

The gunfire ceased.

Cordite lingered in the air.

The pain in Dean's shoulder pulsated with a nightclub-worthy beat.

"We're going in circles," Adams shouted out. "Aren't we?"

Dean shook his head.

Don't reply.

Don't flag down your location.

"Tell you what," Adams groaned, the pain in his voice palpable and thick enough that Dean felt like he could slice through it with a knife. "Let's make this interesting."

Dean heard a metal *ping* resonate in the distance.

Then he heard Adams grunt.

He made out something hard striking the ground followed by a sound on par with a stone rolling across the earth.

Shit.

Dean winced.

You know what that is.

Something solid thwacked the base of the cedar near Dean's feet. He shot a look toward the ground, and his heart shot up into his throat as he ogled the olive-hued frag grenade two feet away.

Dean turned and prepared to dive.

The grenade went off.

A flash of white light blanketed Dean's vision as the concussion from the grenade's blast took him off his feet.

75

Dean blinked his eyes as he rolled onto his back. As his vision returned and a high-pitched ringing registered in his ears, he patted himself down from head-to-toe and then breathed a sigh of relief when he realized the tree had absorbed most of the grenade's fragments when it went off.

Dean got to his feet, raising his SIG in a bid to lay down fire, but when he saw that his hand was empty, terror struck him like a freight train. He realized that his weapon had gotten knocked out of his grip as a result of the blast.

Shit.

Oh, man.

This is no good, Blackwood.

Dean patted the ground for his weapon like a blind man looking for his cane, the darkness around him making it almost impossible for him to pinpoint his weapon. He scurried across the earth like a toddler, swiping his hands in long arcs as he searched for his SIG.

Where is it?

Where the hell did it go?

You better un-fuck this quick, you dumb son of s—

The gut-churning sound of a gun hammer being cocked triggered Dean to freeze.

He looked up.

Then he saw Adams materializing through the darkness from several feet away, a Glock 19 in his hand and the business end trained at Dean's head.

76

Dean tallied that it was the third time his life flashed before his eyes. Memories of his son, Layla, his ex-wife, his late brother, Sheila, his father, his mother, and every person he had crossed paths with in his life flickered in his mind. He held his hands high in the air, tracking Adams as he inched closer, terminated his stride, and then pressed the muzzle of the Glock 19 flush against Dean's head.

This is it.

Despite your best intentions, this is the end of the line.

The soft pattering of something wet hitting the earth tickled Dean's ears. He glanced up at Adams and saw a dime-sized hole in his left shoulder. Adams was wincing and turning pale as he flexed his grip on the Glock.

Dean took in Adam's appearance. It had been a long time since the two of them were face to face. The last time Dean saw Adams was when he was lying up in a hospital bed jacked into a series of machines. Adams was still sinewy, his ripped torso jutting through his flannel, the man not physically degraded in his body, but his face was another story altogether. He was pale, a vacant look in his eyes, his expression placid like he was wearing a mask of his own face.

"Looks like we both hit each other in the shoulder," Adams said. "What are the odds of that?"

"Christ, Tyler," Dean hissed softly, the blood loss from his own shoulder wound starting to get the better of him. "What the hell happened to you?"

"*You* did this to me, brother." Adams held his head high. "I am what you made me."

The lines in Dean's face went taut as he channeled all his hate, anger, and frustration onto the man who was moments away from taking his life. "Just do it," Dean said. "Just pull the friggin' trigger, and get it over with."

Adams pressed the gun harder into Dean's head. Dean's heart was hammering against his chest as he waited for the shot to go off.

One second ticked by.

Two.

Then Adams removed the gun, took a step back, and shook his head. "Too easy," he said. "I want to watch you die like those people I killed. I want to see you *bleed*."

Dean huffed.

What the hell is he doing?

What is he waiting for?

What's this sick prick planning on doing next?

Adams held up the Glock and shook it like he was ringing a dinner bell, flashing a crooked grin as he chucked the weapon aside and took a step back. Adams then reached into his waistband, unsheathed an M3 trench knife and examined it. The blade glinted under the moonlight before Adams tossed the weapon at Dean's feet.

Dean wasted no time.

He picked up the weapon.

Then he shot to his feet and put 6 feet of distance between him and Adams as his opponent pulled out an identical M3 trench knife from the leather sheath hugging his hip.

"Come on, Blackwood," Adams said as he twirled the handle of the knife, spun it twice, and then held it in a reverse grip. "Remember that flick *The Hunted*? Benicio del Toro. Tommy Lee Jones. I watched it like a hundred times in the hospital. They duke it out with knives." His eyes shimmered. "I wanna go out *that* way."

Dean clasped the handle of the trench knife in his left hand, splaying his feet as memories of his old drill sergeant coming at him with a rubber blade played back in his mind. "Let's not do this," he said. "We're both wounded, man. Just put it down. Let's walk out of here." His eyes widened pleadingly. "There's still time to back off of this."

Adams shook his head. "Kill or be killed, brother. The choice is yours."

It's happening.

He gave you a fighting shot.

This is the end of the line.

This is as far as he goes. Or it's as far as you *go.*

Dean nodded.

Adams smirked.

The two men circled one another, arms splayed as they side-stepped in unison like the whole event was a dance. *Ironically*, Dean thought, *Sergeant Mills told me at one point that's what a knife fight was.*

Adams terminated his stride.

Dean did the same.

The two men then charged at one another as Adams emitted a primal growl.

77

The first attempt came from Adams. He took a swipe with his blade at Dean's forehead. Dean ducked under the attempted swipe and slid across the ground as he shot out his hand, sliced across Adam's left calf muscle, and got to his feet.

Adams grumbled as he spun around and faced Dean, switching the blade to his other hand as he punched at his leg like a teenager putting on a display of histrionics.

"Not bad," Adams said as he glanced at the blood flowing freely from the wound in his leg. "Not bad at all."

Dean turned over the weapon in his hand and then held it in a reverse grip. He shook his head, looking at Tyler with a defeated expression, sweat beading his brow. Each breath he drew made him feel like he was slurping down acid.

"Don't make me kill you, Tyler," Dean uttered through hissed breath. "Please, don't make me do this."

Adams gnashed his teeth.

He charged.

Then he took an upward swipe at Dean who stepped back and to his left. Adams took three more swipes at Dean, who ducked away from each attempt by dipping and weaving like a boxer. When Adams attempted to jab Dean in his belly with the knife, Dean cleared out of the way, secured a grip on Adams's wrist, reeled him in like a fish, and then shot his elbow into Adams' nose.

The bones in Adams' nose fractured. His head wrenched back as he cocked back his left hand and prepared to strike a blow against Dean's face. But Dean, slicing upward on Adams' hand and clutching his knife, forced Adams to bail on his attempt.

A guttural growl shot out of Adams as he shot his own right leg and caught Dean in the back of his left knee.

Dean dropped to the ground on one knee.

Adams struck a blow with his right hand against Dean's temple.

Dean lost his grip on the knife, and Adams snatched it away, raised it above his head, and attempted to drive it right into the crown of Dean's skull.

Dean fell to his back as Adams brought the knife down, lunged toward him, and prepared to throw his whole body on top of him. Dean raised his boot, planted a heel kick into Adams's sternum and pushed, kicking his opponent onto his back. Dean scuffled away, put some distance between himself and Adams, and then got to his feet.

Dean scanned the earth beneath his feet.

Where is it?

Where the hell is the knife?

A blood-slicked Adams, the color draining from his face with each second that passed and giving him the appearance of a spector, spit on the ground. He switched the blade from his left hand to his right hand, repeating the process several times over like the weapon was hot to the touch.

"You're doing better than that time in that diner

restroom," Adams said, panting his words like he had just ran a marathon. "Much better."

Find a weapon.

Dean's eyes frantically skimmed the terrain around him.

Find something.

Anything!

Adams inched closer. "Maybe after I kill you," he said, "I'll kill this *wildcat* I've got with me and then go after your sister. Maybe that girlfriend of yours. Maybe your ex-wife. Your *kid*."

Whatever pain Dean was experiencing evaporated into the wind. Hearing Adams' taunts felt like his body had been charged with a million little electrons. His lips pulled back to reveal his gritted set of teeth as his eyes probed the ground for a weapon.

Find a weapon.

Find some thing.

If you don't, you'll—

Dean's eyes widened as he skimmed the area. Several feet behind Adams, scattered among the brush, was Dean's SIG, a sliver of moonlight gleaming off the handle like the weapon was winking.

Get it.

Get your hands on it.

Take this guy down.

"Come on, Tyler," Dean grumbled, every inch of his flesh and muscle and bone squealing like an overheated engine. "Do it for *Kelly*."

The words Dean spoke triggered every part of Adams to tense. The man narrowed his eyes, holding out the knife as he planted his feet, puffed his chest, and ran toward Dean.

Dean pushed off the ground like a track runner, sprinting in a straight line straight for Adams. He could see the whites of Adams' eyes, manic and shimmering with an icy sheen like the blade he held in his hand.

Tyler raised the knife.

Dean jinked to his left and went into a dive.

Tyler brought the knife down as Dean brushed past him, slicing Dean's cheek as Dean dove toward the ground, landed on his chest, and slid across the earth like a baseball player diving toward home base.

Tyler spun around and charged.

Dean shot out his hand as he slid up to the SIG, slapped his palm on it, secured a grip, and turned onto his back.

Tyler brought his knife down in a downward arc.

Dean squeezed off a single shot.

The crack of the shot echoed through the redwoods for close to half a mile.

The shot slapped Adams square in his chest and dropped him to his knees. Adams looked down at the gaping hole in his sternum, the knife falling from his hand as he glanced up at Dean with a relieved expression.

"Good," Tyler said as he batted his eyelids, an air of relief in his tone as blood trickled out the corner of his mouth. "*Good*..."

Dean, clutching his SIG in both hands, got to his feet. He drew down on Adams as he approached him, kicking the knife away as Adams fell onto his back and his eyes rolled into the back of his skull.

"*Easy*," Dean said as he holstered his weapon and applied pressure to Adams's wound. "You're done. Stay down."

"Kelly," Adams whimpered. "I want to see her."

"I don't think that's happening, brother." Dean patted Adams down with his free hand. "You got a phone? Come on, man. You're Mr. Tech Wizard, so I know you've got something on you. I need to call an ambulance."

"I'm dying."

"We can get someone out here. We'll airlift you. I've seen worse hits before, believe me."

"They won't get here in time, Blackwood." Adams closed his eyes. "They won't get here fast enough—and I don't want them to."

"I'm not saving your life because you *deserve* it, Tyler. I need you to *talk*. People need to hear you confess."

Adams slapped his hand on top of the one Dean had pressed against his chest, squeezing it tightly as his eyelids snapped open. "Let it go, brother. I'm tapped out. This was how I wanted things to go." He wheezed. "I got exactly what I wanted."

The pounding of Adams' heart pumped blood in thick waves out of his chest. The crimson glazed Dean's hand to the point that it looked like he was wearing a ruby-colored glove.

Dean sighed, shaking his head as he gripped onto the reality that nothing could save Adams, even if he was walking him into a hospital that housed the best trauma doctors in the world at that very moment. "Tyler," he said, "tell me where she is."

Adams winced. "Who?"

"The woman you kidnapped. The one you took with you. Where is she?" Dean shook Adams's shoulders. "Come on, man. Tell me!"

"You can't save her. The timer is already set to go off."

"*Timer?*" Dean flashed the whites of his eyes. "Tyler, what did you do?"

"*Boom,*" Tyler said weakly. "A big, *big* boom," he smirked. "That wildcat is about to get blown to the heavens."

"Where is it? Where is she?" Dean frisked Adams' entire

body. "Do you have a device on you? Are you triggering it somehow?"

"There's no time."

"Cut the shit! Where is she? Damn it, Tyler, you got one last chance to do something right before you fade away here. Don't let this woman die. Do the right thing, man. What if it was Kelly? What if someone was holding her hostage? *Huh*? What would you do?"

The question prompted Adams to bow his lips down into a frown. He stared at Dean, life retreating from him with each beat of his heart. "Let Kelly go," he said. "Please. Take her away from all of this. *Free* her."

"Then tell me where the hostage is," Dean said. "Tell me now. You've only got a few seconds left, Tyler, so talk!"

Adams parted his lips, shallow breaths coated with a wheeze sputtering out of his lungs. "Close by," he said. "A pickup. She's in the back. She's—" His body trembled. "She's in there...timer is...going off. *Run*."

Adams' body slackened.

His final breath trickled out of him.

His eyelids slowly closed like a curtain lowering on the final act of a stage play.

Dean, his hand still held firmly against Adams' chest, felt whatever was left of the killer, whatever fragments of a soul that was once inside of him, evaporate into the night sky. Dean blinked his eyes as he watched Adams' body go limp, a sense of relief overcoming him that was quickly overshadowed moments later with a palpable dread.

"She's still out there," Dean whispered. "Somewhere."

Dean patted down Adams from head to toe, rifling through his pockets until he located a burner phone in the front of Adams' jeans. Dean opened the flip phone and saw that it was still working, pocketing the device as he got to his feet, spun around in a circle, and shot a glance toward the direction he came from.

"Run," Dean said as he launched into a sprint. "*Find her.*"

79

Dean scampered through the redwoods like his feet were on fire, running toward the dirt road where he had parked before his final showdown with the late Tyler Adams.

There's only one road that comes in this way.

Tyler probably parked close by.

Just keep running, Dean.

Run until you find her!

"Is anyone out there?" Dean hollered. "If you can hear my voice, call out to me!"

Dean arrived at his rental car, slapping the hood as he caught his breath, and turned around in a slow circle. He feverishly scanned his surroundings, pulled out the phone he swiped from Adams, and spotted a NO SERVICE ticker at the top of the display.

"911," Dean whispered. "That'll still work." He punched in the digits, holding the phone to his ear as he continued his run through the woods, his eyes darting around in the hopes that he'd locate Adams' truck sooner or later.

"911 Emergency," the operator greeted.

Dean breathed a sigh of relief. "This is Special Agent Dean Blackwood with the Federal Bureau of Investigation. I am currently in the Redwood National Park, Jedediah Smith Park. I need you to contact all local police and send them to my area immediately. I was just involved in a shooting. The suspect is down, but I have reason to believe that a hostage is nearby, and the suspect indicated that an explosive device is with her."

"Sir—"

"Just forward this through the proper channels," Dean said as he dashed toward a fork in the road. "Get someone out here quickly. Contact the FBI, and get in touch with Special Agent In Charge Kent Wilson. He's my superior. There's no time to waste. We have to move *fast*."

The operator told Dean to wait on the line. As he arrived at the fork in the road that split from east to west, Dean debated which route to take as he made out a *tick-tick-ticking* noise reverberating inside his skull. He could practically feel the bomb close by, the lizard part of his brain registering that the threat was close.

"Where are you?" Dean whispered. "Come on..."

The operator came back over the line, "Sir."

"I'm here."

"Emergency services are on their way as we speak. I'll need you to stay on with me until they get there."

Dean nodded. "I will. And I need you to do whatever it is you do to patch me through to the closest available bomb squad unit. If this bomb threat is real, I might need help dismantling it."

"Have you located the hostage?" the operator said. "Is there any sign of her?"

Time felt like it had sped up to the point that minutes felt like mere seconds to Dean. He ran through the woods, searching high and low for signs of the vehicle Adams had mentioned, the darkness around him narrowing his field of vision. Dean's adrenaline spiked, the wind lapping at his body and making his flesh feel like it was composed of ice as he jogged through the redwoods.

"No sign of her yet," Dean said. "I can't see shit."

"Emergency services are en route," the operator told him. "ETA, forty-six minutes."

Dean gnashed his teeth.

Might as well make it a cool hour.

God damn it.

We're running out of time!

Dean dashed through the woods for a few more minutes, his body tensed, his muscles seared from the exertion, his brain screaming at him to take a break, but he knew that wasn't an option. He continued his search down the dirt road that snaked through the woods. He spun in a circle, feeling that all hope was lost, when the moonlight overhead caught something metallic in the brush about 100 yards away.

Dean broke out into a sprint and made a beeline for the shimmering object. Sweat glazed every part of his flesh, and he felt like he was at a poker table, ready to throw in his last chip.

"Please," Dean whispered. "Please be there!"

Dean was 50 yards away from the object.

Twenty.

Once he burst through the clearing, his smile brimmed from one ear to the other as he laid eyes on a seafoam green Ford F-350 parked in the middle of the woods.

Bingo.

80

Dean slunk toward the pickup with cautious steps, circling it like the thing would detonate if he got any closer, certain that a proximity trigger was something Adams had stored away in his little treasure trove of tricks.

"Slow and easy, Blackwood," Dean whispered. "Slow and easy." He peered into the cab, his eyes widening as he saw a woman's purse resting on the passenger's seat.

"Sir," the 9-1-1 operator said. "Are you still on the line?"

Dean circled the hood of the truck. "I located the vehicle," he said. "Green Ford F-350." He arrived at the rear of the pickup and dished the operator the numbers for the license plate. "Run those numbers. Something tells me it might have been reported missing."

"Is there anyone there? Can you see anybody?"

"No, nothing yet. I can't tell if—"

Something stirred inside of the back of the truck.

The wallop triggered Dean to take a step back.

A moment later, the muffled cries knocking inside prompted Dean to rush toward the back.

"I think I found her," Dean said. "Wait one—" He placed the phone on speaker and reached out for the latch.But then he froze, his instincts sending a signal to his brain indicating that there was a high probability that Adams might have rigged the door.

"*Shit*," Dean whispered as he closed his eyes, cleared his throat, and then said, "Can anyone hear me?"

"Yes," Dean heard a woman say faintly. "Please, get me out of here!"

Dean held up his hands. "I'm FBI, ma'am. Just try to stay calm. Everything is going to be okay."

"*Okay*?" the woman said, her tone making it sound like she was uttering a curse. "That guy strapped something to me, for chrissakes!"

The rhythm of Dean's heartbeat intensified.

Be calm.

"I need you to listen to me closely," he said. "I want to get you out of there, but I need to make sure it's safe. Can you see the door in the back? Are you facing it?"

"No," the woman said. "I'm turned away from it. Maybe if I turn around I can—"

"Don't do that." Dean held his hands higher. "Don't *move*. Just stay right where you are."

"My hands and feet are tied; I *can't* move."

Dean slowly pulled air into his lungs. "I'm going to need you to try to turn your head around as slowly as you can. I need you to crane your neck and see if anything has been wired to the door in the back. I need you to look for wires, devices, or anything that looks out of the ordinary, okay? But don't move too much. It's important you understand that."

Seconds went by as Dean made out a light shuffling in the truck, every noise that emitted from inside of it triggering him to flinch.

"I don't see anything," the woman said.

"You're sure?"

"I can't see a *fucking* thing. Please, get me *out* of here!"

Dean stroked the stubble on his chin, wincing at the back of the pickup like he was attempting to crack a safe.

You can't be sure.

You can't roll the dice on opening it just yet.

"Listen to me," Dean said. "Just stay calm."

"I'm trying," the woman whimpered. "I just want to go home."

Dean edged toward the door. "Just try to take a look around if you can. This is important. I need you to tell me what you see. How well can you see in there?"

"Not a lot. I can only see this thing on my chest."

Dean's eyes widened. "What does it look like?"

"Like a bullet-proof vest or something."

Shit.

You know what it is, Deano.

"Can you see a timer on the vest?" he said.

"Yes," the woman replied. "It says," she took a beat, "it says 5:14, and it keeps counting down."

The fingers on Dean's hand trembled.

The clock is ticking.

The bomb squad won't get here in time.

He closed his eyes.

You're going have to do this on your own.

You need to get eyes on it if you're going to do that.

His eyelids snapped open.

You're going to have to open that door.

"Ma'am," Dean said, his tone cool and even, "what's your name?"

"Morgan," the woman replied weakly. "Morgan Freeling."

"Listen to me, Morgan. Everything is going to be okay. I have people on the phone with me right now who are going to help you get out of there. I just need you to be patient, and I need you to do *exactly* as I say. Do you understand?"

"But the timer keeps counting down!"

Dean nodded. "I know. But we're going to turn it off before anything happens. I just need you to give me one second here to relay what's going on, and then we'll get you out of there. Understood?"

"Okay," Morgan said weakly, tremors cutting through her tone. Dean was certain that he could make out the young woman crying. "*Okay.*"

Dean stepped away from the pickup, took the phone off speaker, and held it to his ear. "Did you get all of that?"

"Every word," the operator said. "And I have Captain Eric Beem on the line. He's the head of the San Mateo County Bomb Squad."

"Put him through."

A quick moment went by before a burnished voice greeted Dean with, "This is Captain Beem."

"Captain, this is Special Agent Dean Blackwood with the FBI. I assume that the operator forwarded you everything I've said thus far."

"She did."

"Listen," Dean edged toward the back of the truck. "We've got less than five minutes before this thing goes off. I don't have eyes on it though. There's a woman locked in the back covered cargo bed. She says a vest has been strapped to her, and she's fairly certain the back door is not wired to blow if I try to open it."

"We need a team to confirm that, Agent Blackwood," Beem said. "You know that."

"We have no time for standard procedure here, Captain.

We need to get eyes on this thing fast, and you're going to have to walk me through disarming it."

Beem puttered out a shaky sigh. "Okay, tell the woman inside to take one last look around. Tell her to do it carefully. Instruct her to limit her movement as much as possible. We need to make sure the truck isn't rigged with something in the way of an anti-tampering device or proximity circuit. Do it quickly."

Dean pressed the phone to his chest. "Morgan," he said. "You need to look around one last time to see if there's anything like I told you before. Do it slowly."

A few seconds passed.

Then Morgan said, "There's nothing." Then she informed Dean that the timer was now at 4:20—and counting.

"Beem," Dean said into the phone, "she doesn't see anything. And we're at four minutes and twenty seconds."

"You'll need to open the back dooor then," Beem said. "It's a roll of the dice, but you need to get in there. Do it carefully."

"Copy that."

Dean pocketed the phone as he reached toward the handle. His fingertips grazed the latch, prickling as though it was lined with barbed wire.

Dean breathed.

He thumbed the latch.

Then he slowly peeled open the door and waited for the bomb to go off.

81

The *pop* of the latch being disengaged sent a shudder up Dean's spine. He felt like it was a fifty-fifty shot that the truck would have been blown sky high the second he opened the door, but it didn't.

Nothing happened.

Adams had given him a fighting chance.

Dean flayed open the door, his face lighting up like a Christmas tree when he saw Morgan curled up in a fetal position. But once he laid eyes on the Kevlar vest strapped to Morgan's chest, rigged with a timer and six packs of Semtex explosive, Dean's smile liquified and dribbled down his chin with heavy pearls of sweat slicking off his face.

"Please," Morgan said, "get me out of here."

Dean took out the cell phone, placed it on speaker, and held it up. "Beem, We're good."

"All right, talk to me," Beem said, his voice registering at a higher octave now. "What do you see?"

"Six packs of Semtex." Dean appraised the tri-colored wires—green, black, and red—tethered to the Semtex blocks and looped into the timer on Morgan's vest. He relayed the information to Beem. "I've seen this before. There's a timer on the front of the vest." Dean spotted a cell phone stuffed into the back of the vest. "Looks like it's looped to a remote, a cell phone. Looks like a burner. Flip style. The thing's been heavily modified."

Dean made out papers shuffling on Beem's end. "You'll have to bypass the remote current with the battery. Can you pinpoint the trip wire?"

"There's three wires," Dean said. "And I've got nothing in the way of tools here, Captain. I don't have a way to redirect the current."

The clock on Morgan's chest blipped, and Dean saw that there were now three minutes left on the timer.

"My purse," Morgan said.

Dean furrowed his brow. "What?"

"My purse. I think he took it. I have a manicure kit inside of it."

Something, Dean thought as he headed to the passenger side of the cab and snagged the purse from seat, *is better than nothing.* He dumped the contents on the ground, feverishly sifting through the wallet, tissues, cough drops, and phone charger until he found a compact, faux-leather, zippered case. Dean ripped the kit open and saw the nail file, two fingernail clippers, a precision cuticle nipper, a double-ended cuticle pusher, and a nail cleaner stored neatly in loops.

Good enough.

Dean got back in the rear of the pickup. Tears were streaming down Morgan's face as she told him two minutes and thirty-nine seconds were left on the timer.

"Beem," Dean said into the phone before informing the bomb squad captain of the implements he now had at his disposal.

"What color are the wires?" Beem said.

"Black, red, and green."

"Which one is tethered into the cell phone on the back of the vest?"

"Red."

A moment passed, Dean making out Beem speaking in hushed tones to whoever was beside him.

"Beem," Dean said, his eyes fixed to the timer that now showed one minute and fifty-three seconds, "I'm gonna need something in the way of an answer here, man."

"We're conferring," Beem said. "The problem is that your boy may have this thing outfitted with a collapsible circuit. If you cut the wrong wire, if you cut *any* of the wires, the thing might go off."

Collapsible circuit

Dean squinted.

I've heard of that before.

He gazed at the vest strapped to Morgan.

God, I've seen this exact *rig before!*

"Blackwood," Beem said. "You still with us?"

Morgan's lips trembled, her gaze fastened to the count-down timer on her vest. "Sir," she said, "it says there's less than a minute left."

Dean chewed on his lip.

Think, man!

Where have you seen this vest before?

It wasn't in real life, so where was it?

He grimaced.

Tyler was taking hints from movies all the way up until he died.

He left clues only I could solve.

Dean squinted at the device on Morgan's chest.

You've seen *this vest before.*

It's from another movie!

God damn it, which one is it?

"Blackwood," Beem grumbled. "We're running out of time."

"Think, damn you," Dean whispered. "What scenario is this from? What is Tyler playing tribute to?"

"Thirty seconds," Morgan said as she closed her eyes, curling up further into a ball and hugging herself tight. "Oh *God...*"

A light flicked on in Dean's brain. "*Wildcat*," he whispered. "Adams called her that twice."

A scene from the movie *Speed* played back in Dean's brain. He saw Sandra Bullock's character—dubbed Wildcat by the film's villain—wandering through a subway station, an explosive device strapped to her body by the villain that Keanu Reeves was able to dismantle by swiftly—and brazenly—pulling out all the wires tethered to the explosive at once. It was a tactic straight out of fiction on the writer's part, a cheap, age-old movie device that would never have worked in the real world. But Dean knew that in *Tyler Adams'* world, one composed of one cinema trope after another, the notion of pulling a "Keanu" and ripping out all the wires on Morgan's vest was something he felt was not far removed from Tyler's way of thinking.

There's no time left.

Dean saw that the device was fifteen seconds from detonating.

Piss or get off the pot, brother.

Dean shot his hand out toward the wires, looking at Morgan as he said, "Do you trust me?" and received a trembling nod from her in reply.

"Blackwood!" Beem shouted over the line. "Talk to me."

Dean spotted eight seconds left on the timer.

He closed his eyes.

He grabbed a fistful of wires on Morgan's vest.

Then he whispered to himself, "Here goes nothing," and ripped the wires clean out of the remote on the back of the vest.

82

White light blanketed Dean's vision as soon as he pulled the wires, his entire body slackening as the bright light in his vision narrowed. He saw himself walking down a tunnel, his late brother Tommy—much older than he was when he died—waving at him from the other side.

"Am I dead, T?" Dean said. "Is this," he looked around the tunnel, "is this what I think it is?"

Tommy shook his head. "No way," he said. "Your time isn't up yet, big man."

Dean squinted through the light, seeing that his fraternal twin brother was close to the same age that he was. Even though Tommy possessed more of their father's burly, Midwestern physique, he had the same hazel eyes that Dean did—identical.

"Where are we?" Dean said. "What is this?"

"You'll get here eventually, brother," Tommy said, "but not yet. You've got miles to go before that happens." He huffed. "And you've got *no* idea the kind of things that are in store for you before we meet up again."

Dean raced toward Tommy, the ground beneath him feeling like it was made of slickened rubber, his feet unable to gain traction as he reached a hand out toward his brother. "*T*," he said. "Wait!"

Tommy shook his head. "Not yet, sport. Go *home*. Live your life." He wagged a finger. "And say hi to my little nephew for me."

Sirens blared in Dean's ears as he felt himself thrust backward out of the tunnel, his heart shooting into his throat as he felt one hand after another pawing at his back.

"Blackwood," someone shouted. "*Wake up!*"

Dean's eyelids fluttered open, his vision a hazy blur of shapes and colors. He blinked several times before his sight fully corrected and he found himself staring at the face of none other than Kent Wilson who was peering down at him with an expression composed of equal parts concern and relief.

"Kid," Wilson said, "look at me."

Dean glanced to his left and made out the inside of an ambulance. His fingertips grazed the railing of the gurney he was lying on, his sights drifting until they became fastened to the tube jacked into his arm that was tethered to an IV drip above his head. He brought a hand to his ear, gingerly stroking the thick gauze that had been placed over the laceration Adams had made with his trench knife.

"What happened?" Dean said as he noted the fleet of police cruisers, sedans, and emergency vehicles parked at canted angles outside the ambulance. Rays from the early morning sun streaked the hoods of the vehicles with a warm, tangerine luminescence.

Wilson sighed. "You passed out. You've been out of it for about an hour and half. I just got here."

Dean parted his chapped lips. "Did the bomb..." He clutched a hand to his chest. "Did the thing...?"

"No," his boss said. "It didn't go off. It looks like that little stunt you pulled ended up playing into your favor." He shook his head. "The bomb squad captain you talked to is still looking at that vest you dismantled. He can't believe that ripping all the wires out like that actually worked."

God almighty.

What were the chances?

"Morgan," Dean said weakly. "Where is she?"

Wilson jutted his chin toward the scene outside. "She's at the hospital. She's getting checked out right now. She's a little shaken up, but she's going to be all right." He patted Dean's arm. "*You*, however, are apparently a tad malnourished and dehydrated, according to the EMTs. The second you pulled that wire, you dropped to the ground, according to Morgan. When's the last time you drank something, Deano?"

"Get me a Gatorade," Dean said. "That'll fix me right up. Nothing blue or red though. I can't stand the taste."

Wilson shook his head.

"Adams," Dean said. "Did you find his body?"

The lines in Wilson's face slackened. "Yeah, we found him. We bagged him up. A press conference is taking place in San Francisco in a few. Everyone over there is elated that we shut this thing down, to say the least. People are practically dancing in the streets."

"Sheila," Dean said. "My family. Have they—?"

Wilson nodded. "They know what's going on. They're all with Sheila as we speak. I got on the horn with your father on my way up here. Everyone knows you're okay. As for your sister, she woke up about two hours ago. Doctors say she's going to be okay. She's a little worse for the wear, but..." He gripped Dean's hand. "She's *alive*, Deano. She's going to make it."

Tears welled in Dean's eyes.

It's over.

It's finished.

Aside from a mountain of paperwork and debriefs, he sighed, *it's done.*

"We gotta get you checked out by a doctor," Wilson said. "After that, the next few weeks are going to be spent talking to everyone back in Washington, including the guys over at Behavioral Science. After everything that happened with Adams, they'll have to rewrite a lot of their profiling playbook from scratch."

"It's all about the bottom line with those fucks."

"*Always.*"

"Whatever," Dean groaned. "Let them pick my brain, but I want to see my family first."

"Of course." Wilson leaned in close. "You got a guardian angel or something looking after you, Deano. I can't count how many times you've stared death in the face and told it to go screw itself."

"More times than I care to count, Willy." Dean thought about the vision he had earlier of his brother Tommy. "And I think you're right. Someone *is* looking after me." He shot off a grin. "I think he has been here this entire time."

"Let's get you home, kid." Wilson patted Dean's arm. "I think we've had enough fun for one day."

Moments later, the EMTs entered the ambulance, did an appraisal of Dean, and informed him that they were en route to the local hospital. Dean asked Wilson to relay where he was going to his family before he fielded a few questions from the local police and Captain Beem. Wilson eventually shooed them all away and told them there'd be plenty of time to pass Dean around for a few interviews when he was back on his feet.

"I'll follow you to the hospital," Wilson said as he clapped his hands on the swinging doors to the ambulance. "It's about an hour drive. Try to get some sleep in the meantime."

Dean nodded as Wilson closed the doors to the ambulance. The vehicle then lurched forward as the EMT behind the wheel triggered the sirens.

Dean sighed as he lifted his head and fixed his sights out the back window, watching as golden rays of morning sunlight filtered through and cast a warm glow across his face before he closed his eyes and fell into a slumber.

83

"*Speed*," Sheila said incredulously, propping herself up in her hospital bed on her elbows, a sizable amount of color in her face now compared to the last time Dean saw her. "You had a hunch that Adams was paying tribute to another movie and just—" she threw up her hands—"pulled the wires on the explosive?"

Dean wrinkled his brow. The series of cuts and scrapes seared on his face after two days of healing. "Adams referred to the woman he took as hostage as a wildcat," Dean said. "That was from the movie. He also crafted the device he strapped to her after the same one Dennis Hopper's character made. I guess it was just a matter of me putting two and two together to figure out what cues Adams was taking."

His sister sighed. "It was a shoddy move on Adams' part. Why would he construct the vest like that? It was flawed. He made it way too easy for you to dismantle. I mean, sure, you still had to figure out that he was referencing that movie, but still."

"Part of me thinks that maybe Adams couldn't go

through with it," Dean said. "Or maybe his penchant for cinematic references got the better of him. I don't know."

"He was bound to get caught sooner or later," Sheila shrugged. "It was just a matter of time. Regardless, he still had one last chance to kill you *and* that woman, but he didn't. I can't help but wonder what drove him to give you a fighting chance during the knife fight and what happened with the bomb afterward."

"We can only have the luxury of speculation on that one," Dean said. "If Tyler were still alive, we could pick his brain until eternity to come up with an answer. Maybe it *was* deliberate on his end. Maybe it was oversight. We'll never know. Luckily, I'm old enough now to accept that lack of closure is one of the many tenets that life has to offer."

"You got lucky," Sheila said. "I think that's the takeaway from all of this." She gestured to the sling holding up her arm. "We both are. I mean, Adams had several opportunities to kill you, to kill me, but didn't. Maybe it was hubris or something, but I guess your colleagues at Behavioral Science will have to figure that one out."

"I'm supposed to meet with them a few days from now," Dean said. "They're flying out to LA to pick my brain. I'm sure they'll draft up a final report that states why Adams did what he did, including what drove him to give me those handful of chances to live."

"Maybe you'll find comfort in that."

"No, She." Dean shook his head. "There's no walking away from this feeling 100 percent. People are still dead, and that's unacceptable."

"Well, what about Kelly Mayer?" Sheila said. "What happened to her?"

"Let's just say the FBI dipped into one of its 'expense accounts' and paid her off handsomely for her efforts."

"They can do that?"

"It's the federal government," Dean said. "They tend to do whatever the hell they want." He smirked. "It's funny, even after all that went down, after everything we put Kelly through, she's staying in her same job and in her same town. Kelly told Wilson she was just happy that there was an end to Tyler's story, as macabre an ending as it may have been."

"She's a strong woman. God only knows the kind of courage she had to display to get through all of this."

"So are you, She. You went through the ringer on this one."

"We both did." Dean's sister motioned to the cuts on his face. "We went through the ringer and then some. But it's over now. We're still in one piece, for the most part. I guess there's a victory in that."

"What did Dad have to say when he came here?" Dean said. "I'm curious what words of wisdom the old man had to offer."

"He said, 'Stop getting into arm-wrestling matches with psychos, Sheila. The last thing I need is to bury you before the lot of you bury me.'"

"Having a decent bedside manner was never one of Pop's staples."

"It's his way of coping. You know that."

"I guess you're right." Dean picked at the callous on his palms. The guilt from what happened made him feel like a tar-coated brick was lodged in his chest. "I don't like how this all went down. I have a hard time stomaching that all of Tyler Adamss victims will become nothing more than footnotes after all of this. It's not right, and that's the way it always tends to be."

Sheila adjusted her weight on the bed. "You should talk to

Layla.When she called me earlier, she said she was planning to pen an article dedicated solely to the victims. She said she wants to jockey the narrative pertaining to their lives out there in front of Tyler's story. Layla said she's set on eclipsing the media talking about Tyler's end of the ordeal 24/7."

Dean's lips bowed up into a proud beam. "If anyone deserves a medal of merit in this world, it's that woman."

"Start by buying her some flowers or something."

"I was planning on it."

"Good," Sheila said. "Because after everything that happened, it should serve as a reminder that life is short, and time is finite. Don't shortchange what's right in front of you."

Dean nodded. "You're right. Hell, we almost bought the farm on a handful of occasions the past couple of weeks. Like you said, we got lucky. I guess sometimes you can't quantify how these things happen. Sometimes a bullet misses hitting you. Sometimes a guy can get shot ten times but still manage to survive. I don't see that as fate or an odds thing." Dean's gaze drifted as images of Tommy flooded his mind. "Hell, maybe there's something to be said about the whole guardian angel thing."

Sheila laughed. "Since when did you become religious, Father Blackwood?"

"I wouldn't go that far. I'm still trying to scrub off that Catholic guilt still clinging to me thanks to all those times Dad dragged us to Mass."

"Remember that one time during communion when Tommy broke wind when he took the body of Christ?"

Laughter stitched Dean's rib cage. "*Oh yeah*," he said. "I remember it well."

Dean put his focus on the window outside of Sheila's

room, fixated on the horizon off in the distance, contemplating what was waiting for him down the road.

"What's next?" Dean said as he motioned to his sister. "For you, I mean."

Sheila rested her hands across her belly. "I'm not sure. After everything that went down with SFPD, I'm itching to pivot to something else."

"Something *not* law enforcement related?"

"No, just," Sheila shrugged, "something simpler. I kind of feel like I should take a step back and really think if this is the career I want—being in charge of a whole division, I mean."

"What would you do?" Dean said. "I mean, if you had your choice."

His sister smirked. "Maybe I'll move to Oregon. The idea of shifting down into second and watching over a small town sounds comforting."

"It would suit you."

"I think so too," Sheila said. "And what about you? What about the Bureau?"

"Dunno." Dean flexed his brow. "I still have time left on this bullshit contract, and now that I took down Adams, they're more jazzed than they were before at my"—he thought of a way to phrase it—"*knack* for taking down the bad guys. All I can say is the next time you pick up the phone and tell me you've got a serial killer in your midst, I'm gonna turn down the offer to come your way. Based on what you're telling me about the life choices *you* plan on making, you should do the same."

"Oh, I will." Sheila's expression screwed into a grimace. "Believe you me."

Nothing was said for several moments. Dean relished the first bit of silence in what felt like months. He closed his eyes, the brisk A/C unit above his head licking at his skin.

Time to find a beach somewhere.

Time to heal, time to do anything but think.

"Sheila," Dean said as he opened his eyes. "I know I said it before, but I have to say it again." He perched forward in his seat. "I'm sorry for what happened to you. For all of it. I don't want my relationship with my family to be defined by nothing more than enduring chaotic mishaps masquerading as family reunions."

"I agree," his sister said. "But we did a damn good job of solving this thing, little brother." She chuckled. "Until I got knocked into a coma, that is."

"I just wanted to take all the credit," Dean said. "I couldn't live with the idea of getting one-upped by my older sister."

"Even though you won, don't ever forget that I'm the smart one."

"Smart-*er* one."

"Smart-*est* one."

Dean winked. "When you're right," he said as he stood up from his chair, "you're right."

Sheila reached out her hand.

Dean took it.

The siblings squeezed each other reassuringly.

"Love you, kiddo," Sheila said.

"Love you too, She." Dean moved toward the door. "You sure I can't stay? I've got nowhere to be for a little while. I could sit here and binge whatever crappy show you were watching before I walked in here."

"I think I've had my fill of your rugged mug for a little while," Sheila said. "I'll be out of here in a few days. But call me before then. I was eyeballing tickets for Disneyland in a couple months. You, me, Layla, Jeremy, all of us. I figured we could get a jump-start on learning this whole 'normal family' bit sooner rather than later."

"And you thought going to a cramped theme park with a million other people is the way to go?"

Sheila laughed. "It's a start."

"I'll let Jeremy know," Dean said. "He'll be glad to see you." He rapped his knuckles on the doorframe. "Be good."

Sheila said, "You too," and waved goodbye to her brother as he exited the room. "And do me one more favor," she called out.

Dean huffed.

Took out his pack of nicotine toothpicks.

Gave the package a once-over and tossed them in a waste basket.

Puffing his chest, Dean hustled toward the elevator, the bright wash of lights overhead illuminating him just like the vision of Tommy he had a few days before. Even though he was bruised, exhausted, and in desperate need of reprieve, he was relieved for the first time in days, despite how battered he felt.

"Live your life," Dean could hear Tommy whisper. "Be happy, and don't forget to tell that woman that you love her."

"I will," Dean replied as he pushed through the door that opened up to the stairwell. "I'm on my way right now."

EPILOGUE

Two knocks sounded on the front door to Dean's residence. Layla was slicing up carrots in the kitchen. Dean's dog Willy was inching toward the cutting board with his nose turned up and a devious twinkle in his eyes. "Back off, bub," Layla said. "I'm onto you." Willy hung his head sheepishly, grunting before he made his way to the living room.

Layla put the knife down, wiped her hands on the towel, and moved toward the door to answer it. She smoothed the tangles in her hair, palmed the door handle, and opened it. Standing on the porch was Dean with a bouquet of lilies clutched in his hand.

Red tints flushed Layla's cheek. "Agent Blackwood."

Dean held out the flowers. "Miss Adrian."

The two embraced as Willy rushed into the foyer and poked his nose in between them. The mutt was fighting for a slice of the affection being exchanged until Dean got down on one knee, hugged him, and then scratched him behind his ears.

"I feel bad," Dean said. "For Willy, that is."

Layla held the flowers up to her nose and took a whiff. "What for?"

"Because." Dean got to his feet. "He's not going to be too thrilled that I'm home tonight just to hop on a plane tomorrow."

The comment prompted Layla's grin to slacken. "You're working again?"

"No." Dean shook his head. "Not unless going to Hawaii for two weeks to stare at the waves counts as work. I suggest you pack accordingly, by the way."

Sheer elation washed over Layla, her face glowing as she threw her arms around Dean's neck. "I'm sure we can find someone to watch Willy for a little while. Your dad even mentioned looking after him when we were visiting Sheila."

Dean shot a look toward his dog. "You hear that, you miserable ingrate? You're spending the week with Gramps."

Willy angled his rear end toward Dean, kicked out his back legs one at a time like he was stirring up dirt, grunted, and then padded his way into the living room.

Dean pulled Layla in closer and nestled his face in her cheek, his posture slackening like he was butter melting in her arms. "I should have said it before, but I'll say it now."

Layla pulled back and looked deep into his eyes.

"I love you," Dean said, feeling as though the words elicited a sweet taste when he said them out loud. "A million times over."

Cupping his face in her hands, Layla replied, "I love you too," before pressing her lips firmly against Dean's.

The two held onto the moment for as long as possible. All of Dean's cares, worries, and concerns drifted away as he held the woman in his arms, close to him like a life raft.

Something else will come up.

There will always be another case, another bad guy, or another problem to remedy.

He reached behind him and palmed the door handle.

That may happen soon.

Dean closed the door and wrapped his arms around Layla again, his focus solely on the woman he loved.

But not today.

AUTHOR'S NOTES

Thank you for reading *Midnight Kill,* book 2 of 5 in the Dean Blackwood series.

Be sure to check out Book 3, *Desert Kill.* I've included a sneak peek on the next page.

As an independent author, reaching more readers can be challenging, and that's where I could really use your help. If you enjoyed the story, I'd be grateful if you could leave a brief review on Amazon. Your support makes all the difference.

Go to: www.amazon.com/dp/B0DCKC5C23

SNEAK PEEK - DESERT KILL

Introduction

If Mad Max and Die Hard had a baby, it would be called *Desert Kill.*

In the desert, there are no rules, except one:
   Never transport psychotic criminals.

When the U.S. Marshals asked me to escort public enemy number one through the Arizona desert, saying no wasn't an option.

If I'd known car chases, explosions, and runaway prison buses were on the agenda, I'd have called in my old Army Ranger buddies for backup.
   But I'm no ordinary prison guard.
   And this bastard chose the wrong FBI agent to threaten.

If it's the wild west he wants, it's the wild west he'll get.
   But out here, I'm the law—judge, jury, and executioner.

PROLOGUE
DEAN

I'm about to get shot in the head—and the guy with his finger on the trigger is as *fucked* in the head as it gets.

It's the third time in my life that I've had a gun pointed at me. You would think I'd be used to this by now; not worried by the business end of a pistol being pressed to the back of my skull, but I'm not.

For the first time in years, I'm scared.

I'm downright *terrified*.

Trust me when I tell you that guy in the back seat jamming the gun against my skull isn't bluffing; he's *itching* for an excuse to blow my brain across the windshield, and after everything that's gone down between us the past few days, he's got plenty of reasons to send me to my maker.

If there even is such a thing.

I never took the time to figure out where I landed on that.

Probably won't be able to now, if I'm being honest with myself.

I see the fleet of police cruisers parted at canted angles through the windshield. Officers stand with weapons drawn, dipping in and out of cover behind their vehicles as they try to talk the guy down in the backseat.

"Let him go," one of them says.

"Put the weapon down," another guy chimes in.

After a while, the uniformed officers' attempts at moonlighting as hostage negotiators become so nauseating that I'm tempted to holler at them to shut the hell up. Whatever they're doing, it's not working. I squint as the streaks of crimson and blue lights on top of the cruisers strike me in the eyes, teasing the start of a migraine that's snaking up the back of my neck. As this all plays out, the car radio is pumping out The Rolling Stones's "Fool to Cry" at the request of my would-be executioner.

The cell phone resting on the center console chirps to life.

I draw a breath.

I hold it and then slowly puff the air out.

I eyeball the guy behind me in the rear-view mirror and ask him if one last phone call can serve as my final request.

"Fine," he says. "Just make it quick." He motions at the cell with his piece. "And put it on speaker."

I reach my hand out slowly toward the cell phone, the rest of my posture rigid to ensure my captor that I'm not about to make a move for anything other than the phone.

I pick the phone up.

I answer it.

Then I place it on speaker and feel my body deflate the second that I hear Layla's voice.

"Dean? " she says. "Are you okay?"

I snort. "All things considered."

"I can see you." Layla's tone is curt, strained like her vocal cords are cinched with rubber bands. "I'm right outside of the car."

I try to make out Layla among the congregation of cops outside, but it's too difficult. The fact that it's the dead of night, coupled with the flashing lights and the sheer number of people outside, makes it damn near impossible to make out anyone in particular.

"Everything's okay," I tell her, flinching as I utter the words out loud because I know it's complete and utter horse shit. Everything is *not* okay.

I'm just five pounds of pressure being applied to a trigger away from being turned into a memory.

"Dean," Layla says, tremors snaking through her voice, "there's something you need to know. There's something I have to tell you."

The guy behind me burrows the gun harder into the back of my head, the barrel scraping the occipital bone right where my spine connects to the base of my skull.

"Baby," I whisper to Layla. "I just wanted to say that I love you, that you mean everything in the world to me."

"Dean, wait!"

The guy behind me nudges my seat. He tells me that's enough. Then he demands that I hang up the phone and hand it back to him, so I comply because the guy has a fucking piece to my skull.

I shake my head. I wish I could have said more to Layla. I wish I could have told her that every second I've spent with her has been a moment that I wouldn't trade for anything. If the guy in the backseat had given me more time, I would have rattled off some romantic soliloquy that would make The Bard bat an eye, but there's just no time.

The last of the grains in the hourglass have dwindled.

I'm about to die, and there's no two ways about it.

"This is it," the guy sneers, ice glazing his tone, speaking to me like the tried-and-true killer that he is. "Last call."

"Yeah," I tell him. "I kind of had a feeling."

"You wanna say anything?

I shake my head. "Nope."

A few moments tick by.

The guy shifts his weight in the backseat.

He sighs.

Then he instructs me to close my eyes.

I do as the son of a bitch says. Hell, I was going to do it anyway. The last thing my eyes register is the fleet of cops outside before all the memories of my life play back at high speed. Again, just like the gun being held to my head, this is not the first instance in which this has happened...but this time I know it's going to be the last.

I think about Claire, the mother of my child.

I think about my son, Jeremy.

Then my sister.

My father.

My late brother Tommy, God rest him.

Then I think about Bazz.

Willy.

About all of the friends and family who have come and gone over the years, and as I go to draw in what I know is going to be my final breath, I hear the guy in the backseat cock back the hammer of his weapon.

Euphoria sluices over me like a tidal wave.

The last thing I think about before the guy pulls the trigger is the last time that I hugged my son.

Made in the USA
Las Vegas, NV
21 December 2024